ALSO BY JEFF JACOBSON

Wormfood

Foodchain

FOOD4U!

FOOD4U!

THE SUTTER FAMILY LEGACY OF EVIL

BOOK 3

JEFF JACOBSON

FOOD4U!
Paperback Edition

Dark Wolf Books
An Imprint of Wolfpack Publishing
1707 E. Diana Street
Tampa, FL 33610

www.darkwolfbooks.com

Edited by My Brother's Editor
Cover Design by Safeer Ahmed

Paperback ISBN 979-8-89567-919-7
Ebook ISBN 979-8-89567-918-0

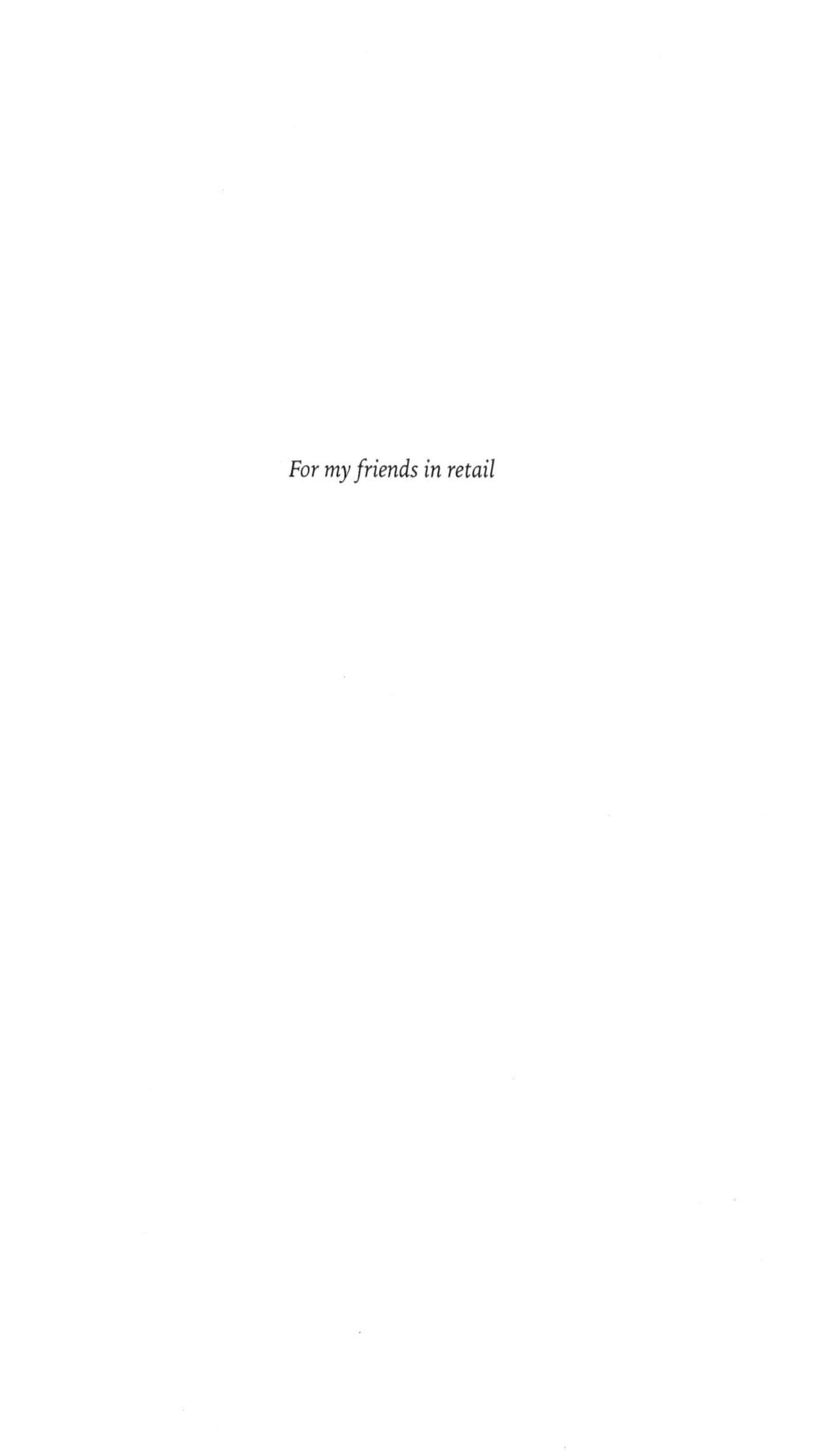

For my friends in retail

FOOD4U!

1

INTERVIEW TRANSCRIPT-SUBJECT:-REDACTED-

Transcribed by: Ofc. -REDACTED-, Berwyn, IL PD

AGENCY: DEPT. HOMELAND SECURITY

DATE: 29 July 2026

LOC: Berwyn Police Department, 6401 W. 31st St, Berwyn, IL 60402

TIME: 2:49 AM

CASE: 47-5190-0043

PRESENT:

Special Agent Fred Jackson—Department of Homeland Security (DHS)

Special Agent Alex de la Iglesia—Department of Homeland Security (DHS)

Joseph Sutter—FOOD4U! Employee

Unnecessary sounds, such as "um" and "ah" have been omitted from the following statement for the purpose of making this statement easier to read.

BEGIN RECORDING-

JACKSON: Okay, let's get started here. We are using both audio and video to record this interview today. This is Special Agent Fred Jackson with Special Agent Arturo de la Iglesia, DHS. It is approximately two forty-nine a.m., on Wednesday, July 29. We are interviewing a Mr. Joseph Sutter, aged thirty-three. Driver's license lists your address as 3114 West Rosemont, Apartment 8G, Chicago, Illinois. Is this correct?

SUTTER: …What?

JACKSON: Your address. Is it correct?

SUTTER: I don't…

JACKSON: I know you've had a hell of a shock, but like we've been saying, we need some information. This situation is…well, this is something most unusual, and we need to understand what happened. Now, you've been cleared by medical personnel for a preliminary interview. Can I get you another blanket? I'm afraid we don't have the time for another smoke. Would you like something to drink? Eat?

SUTTER: …Fuck.

DE LA IGLESIA: Get it together, big guy. You have a metric shit ton of explaining to get through.

JACKSON: What my partner is trying to say, is you being a survivor of a major incident, we need to know exactly what happened prior to the… incident. Now we need to establish your identity so we can proceed to the other matters. So then. 3114 West Rosemont. Is this your current address?

SUTTER: Yeah.

DE LA IGLESIA: That a basement?

SUTTER: Yeah, garden-level apartment.

DE LA IGLESIA: Basement.

JACKSON: Okay. We're officially getting started now. We are speaking with Mr. Sutter today with regards to the, well, I guess an incident at the FOOD4U! on Machen Avenue. You are not under arrest at this time. As I explained, this is simply a preliminary interview to try and get a handle on the…explosion?

SUTTER: Is that what you guys are calling it? An explosion?

DE LA IGLESIA: What we're calling it isn't your concern right now.

JACKSON: We don't know what happened. So we don't know what we're calling it yet. That's why we're talking to you, boss. What would you call it?

SUTTER: A fucking nightmare.

JACKSON: I can't exactly put that in the report.

SUTTER: Why not? It's the only thing that'll make sense. And besides, I wouldn't worry too much about your report. I don't think anybody's gonna read it.

JACKSON: Well, we all have our responsibilities. That's why we're here. At the moment, the working theory is a gas leak, spark, and subsequent explosion.

SUTTER: You saw what happened to the store. Did that look like a gas leak to you?

DE LA IGLESIA: It doesn't matter. That's not our department. We're getting sidetracked. Our job is to talk to survivors, get a clearer picture of what actually did occur.

SUTTER: Are there any other survivors, besides…

JACKSON: We can worry about that later. Right now, we're here to find out what happened. Experts are combing through the site, gathering evidence, and we'll have concrete answers soon. In the meantime, we're trying to talk to as many people as possible to find an explanation. And frankly, there's not many.

SUTTER: People or explanations?

JACKSON: Both.

SUTTER: Don't you guys need to read me my rights or something?

JACKSON: Once again, you are not under arrest. There is no need for a Miranda warning.

SUTTER: Sure. Just a friendly chat. Me and two junior G-men. And Big Brother watching and listening to everything up there in the corner.

JACKSON: The camera is automatic. And we're not FBI. Homeland Security. See?

SUTTER: As if that makes any kind of difference between you government pricks. Fuck off.

DE LA IGLESIA: Annnnnnd I've hit my limit already. Listen up, you fat, four-eyed slob. I don't know exactly who you think you are, but I gotta tell ya, from where I'm standing, I'm not impressed. I didn't know they could stack shit that high. I mean, look at you. When's the last time you had a salad? An actual vegetable? Time to wake up and smell the roses. A state of emergency has been declared, and I don't care about your delicate sensibilities. You've had plenty of time to get yourself together. So, you either start talking, or I'll knock a few teeth out, see how smart you are then.

JACKSON: Art, we're recording.

DE LA IGLESIA: I don't care. A whole store, destroyed! What the hell happened there? Nobody even knows how many are missing? And the remains we did find…whatever that is, it's not normal. You know something! I can smell it. So cut the horseshit and tell us what the hell happened.

JACKSON: I'm afraid we need your cooperation, Mr. Sutter. Joe. Please help us out. We're not the enemy here. We're just trying to find out what happened. I seriously doubt that you, or any employee for that matter, had anything to do with…whatever occurred. I wish there were more survivors we could talk to, but we simply don't have many choices. It's time to belly up to the bar, big guy.

SUTTER: I…I know what you guys want. You want an easy explanation, something you can put down on your reports, and it'll make sense and fit neatly into your reality. I wish I could give it to you. I really do. But look, you gotta wrap your head around this, that in my life, nothing's that clear. My family history…you have no idea. So I don't know, man. I don't think it's gonna work. I tell you what really happened, what I saw…well, what we *think* was happening…you won't believe me. You'll throw me in a rubber room. I can do without shock treatment, thank you very much. Drugs…well hey *maybe*? The PTSD from all this is gonna be a bitch. But no, no thanks. You boys hear this story, everybody that watches this video, you'll come to the obvious conclusion, the only conclusion really, that I've lost my goddamn mind. I'm a danger to myself and others. You'll ship me off to the laugh factory.

JACKSON: I get your concern, I really do. This whole thing, I've never seen, never even heard of anything like it. The eggheads, the guys in the white spacesuits, nobody knows what to think. Well, you were there. You know. But please understand this, me and Art, we're not here to judge you. We're not here to evaluate your mental capability. Not our job. We just want to know…what on earth happened to that store?

DE LA IGLESIA: Just start at the beginning. Easy.

SUTTER: Easy? We're a long way from easy. For example, the beginning? When did it start? I'm not exactly sure, you know?

DE LA IGLESIA: Oh, for God's sake. You better take this seriously.
SUTTER: I am! I get it. People, well I guess they died. A lot of people. But… *when*? When did it start? Hell if I know. You talk to the Professor, man, he'll tell you it started at the beginning of time, the big bang or something, you know. You push him, though, and you might get him to admit it started in the 1800s, and all the little things up to now. But recent history, I dunno. I mean, maybe the vandalism thing with the chalk. But I never saw it. Just heard about it. That was even before the suicide, and that was what, at least a couple weeks ago.
DE LA IGLESIA: Suicide?
SUTTER: Yeah. Dude blew his head off with a shotgun in front of the store before we opened one morning. That's gotta be a part of this. I wasn't there when he did it, thank fuck. So then you know, it follows you gotta look at what made him do it, right? To get to the beginning. Man, I don't know exactly.
JACKSON: Let's not make things more complicated than they need to be. For right now, just start with the first person that you know who disappeared.

Start when you guys called the cops. We'll go backward if we need to.

SUTTER: Again, man, I wasn't paying attention. I didn't really care. Don't look at me like that. I know it sounds cold and heartless, yeah, yeah. What do you want me to say?

JACKSON: We have a call record. Someone, a Wanda Bonansinga, I believe, from the store called the central desk at the nearest police station yesterday, at, let's see…eleven oh nine a.m. The sound was garbled, but there was a definite report of a missing woman. A report was logged at the time, but no officers were readily available to investigate, to look for a Mrs. Merriweather.

SUTTER: Who?

JACKSON: Mrs. Merriweather. Elderly woman, seventies. In the call, her vehicle was reported as abandoned in the parking lot of the store. Eighty-seven Jeep, if I remember correctly.

SUTTER: A Jeep? Oh, oh yeah. Mrs. Toenails.

DE LA IGLESIA: What? Who?

SUTTER: Mrs. Toenails. I… No, before we get to her, before we go any farther, you gotta understand this. You gotta wrap your heads around this concept. It's important, I think. So if you don't at least accept this one basic idea, this one *thing*, nothing is gonna make sense.

JACKSON: Okay. We're listening.

SUTTER: You need to understand this. The employees and the customers…we're *different*. Two totally different sets of mentality, of perspective. That's as clear as I can make it. We weren't like them, the customers, see?

JACKSON: Not really, no.

SUTTER: This job… I can't speak for most people that gotta work retail I guess, 'cause I can't really prove it, but I'd bet that most of us, we hate our jobs. I mean, we fucking *hate* our job. Hate being there, hate breathing that recycled air, hate the people we have to work with, but most, most of all, we hate the customers. No, no, no. Fuckin' relax, man. I can see you guys getting all excited because I'm admitting that I hated the customers. But whatever conclusions you guys are jumping at, you're wrong. See, if the rest is gonna make sense, you gotta understand this first, what it's like to go to a soul-crushing job that makes you want to claw your eyes out every goddamned day.

DE LA IGLESIA: If you don't like it, can't cut it, quit. Find another one.

SUTTER: Must be nice. Good for you. You're dripping your entitlement all over the floor, man. What's that feel like, not being trapped? Huh? And what am I gonna do, huh? Go out at thirty-three and find myself another entry-level job? That's a hell of a solution. You never had to work retail? Lucky you. Must be fucking nice. Didn't you guys ever have a job that you *absofuckinglutely* hated?

JACKSON: We're cops. Don't you dare lecture us.

SUTTER: I get it, and I'm not. I'm not talking about somebody that deliberately signs up for a job where they know damn well they're gonna be facing actual criminals and pissed off people all day long. No. I'm talking about somebody that just needs a job. Maybe it was all they could do to graduate high school. I'm talking about somebody that just needs health care, you know? Not everybody's got a support system. I bet you guys still talk to your parents, brothers, sisters. Cousins. Not everybody's got that.

DE LA IGLESIA: I don't need to listen to a lecture from some wannabe socialist. Get back to Mrs. Merriweather.

SUTTER: I am talking about her! I'm talking about everyone like her. I'm talking about the fucking customers. Those mindless, soulless vampires never stop coming, man. And the thing about the job, man, it never changes. Ever. That's why I can't say when all this started. The weeks and months, they just blend and get all smeared together into one long goddamn day that feels like you never go home. It doesn't end. So you get numb.

JACKSON: Okay.

SUTTER: You go more than numb. You get…distant, you know? Things happen in slow motion, far away. The customers, you kinda stop seeing them. They become abstract shapes to avoid. You interact with them only if absolutely necessary.

DE LA IGLESIA: So, is it fair to say you wanted the customers dead?

JACKSON: Jesus, Art.

SUTTER: Nah. Of course not. Maybe *hate* isn't the right word. I just stopped paying attention to them. They come. They go. It's endless. When I get to work, I think maybe my brain says fuck it, good night, and it goes into a coma on purpose just to save my dumb ass. And that's why I don't know when this really started.

JACKSON: Just do your best. Mrs. Merriweather?

SUTTER: I don't know if she was the first or second senior citizen that went missing. She was just the first one that anybody noticed. Anyway, I don't think any of this matters. What you're doing here. Not really. We're all fucked.

JACKSON: We just need your side of the story. That's all.

DE LA IGLESIA: Spill.

SUTTER: Fine. Okay, fine. It doesn't matter. None of this does. I don't care if you believe it or not. I…don't think we're going to get through this, just so you know. But okay. I'll tell ya what happened.

So. Mrs. Toenails. I'll tell you what happened, sure. I'll tell you everything. But I gotta say right off, hey, spoiler alert. We never did find her, just so you know. And then when things really went sideways, we tried to call, but we had other shit to deal with then.

Gloria's the one that ultimately took charge of looking for Mrs. Toenails because, let's face it, Kyle, the store's actual general manager, was useless. Gloria's the assistant general manager. Black, 50s. South Side to the bone. Smartest person in the store, no doubt. Maybe the smartest person I know. And that's why, most of the time, I'd go out of my way to avoid her. She always had a special chore for me to do. She's one of the reasons why I deliberately chose the job lowest on the store food chain, which was out in the parking lot at FOOD4U!.

Outside, there's less people I gotta talk to.

See, I'm the kind of person that would rather deal

with psychotic midwestern weather than people. Especially customers. You only talk to 'em when absolutely necessary, like only when you're worried they might get pissed off and go to a supervisor and word would get to Gloria, and then you'd be in for another stifling lecture about responsibility and obligation and cooperation until you just want to bang your head sideways into the file cabinet. So out in the lot, you only speak if asked a direct yes or no question but never say anything else to customers if you can help it. It just leads to hassle you don't need. It's easier to turn your brain off and endure the weather.

And let's be honest here. It isn't as if I really have to *think* a whole lot when I'm doing my job.

I push shopping carts.

There's not a whole lot to it.

I mean, it's not exactly complicated.

A badly trained baboon could do my job.

How hard we actually have to work depends on how many people show up to shop. Sometimes there's only a dozen customers an hour. Sometimes there's hundreds. They pluck one of the rusty, lunging metal baskets on wobbly wheels out of the snaky rows in the vestibule of FOOD4U!, do their thing in the store, and dump their shit in their car. Once the cart is empty, they might take the time to do the right thing and push it to one of three corrals spaced around the lot, but usually they just shove it in a random direction away from their vehicle and drive away as if they were the only sentient beings on Earth that mattered. I'd read about a theory online proposing that taking the time and effort to place a cart in a corral was really an ethics test. There's no obvious, immediate reward for doing the right thing, and therefore, if someone went out of their way to bring the cart back for the good of the community, they "passed." If this theory was correct and truly served as some kind of halfway accurate thermometer of humanity's moral compass, more people than you want to think about failed. Spectacularly.

My job is to march out to the corrals and collect all the strays and bring all the carts back.

And the cycle repeats itself.

Over and over and over.

Ad nauseam.

Only the weather changes.

The parking lot covers five acres of pockmarked asphalt that grows soft as stale gum under the Illinois summer sun and stiffens up, brittle and cracking, in the icy winters. Highway 112 stretches along the southern edge. There are three entrances or exits to the highway, but for some reason, they're only wide enough for one vehicle at a time. And nobody bothered to paint any directions or anything either. Slow times, like Monday or Tuesday mornings, there wasn't much trouble. Weekends, though, were chaos. Vehicles clogged the highway and parking lot like slowly clotting blood. Across the highway was a tired strip mall with a taqueria with a permanent CLOSED sign in the window and a dentist that everybody was too scared to visit.

This particular FOOD4U!, one of 22 or 23 left nationwide, depending on if you believed the rumors that yet another store had closed, was nestled in an industrial wasteland and maze of railroad tracks that provided a buffer from the western 'burbs and the big bad city of Chicago. The parking lot lay to the east and west. There was an access road around the north side for the trucks and loading docks. Outside of that there wasn't much, just railroads and factories.

We might walk anywhere from two to fifteen miles in a day, wandering out to the corrals and hauling the carts back to the stacks in the vestibule. I burned through a pair of hiking shoes every summer. Boots are generally tougher, but they still wouldn't last more than a winter and a half if I was lucky. Proper gear was essential. I tended to get a little OCD about my outfit, especially my shoes. I'd never come out and admit it at work, but I couldn't focus on anything until my shoelaces had been tightened to a precise tension, just shy of a tourniquet really, then triple knotted. For whatever reason, it made me feel secure, like it gave me a solid foundation for whatever came my way. If both shoes weren't equally tight, I might as well have been wearing clown shoes, and my brain couldn't function.

I suppose we all find our own methods to get through the hours.

Covering your head when winter locked the Midwest in ice was also key. Thick woolen caps under my Carhartt jacket hood kept me snug, while in the summer I traded the wool for a giant Party City sombrero that someone left behind in a cart. It helped to keep the unrelenting sun off my face and neck. The fact that this was a blatant violation of the employee dress code was the cherry on top.

Music is my life, and so that was the other reason I'd rather be outside. The store couldn't stop you from listening to whatever you wanted when out on the lot.

Well, they tried. Believe me, they tried. For the first few years, I fought with management daily over wearing earbuds. Anytime we had a walk, where a gaggle of corporate clones would come sniff around the store every few months to make sure everything was up to their incomprehensible, inconsistent standards, the attorneys would gnash their teeth at what they perceived as unsafe behavior that might, god forbid, open FOOD4U! up to a lawsuit. So, after a lot of back and forth and more than a few threats of termination, I finally found a compromise.

Or rather, technology caught up with our feud, and now I wore a kind of thin, wraparound headphone thing that hooked over my ears, sending vibrations to the bones in front of my ears and just behind them, all while leaving my ear canals completely open. I didn't really understand the tech, but it worked. Kinda. I mean, it did sound a bit like you were listening to the music from a portable, mono AM radio from the far end of a bowling alley, but it was better than nothing. I gotta be honest, though. The attorneys were right, but don't tell 'em. Even if my ear canals were wide open, when I was blasting Motorhead, I couldn't hear any other damn thing.

I think they eventually just got tired of fighting with me.

The only tool we used was a thick canvas strap, around twenty feet long with steel hooks at each end, to snag the catches built into the carts and connect a dozen or so in a train. That way, you could push a stack back into the vestibule with a reasonable amount of control. Usually, while walking out to the corrals, we'd sling the ropes around our shoulders so much that it left more or less permanent stains on our faded orange hi-vis vests.

As there was a fair amount of physical labor involved, you'd think me and Sammy would be the leanest dudes in the store.

Alas, we were not.

I suppose it is possible folks started disappearing before you guys got involved. Lots of homeless guys in our neighborhood. But again, I don't know exactly when. I said, stop looking at me like that. If there were any cars left on the lot, I never noticed. I mean, outside of the Professor's car. Because, again, I wasn't paying much attention. Babysitting customers, not only isn't included in the job description, that's above my pay grade, you know?

But come to think of it, there were more than the usual number of people these past few weeks who, when they walked out of the store, couldn't remember where the hell they parked their car. A lot more. Back in the day, we had a customer every once in a while who'd wander around, up and down the lanes of the parking lot with increasingly disbelieving anger crawling up their faces because they couldn't find their car. Me and Sammy always thought it was because the entrance was on the corner of the giant rectangular building, and that's what threw people's internal geography off, but you know, now with everything that happened, I wonder if it was really because...well, you know.

See what I mean? Who the hell knows when it

started. I mean, really started. When I first noticed, a customer might lose track of their car maybe once a week. Then it got to be almost every damn day.

Yesterday though, nobody suspected anything. Life was normal. The car alarms going off all over the place all day long were normal. Nobody locks their car and activates the alarm to stop thieves anymore. Car alarms are homing beacons now. I'm forced to endure those fucking digital screams all damn day, every day. If security was the issue, you'd think half the customers' cars were being stolen while they were in the store. Nope, no such luck. Customers stumble out into the lot, blinking in the searing sun, and when their vehicle isn't where they think they left it, out comes the damn key fob, stabbing at the little alarm button until their car shrieks at them. Eventually, they'd figure out where it was and go trudging away to dump their shit.

I'm telling you, something happened to their minds while they were inside.

Okay, okay fine. I'll get on with it. But I'm convinced that's a big part of what happened.

Mrs. Toenails was a regular. Every damn Monday. She used to come in with her mom, if you can believe it. That was a treat, the two of 'em demanding attention nonstop. Haven't seen the mom in about a year though. Figure she isn't mobile enough anymore. Or she's dead. Thing I remember most about Mrs. Toenails was she'd always want help loading her car. Didn't matter what she'd bought. Could be just a couple of silicone ice trays. I think she just wanted somebody to talk to. She had to prop the gate on her ancient Jeep Wrangler open with a broom handle 'cause it wouldn't stay open on its own. And no matter how cold it got, her feet would be bare, and she'd wear the same nasty ass pair of flip-flops. You couldn't help but stare with horrified fascination at her uncomfortably thick, jagged toenails. I suspect she had to go to like a tractor mechanic or something just to get 'em trimmed.

Mrs. Toenails always parked in the closest handicapped spot to the front doors, and her car was still there on Tuesday morning when Boris the Rattail showed up. He was a guy who wore stiff braces on his legs that locked his knees into place, and he'd kinda crab walk along, using two of those canes that wrap around your forearms. He had a super impressive mullet haircut, with a braided tail that hung out of the bushy squirrel tail another two whole feet. He was quite proud of it, and when he really got going on his canes, that rat tail would swing back and forth like a whip.

He came in every Tuesday soon as we opened. He was also the kind of guy who would get possessive over public spaces for some reason. He truly thought of that closest handicapped spot as HIS, like his name was on the damn sign. At least on Tuesday mornings anyway. He was pissed about having to park an entire spot over because the Wrangler was in the way. He should have known better to come early. All the handicapped spots were taken by seniors every morning.

I knew enough to avoid Boris because he had a shorter temper than a hungover honey badger, so I usually found something on the other side of the lot that needed attention. I'm guessing once Boris found his spot blocked, he went inside and raised holy hell. And let me tell you this, Gloria's a lot of things, believe me, but dumb ain't one. She knew damn well it was Tuesday morning and like me, was smart enough to keep busy with something else just in case Boris had a problem. Often, that task could be something truly awful, like emptying the grease trap on the chicken rotisserie. So, if Gloria was willing to subject herself to rancid chicken fat, that should give you an idea how much fun it was dealing with Boris.

Yann was the supervisor on front-end duty that morning, and while I got nothing against the guy, he wasn't the best at multitasking. Give him a single simple job, and he'd be just fine. I think he'd been chewed out too many times by old managers and now was terrified of making a mistake. So he tended to only focus on one thing at a time. And if things got even more complicated, his gestures got even more frantic and his already nearly undecipherable accent would become downright incoherent. Then when people asked him to repeat what he'd said, he'd really lose his shit. If I was in the right mood, it was pretty entertaining to watch.

Kyle had offered me a supervisor position my second year at the store, and I told him I'd rather staple my tongue to the asphalt. Supervisors are forever caught in the vise between customers, management, and lowly basic hourly employees like me. No fucking thanks.

Anyway, I have no doubt Boris lit into Yann like it was Yann's fault that Mrs. Toenails had parked in

Boris's own personal spot. I heard from Wanda that Yann was busy at the time trying to explain in English to a customer whose own grasp of English was tenuous at best that no, the store couldn't accept soiled bed linens as a return, especially since they also carried what appeared to be quite lively bedbugs. Add Boris to that tinder and you might as well toss a hand grenade into a cave of bat guano for poor Yann.

All the yelling got Kyle's dandruff up, and he must have gotten tired of waiting for Gloria to solve the situation because he eventually emerged from his office to see for himself what's what. Boris insisted on dragging him outside to show him the war crime right there in broad daylight. Kyle only comes outside personally during business hours only if it's absolutely necessary. I know that Kyle's the general manager and all that, but I'm gonna let you in on a little secret. Pretty sure he wasn't the brightest bulb in the FOOD4U! leadership marquee. It wouldn't surprise me if his wife still helped him tie his shoes.

He came outside, holding up his hand to his forehead to block the glare like some explorer surveying a vast landscape. It only really served to confirm that, yup, the Wrangler was sitting there in the closest handicapped spot, big as life. Still, he walked out to the Jeep to investigate. I'm not sure if he thought it was a mirage or what.

I should have known better and followed Gloria's lead, found something to do somewhere else, but I had the bad luck to be grabbing a water from the cooler at that moment. I was watching him from the cart crew corner and didn't duck back inside fast enough before he caught sight of me.

"This Mrs. Merriweather's vehicle?" Kyle asked.

I shrugged. Along with customers, I try not to talk to management if I don't have to, you know? At the time, I had no idea that Mrs. Merriweather was her name. If he'd asked if the Jeep belonged to Mrs. Toenails, then I probably would have nodded.

He frowned. This was not part of Kyle's daily routine, and Kyle was not a fan of anything that deviated from routine. His big pale head swiveled back and forth, as if searching the lot for Mrs. Toenails. Maybe she'd popped over to the dentist to have her teeth cleaned. He liked problems with an easy answer, where a quick glance could reveal both the issue and solution, and he could impart wisdom from his lofty position as general manager. He took off his glasses and rubbed his eyes against the glare. I knew what he was thinking. Corporate was coming in for a walk tomorrow, and this was the last shit he needed to be dealing with. Didn't people understand he had registers to wipe down?

He replaced his glasses but still didn't know what to do so he fiddled with his American flag lapel pin, something he considered a part of his work uniform for some reason. Almost positive it wasn't a requirement of the regulation manager outfit, but it seemed to fit right in along with the cutting-edge tan khakis, white New Balance sneakers to show he was one hip motherfucker, and of course the FOOD4U! emblazoned pale-blue polo shirt.

By now, we were drawing a crowd. There was Boris of course, since he wanted his parking space back. For a guy that needed two canes to get from A to B, he sure couldn't stand still, clacking all around the Wrangler. Maybe it was the meth. Now that I think about it, how fucking sad this whole thing is that the only reason anybody started noticing anything was because of simple, petty jealousy. Over a stupid parking spot.

I knew Sammy had joined me watching the sideshow unfold because I heard him breathing off to my right. It was nothing out of the ordinary, but I guess it did sound like a manatee with a bad cold. Sammy the Samoan was a giant, perpetually smiling Buddha, only with a shock of scraggly black hair that looked like it might forever entangle any comb that dared to get too close. He was only twenty-two but could've passed for anything between fifteen to forty-five years old. He weighed over 300 pounds easily and was several inches shy of six feet. He wasn't Samoan. At least, I don't think so. Sammy was one of those guys whose deep, squinty eyes and dark, tanned skin made him look like he could have been from damn near anywhere in the world. He could've been Hispanic, maybe Filipino, Native American, maybe Chinese. This, combined with his eternally cheerful nature, made him the adopted mascot of nearly every clique in the store.

If you saw him wandering around the store, maybe taking his time delivering trash from the lot back to the compactor, you'd think that by most standards, hey, maybe that guy needs to hit the gym. But if you caught him in action, out on the lot, he moved downright smooth, not quite a dancer, more like a diesel tugboat chugging serenely along on a placid surface. I mean, he had a trick that made me laugh. Every once in a while, word would come down that corporate was tightening everybody's belts, and water for the cart crew was a luxury. Sammy would simply take his time going to the food court, getting one of the ridiculously tiny cups they hand you for complimentary lukewarm tap water and a long straw. He'd nestle the cup in the right chest pocket of the faded orange hi-vis safety vest with the straw up around his collarbone. Then, swear to God, he'd ease around the entire lot, pushing in enormous stacks of carts, so fluid and gentle he never spilled a drop. Every once in a while, he'd pause, tilt his head slightly, and take a sip, then he'd heave a satisfied sigh and continue.

He was known as Sammy the Samoan mostly because the alliteration was fun. And at this job, you grab hold of whatever makes you halfway chuckle and hold on tight.

We bumped fists.

"Mornin'. How's it going?"

"Living the dream."

"That's Mrs. Toenails's Jeep," Sammy said. "Why's it still here?"

I shrugged and said, "At least Kyle's on the job. Everybody can relax now."

In a lot of ways, Kyle was the best manager you could ask for. For one, you never saw him much. He'd lurk in his office, creating colorful signs that featured a lot of blurry stock photos and badly cropped motivational quotes ("TEAM: Together Everyone Achieves More") on a twenty-year-old computer. The printer was even older. Somebody had shown him how to do it with some ancient, clunky software, and he took to it with such fervor, you'd think designing these 8.5 X 11" sheets was his primary responsibility. That and rearranging the bottles in liquor. It was an open secret throughout the store that he regularly 'forgot' to pay for bottles of cheap Zinfandel. Now he was cupping his hands against the dusty Jeep windows and peering inside. Maybe Mrs. Toenails was hiding in the back seat or something. Maybe he thought she might have left a note.

"Tow it!" Boris shouted. "Get that piece of shit outta here!" Personally, I thought that Boris had a lot of balls calling Mrs. Toenails's Jeep a piece of shit when he himself drove a maroon PT Cruiser with a mint-green passenger door.

Next outside was Gloria, doubtlessly coming outside to keep Kyle on track. She had a sixth sense whenever stuff went sideways at the store, which was often, and undoubtedly realized it would only cause her more headaches in the long run if she hid out in back with the chickens. I think she might have suspected that this wasn't Boris's usual bullshit. Gloria had a way of looking into you with a gaze that pierced your flesh, your bones, your mind, your soul. Like I said, I tried to avoid her. All I knew was she was a widow, a lifelong White Sox fan, and a devout Baptist. That was more than enough to avoid her. Because she was my *real* boss, you know? But credit where credit's due. As dumb as Kyle was, Gloria was smart. Anything that went right at this particular FOOD4U! location was more than likely a result of her hard work. I don't think anybody worked with more determination than Gloria. Nothing got in her way. Where most employees at the store, like me, would wander away from a task if we got bored or tired, whatever it was would just give Gloria more focus, more grit.

So that was a *third* reason to constantly duck under her radar.

But again, she was the only reason this location functioned at all.

As usual, Kyle deferred to Gloria. "You know whose car this is?"

"I don't know her name," Gloria said, taking a long look around the parking lot. "But I remember what she looks like. Elderly woman, usually by herself."

Sammy pitched in. "Flip-flops!"

"True. She does seem to prefer flip-flops."

Kyle nodded at me. "You've seen her?"

I nodded back. "Sure."

"This morning?"

I shook my head. "Not this morning."

"I don't need this headache," Boris said, like he was worried we might be forgetting him. "I'm on a schedule. And this is right in my way. Look at it! Nobody gives two shits about the handicapped," he said, slamming his canes against the asphalt as he circled Mrs. Toenails's Jeep a third time.

"Well, sir, I can understand—" Kyle started, but Boris was just getting warmed up.

"Do something about this piece of shit!" Boris cracked one of his canes across the Jeep's hood.

Kyle said, "Now sir, I'm afraid we can't have you—"

"All I hear is excuses!" Boris yelled and hit the Jeep again.

Gloria turned to me. "Was she here yesterday?"

I shrugged again. "I guess so? I don't know."

Gloria turned back to Boris and clapped her hands

with shocking force. Once, twice, three quick deep POPS that cut his rant off mid-sentence. He blinked and looked confused, as if she'd unleashed some kind of spell on him. Really though, he was just a toddler that had been outsmarted the way you'd distract an excited dog in order to grab their favorite toy. "Thank-you-sir-for-bringing-this-to-our-attention," Gloria said in a toneless, unbreathing voice that she reserved for the truly deranged customers. "We will take it from here. Have a pleasant day."

Without giving Boris or Kyle a chance to respond, she turned and headed back to the store. As she passed me, she said, "Joseph and Samuel, follow me. I will require your assistance."

As Kyle and Boris looked at each other, unsure of what to do next, I groaned inwardly. Nothing good could come from this new assignment. Unless Gloria had us testing video games in our sparse Electronics section, something I highly doubted, the day was getting off on seriously the wrong foot.

Like most Tuesday mornings, it was fairly quiet, with only a few dozen customers shuffling in and out. Some we'd see often enough to recognize, like an old guy in a Vietnam War baseball cap and a perpetual scowl. He never said a word to anybody, and that was fine with me. Some were new, thankfully. Like a plump lady trying to hold onto a squirming rat dog in a pink harness that proclaimed *Service Dog* in stern letters. If that dog was an actual support animal of any kind beyond some narcissistic entitlement, then I'd eat my shoes.

I had a feeling that, like most of us, Gloria didn't want to spend any more time outside at the front of the store than absolutely necessary. Not since the suicide. Like I said, I hadn't been at work when it happened. I'd been told it happened around dawn, some poor homeless guy put the barrel of a shotgun under his chin while kneeling in front of the ENTRANCE door. I know some employees had recordings of the security video on their phones, but I'd decided I didn't need that in my head. It was bad enough coming to work and getting a daily reminder. Somebody, maybe Don, had tried to power wash the blood away, but the process left faint, bleached stains on the concrete and stucco wall, and it was impossible not to notice.

Once we were inside the vestibule, Gloria turned to me and Sammy. "We are going to search the store for this customer. I trust you know who you are looking for?"

Sammy nodded.

I said, "All we gotta do is look at their feet."

I swear to the baby Jesus, Gloria could drop the actual temperature around her when she wanted with just a naked stare and a faint thinning of her lips that erased the very idea of humor in the universe. She took a moment so we all could register that she was pointedly ignoring my suggestion, then continued. "Joseph, you take the south side of the store. Samuel, the north wall." She caught his perplexed expression and pointed off to our right. "There. That side. I'll take the middle. Check along the walls first, then come back along each aisle. Make sure you look behind any displays, especially in Hardlines. This wouldn't be the first customer to fall asleep on the furniture."

Boris passed us with a baleful glare and machine gun clatter of canes.

Kyle was next. "I'll be in my office. Let me know if you find her." He walked inside, no doubt calculating how long he could stall in his office before slipping back to liquor.

Gloria said, "We will meet up at Receiving. Any questions?"

Me and Sammy shook our heads.

"Okay then." Gloria walked through the EXIT, calling over her shoulder, "And Joseph, please leave your ridiculous sombrero out here."

The only FOOD4U! location in Illinois used to be a Crafty Beaver, a lumber and home DIY big-box branch location that died out in the early '90s, killed in action between skirmishes between behemoths like Home Depot, Lowe's, and Menards. The big building was constructed in the early '40s, first for the war effort, then was used as some kind of factory until the '70s, where it went through a wildly varied list of owners until the Crafty Beaver folks gave up on it. The place sat vacant until the '08 real estate crash, when FOOD4U!, a discount surplus little upstart with maybe a dozen stores in the Southwest, took advantage of plummeting property values and bought the massive building in the middle of an industrial wasteland crisscrossed with endless miles of railroad tracks, betting the cash-strapped residents of the distant western Chicago 'burbs would crave cheap shit.

FOOD4U! was right. Customers, especially those with little or nothing extra to spend, were drawn to the store like moths to a deadly bug zapper. At first, the store mostly carried cut-rate food like generic boxes of mac 'n cheese that had been on the shelves for *years* and discount produce that had been already turned away by the local Jewel and Mariano's, after altering the sell-by dates by a few days here and there. Customers didn't care. Price was more important than quality.

As profits grew, FOOD4U! expanded its merchandising base. Corporate buyers lurked in the gray areas of international commerce far, far away from the food end of things, uncovering vast quantities of whatever junk had either been overproduced somewhere overseas or might violate EU safety laws in some way, and now it was here in the States, costing money every day it took up valuable space. So the product was sold at a steep loss to the original producer, repriced to cover costs with a sliver of profit for the shipper, then trucked out to FOOD4U! stores where people couldn't wait to get their hands on it. It didn't matter what it was, or if the customers even needed it or not, the only thing that mattered was that it was cheap. A deal is a deal. Fifteen plastic spatulas for two bucks? Fuck yeah! Sure, half of 'em will melt when exposed to any heat above 100 degrees Fahrenheit, but...*two bucks!*

FOOD4U! sold plenty of standard big-box garbage too, not just food where it might be dubious if it was actually legally edible, just like your Walmarts, your Costcos, your Targets. Crap for every room in the house. And garage. But FOOD4U!'s merch was always off brand, from something that sounded *almost* like a solid, trusted company. *Frigid-Air* refrigerators. *Whirlingpool* washing machines. *FG* TVs. *Maitag* microwaves. *Dison* vacuums. Some of the younger employees called the store TEMU4U! when no managers or sups were around, but I'm not sure I got the joke.

Customers grabbed a cart in the big drafty vestibule out front, then had a choice between two large doors with rolling metal gates that were dropped and locked each night, ENTRANCE off to the left and EXIT on the right. Should be easy. But if you've never worked retail, you'd be surprised at how many people couldn't figure it out. The design was supposed to guide customers through the store in one smooth clockwise direction. It won't surprise anyone, of course, that real life usually scrambled the basic plan, and customers ran around in nonsensical directions like their hair was on fire.

Thick, rough cinderblock walls contained over 105,000 square feet of halfway organized piles of *stuff*, almost more than my brain could comprehend. It was like contemplating a concept like outer space or infinity, utterly incalculable, too much for me to wrap my head around. At least to me anyway. Truth be told, the whole store made me uncomfortable, gave me vertigo. The air and light in the store didn't feel natural. It gave off a vibe so artificial it felt like it was slowly poisoning me, scrambling my thoughts. It felt...*wrong* somehow, going to work for a store that sells nothing but garbage you suspect is slowly killing the planet, where day after day you face hordes of people that treat the place as a theme park, open-air toilet, city dump, personal living room and/or kitchen, and a flea-market that deals mostly in stolen goods.

So I'd only venture inside the store for absolute necessities and nothing else. Time clock. Restroom. Locker. Vending machine in the break room. Breaks themselves were taken outside in the shade in the summer or hiding in the vestibule in the winter. That's all, until something unexpected came up. And around once a week or two, something usually did.

Like now. Sammy headed off to the right, saying hello to John, the guy who waited at the EXIT door to check customer receipts, and disappeared inside the store. Another reason I didn't like being inside was because I ended up getting tired of squinting at shit I couldn't see, so I'd end up having to wear my regular glasses inside. Sunglasses hid your eyes so people couldn't see what you were thinking. I tried a few times with my prescription sunglasses, but it felt too much like stumbling around with the lights off. I reluctantly switched 'em.

I couldn't put going inside off any longer, so I gritted my teeth, slung my rope around my shoulders, double-checked my name tag was flipped backward because when people I didn't know called me by my first name, I wanted to stomp on their toes, then joined the trickle of customers going through the ENTRANCE.

Kyle liked staging whatever new merchandise the buyers had dropped in our lap right up front just inside the ENTRANCE, and that always created traffic jams as customers clogged the wide doorway, staring dully at the fresh, gleaming stacks of crap. It was as if some kind of mass hypnosis hit them as they stepped under the erratic combination of outdated, ultra-bright sodium vapor lights and flickering fluorescents that bounced off walls painted an industrial tan the same shade as an undercooked pancake. Customers had been drawn to the store by that irresistible lure of something shiny and new, no matter how useless. The place enchanted shoppers, dulling their self-awareness, choking out their sense of logic and reasoning.

A length chain-link fence that stretched almost to the ceiling bisected the store for about forty feet, splitting the ENTRANCE and EXIT. Corporate psychology decided this design would gently herd customers deep into the store where they'd find themselves surrounded by literal acres of merchandise, and somewhere along the way they'd inevitably succumb to the seductive lure of that sweet, sweet burst of dopamine when buying anything, especially if it was worthless crap. The idea again was that customers would eventually complete a clockwise circuit of the store, ending up in Front End. Once they'd purchased their shit, they'd head out, guided to the EXIT on the other side of the fence.

On the ENTRANCE side, the merch boys would stack whatever new arrivals along the fence and in various piles or displays, taking up so much space it was guaranteed to piss off the fire marshal. This week's collection included stacks of possibly used tires, shrink wrapped in pairs for some reason. Toddler snowsuits that felt a little too slick, almost damp somehow from something that wasn't water. I suspected they might burst into flames if they got within a couple dozen feet of an open flame. Golf shirts with combinations of colors and patterns that should be a crime, or at the very least carry a heavy fine. Size 13 and 14EEE imitation snakeskin cowboy boots made in Taiwan, clearly sent to the wrong part of the country. Twenty-gallon buckets that honestly, if you filled with anything heavier than Styrofoam, you wouldn't be able to haul very far. Indonesian Region 3 DVD players. And much, much more.

I closed my eyes and bowed my head in appreciation to the gods, both for the halfway sparse Tuesday morning crowd today and the daily thanks that Kyle hadn't bothered to fix the loudspeaker system so there hadn't been music inside the store for over three years. Well, for nine or ten months out of each year, anyway. Until fucking Christmas. Kyle was a big Yuletide fan. Not only was it the absolute center of the retail universe, but our general manager loved every ritual, every single decoration, every bizarre pagan element associated with the birth of his beloved baby Jesus. Yes, it's true that Gloria was a fellow Christian, but let's face facts here. There's a world of difference between her staid, orderly Baptist church and the free-wheeling, almost sacrilegious cult of Kyle's Pentecostal wildness. Gloria quietly loathed the outlandishness, the gaudiness, the waste of retail Christmas decorations. She believed in a firm separation of church and commerce. It wasn't a whole lot different than keeping church and state far away from each other.

I'm not sure Kyle understood the whole work/life balance thing. I don't think he could separate anything in his life. Maybe that took too much brain power.

Anyway, as soon as October rolled around, Kyle set up a big ass karaoke speaker in Front End that he'd gone out and bought at a reputable store with his own money, playing one single holiday CD that contained twelve soul-killing Christmas carols over and over. It made going inside unbearable. A buddy of mine who owned a record store where I used to work had a gift for being able to dissociate from almost any audio around him, this superhuman skill of simply dialing any music he heard down in his head. Nothing fazed him. Not Christmas music, not piped-in elevator music, none of that god-awful modern country pop, or whatever monstrosity being forced on you from inescapable advertisements. I envied him.

Music was the thing that made me the most happy if I'm being honest with myself. Definitely happier than my last girlfriend anyway. Nothing else came close. No beer, no whiskey or tequila, not even any illegal drugs I'd ever tried. The right music at the right time revealed truths, helped you understand yourself and your world on a core level. Music moved me. Made me feel like an actual living, breathing, conscious entity. I don't know how else to describe it. The drawback to being able to pull that much power from music was that it also left me vulnerable and exposed to any halfway catchy earworm. When these advertising jingles or pop melodies squirmed into my head, I couldn't escape or release the plodding predictability, especially prevalent in Christmas music, and as they kept echoing, tumbling over and over in my skull, I went quietly crazy.

Sometimes not so quietly.

Once you slogged through the swamp of all the new crap, dodging people where you can literally see their consciousness fall apart in real time, watching that light slip away in their eyes, you're in Hardlines, also known as House Shit. This is all the electronics, the appliances, mattresses if we have any, furniture, stuff like that. I lingered on the row of recliners. Gloria hadn't been joking. Customers had been known to fall asleep on the furniture with alarming regularity. It tickled a part of me that there was a chance one of them had simply up and died while taking a short break, and unaware shoppers continued brushing past the corpse.

No luck spotting Mrs. Toenails, living or dead. Except for a family giving a bunk bed a thorough inspection, everything else was empty. I passed them while the father shook the bed like they were in an earthquake, the two boys having a ball. I clapped my hands and offered them up in a thank you prayer motion, grateful and feeling a strong urge to acknowledge it whenever I get to experience those simple moments hearing peals of children's laughter. It didn't happen often. And all I can say is when you listen to kids being giddy and loud because something cheap and easy is giving them joy, if that doesn't at least make you smile, you might wanna go talk to somebody. Maybe it's another retail survival skill. I tended to seize on moments like that and squeeze 'em for all their worth.

'Cause I'm telling you, it's a hell of a lot better than hearing 'em cry. Or scream.

We got to hear that a lot.

And it wasn't just kids whining, kids being tired, cranky. Having temper tantrums. Sometimes, sure. That's not so bad. It's understandable. It's when the parents hate their kids I can't listen. Sometimes when you see how people treat their own children, you can start to truly understand why we're so fucked up as a species.

After House Shit, there were the heavy-duty chemicals, all the cleaning soaps and all that, the detergents, the bleach. That aisle always made my eyes water, but no matter much how deep breathing I gulped down, I never got high. Not enough so that I noticed, anyway. Next was soft goods, stuff like Styrofoam plates and cups, all the disposable shit in our lives that will eventually fill the gaps between all that metal and plastic in the landfills.

I passed a motionless young guy in one of those Anti-Social Social hoodies staring with what appeared to be absolutely no comprehension at a package of plastic forks in his hand. I figured he had specific instructions from his mom or girlfriend and was now weighing the consequences of bringing the wrong utensils home. I didn't envy him.

Near the back of the store, I had to dodge a giant display of wind chimes that more or less blocked the aisle because management couldn't figure where else to put it. Somebody in the acquisition department in corporate had stumbled over a deal too good to pass up liquidating a wind chime company. So now we, and most other FOOD4U! branches I assume, were stuck trying to sell a crazy huge assortment of wind chimes. These things were built out of bamboo, metal, wood, ceramic, and plastic, ranging in size from cigarettes all the way up to monsters over six feet long, big around as a tree stump. They'd gone to the trouble of erecting a heavy-duty steel rack, hanging as many display models as possible, and lacking any other space for storage, had simply stacked the hundreds of boxes around and behind the display. The chimes had been bought for pennies, and everybody knew it. The boxes had been tossed around so many times the cardboard was shaped more like bean bags than actual rectangles. Sammy and I had a bet on how long it would take for a customer to pull a box from the bottom and bring the whole damn thing crashing down on them. I bet a protein bar it would happen in under two weeks.

So far, disappointingly, nobody'd been crushed.

"When are they gonna get rid of this shit?" the vet in the black cap asked me. His cap read "1st Marine Division-Recon-Vietnam 1967-1978." He nodded to the haphazard jumble of wind chimes in case I wasn't sure what he meant, all while giving me a look that made me feel like a bug impaled on a pushpin in a museum pegboard.

His attitude immediately raised my hackles, and I reacted automatically, primed by a million other asshole customers, starting with something about how we'd be fucking thrilled to carry his lordship around the palace at his behest. He didn't even let me get my first word out before cutting me off brutally with, "Getting kinda sick of this shit, having to dance around this mess. I'm not dead yet, but I ain't a spring fucking chicken neither. Somebody needs to do their job."

I inhaled through my nostrils, nodding the whole time, and even managed a grin while I said, "Absolutely. I'll bring it up at the next board meeting."

"That supposed to be smart?"

Listen, I know damn well I'm not particularly intelligent. Every once in a while, though, I think Darwin's ghost takes pity on me and shoots me a warning that I can't ignore. This time, a realization burst inside, and as it soaked into my very bones, I knew that even though I had at least a foot, over a hundred pounds, and thirty-five, forty years on this old guy, he'd wipe the floor with my ass without breaking a sweat. And judging from his expression, he looked like he was ready to go to town, ready to fucking rumble, more than ready. It didn't matter that he was dressed like some senior citizen in a cartoon, slacks up to his belly button, long sleeve shirt, and black windbreaker. Sensible brown shoes. He stared at me, daring me to keep being an asshole. He just needed a second excuse, a confirmation that I deserved it, and then he'd gladly tear me apart. Thank holy fuck I was smart enough to see this. Despite his deceptively harmless looks, his smaller and older stature, I'd be damn lucky if parts of me didn't up in the Emergency Room.

"Ah, uh no. No. Not trying to be smart."

"I hope not."

The second follow-up realization to hit me was that this anger might be directed at me, but my behavior wasn't the root cause. Sure, I was being an asshole, so you can argue among yourselves long as you need whether I deserved an ass-kicking or not. I was just in the wrong place at the wrong time and dumb enough to put a target on my stupid fat face. Something else was eating at him, waiting impatiently for any opportunity to justify erupting in boiling fury. Retail employees run into folks like this all the time, folks with ticking time bombs in their brains, looking for any chance to lash out. The best and safest course of action for me was to keep moving. I gave him a quick, respectful nod as I skirted the simmering psycho and the potential legal catastrophe, giving both as much space as I could.

He glared at me the whole way.

Next aisle. Nobody.

I looked toward the back wall. No Mrs. Toenails.

I wondered if Sammy was having any luck on his side of the store. He had HABA, Health and Beauty products like toothpaste and shampoo, Dry Food, and all the crazy candy and chips and snacks from all over the world that had already expired last century or would sometime far off in the next one. I didn't think he would find her. Morning merch would probably have noticed an old woman as they stocked the aisles.

Maybe not though. I knew the store's lone forklift driver would happily run down anyone if they lingered too long in his way. His name was something that was pretty much all consonants, and since I couldn't sound it out in my head, I couldn't remember it. He had a habit of grinding his back teeth together, forever chewing on an imaginary cigar. He treated the aisles like an F1 track, and he'd get a bonus if he finished early. Of course, there was no such thing as a bonus anywhere to be found for hourly employees at FOOD4U!, but that never stopped some people going above and beyond their duties for reasons I never could fathom. Still, even if the forklift driver had hit her and was somehow unaware of it, customers would eventually trip over her. If nothing else, they'd track down an employee and complain they couldn't get their carts down an aisle because it was blocked with a lifeless body.

Out of the three of us, Gloria might have a better chance at finding someone lost in the maze of clothing racks and endless shelves of shoes in the center of the store. It was far too easy to get stuck behind older women who waddled through those tight aisles in perpetual slow motion like sleepy penguins lost in a blizzard, so I tended to go the long way round when hauling trash to the back of the store at the end of the day. I'm the poster child for stretching out the clock while doing as little as possible, but even I had limits to my patience.

At the back of the store, the basic shelves of merchandise were replaced by much taller, industrial warehouse racks that reached almost to the ceiling. Excess merch was stored up in these heavy steel racks in shrink-wrapped pallets. I'd heard of stupid but at least halfway harmless internet trends where teenagers would hide among the toilet paper or whatever until the store closed at night, then have the place to themselves, but I didn't think Mrs. Toenails was overly worried about her followers on Insta.

I was right. Or at least, she wasn't hiding behind the toilet paper.

I turned right down the last aisle and almost collided with the plump woman with the patently phony service animal. She'd planted herself in the middle of the aisle, clutching the squirming rat with one hand while pointing at me with her other hand in an attempt to stop me. She wore an unflattering white sweater plastered with some name that I guessed was the designer, Marc or Mare or something. I never understood why people loved wearing clothes with various mystifying names in pompous fonts all over the fabric. I always felt like I was missing something, like there was special information out in the world that was not meant for me. For example, the guy staring at plastic forks was wearing one of those Anti-Social Social Club hoodies I see everywhere. Fuck does that mean? All I heard every time was the Anthrax song.

The lady with the dog demanded, "Do you work here?"

I said, "No," and kept walking.

To make that work, you have to mean it. No eye contact. And never, ever stop moving. Usually, the customers don't know what to say next, because "Do you work here?" is not a genuine question. They're not actually interested in the answer. They know it already. It's just an opening, a way to get to, "Help me. I need..." So, if an employee doesn't immediately acquiesce, the customer usually doesn't have a follow-up.

The lady with the dog watched me walk past with her mouth open.

I didn't care. The vet had me feeling rattled. I didn't think this woman would kick my ass or anything like that, but I didn't feel like dealing directly with any customers anytime soon. I kept going along the back wall, holding my breath when I passed the chicken room. At some point, FOOD4U! wanted to emulate Costco and Sam's Club, deciding that hot, roasted chickens was just what they needed to recover from the ice cream and frozen yogurt counters they'd tried installing as a kind of high-fat version of Starbucks inside most of the bigger stores. The sweet ice cream and yogurt didn't quite work out because while people could shop and drink coffee at the same time, most lacked the hand-eye coordination to shop while eating an ice cream cone. Employees were the happiest to see the whole endeavor end, since everything in the store, *everything*, had been coated in sticky smears.

Now we had a chicken rotisserie machine. FOOD4U! had gotten two dozen of the creaking behemoths for next to nothing when a fast-food franchise went under in Georgia. The chickens, raised on some factory farm God knows where, arrived more or less frozen, minus all the interior organs and feathers. For reasons that nobody bothered to explain to the hourly employees, our particular rotisserie machine had been installed in a tiny, metal-lined room at the far end of the store, instead of near the front doors. The giant rotisserie machine filled most of the space, capable of roasting up to 120 chickens at a time, sink on one side and drying rack on the other, with a connecting door to Receiving and Trash.

The chickens were impaled on long spears that slotted into a revolving chain and slowly rotated for about an hour. Each fully roasted chicken was dumped into a cheap plastic container that snapped shut, sealing the heat inside to maintain a steady few thousand degrees Fahrenheit. These were shoved through the back of the heated display case that faced the back aisle. Customers could then grab whichever chicken took their fancy from the front. This glass display was kept so ridiculously hot, the bird carcasses had a tendency to melt the plastic containers, soldering microplastics to chicken fat. Most employees had sense enough to stay far away because of the overwhelming heat, but Abid seemed perfectly content to roast along with the chickens, suspiciously cheerful even. He had to use three hair nets to cover his entire beard.

Today, it looked like there was some kind of trouble with the rotisserie machine. While Yann struggled with the doors, Abid proved he was no idiot. He happily let Yann take charge and stood well back, chatting with a customer. The customer was a thin little guy with round John Lennon glasses that made his eyes look uncomfortably small, especially since right underneath the glasses was a startlingly large handlebar mustache that must have taken half an hour every morning to tame. They seemed to be talking about all the kinds of spices that Abid wanted to use, but his hands were tied because the chickens arrived at the store already preseasoned. While the two were chatting, Yann kept impotently yanking on the doors, quietly cursing the machine in his native language. He held a crescent wrench and screwdriver in his left hand but didn't look like he knew what to do with them.

If Yann was the guy management had sent back here to fix something mechanical, then that meant that Don had called off again. Don was the maintenance guy, corporate speak for a janitor. He was a solid enough employee for going around the store, collecting garbage and replacing the bags with his big gray tilt truck, sweeping once in a while, but his chance to really shine was when various components like doorknobs, paper towel dispensers, broken carts, and the like around the aging building fell apart and needed repair and rebuilding. These assignments tended to take a while, but he knew what he was doing, and once he was finished, things usually worked better than ever. I tried to keep at least a yard or more between us, since Don's breath smelled so strongly of his "medicine," I was worried about the inevitable massive fireball if he exhaled near an open flame.

He called out on a regular basis. He had more food poisoning than anybody I'd ever known. I was usually the one Gloria would track down in order to formally pass along the responsibility of collecting garbage. The first few times, I'd try and counter by saying that I was part of the cart crew, not maintenance. Gloria would give me one of her thin smiles and recite the corporate line about how all employees of FOOD4U! were part of the maintenance crew as everyone was responsible for picking up trash. I didn't bother to argue anymore and tried to make a mental note to check for the maintenance truck near the restrooms, where Don would usually abandon it near the end of his day. This was a utility trash tilt truck, a big gray plastic wedge on two wheels. Sometimes though, nobody knew where he'd left it, Don included. You'd have to wander through the store to find it. Apart from being inside, I didn't mind that much. Another way to squeeze the clock.

It was only too easy to picture the gelatinous chicken ooze that had gummed up the rotisserie doors, so I moved quickly past the empty case to wait for Sammy and Gloria at the wide swinging doors that led to Receiving in the middle of the back wall. There weren't many customers this morning, and they were easy to ignore. Looking straight down the main center aisle, I couldn't see Gloria, just a few people wandering around in the typical shopping daze.

Sammy came around the freezer. This was one half of a large, sort of separate building inside the bigger FOOD4U! with glass doors on three sides so customers could find their frozen TV dinners, chicken nuggets, fish fillets, ice cream, tater tots, and the rest of the cheap processed garbage that tasted so good. The cooler was on the other side, a big ass refrigerator where we kept the milk and eggs and yogurt and about four tons of cheese. Employees used a corridor just wide enough for pallets and a forklift behind these two structures to stock everything from the inside. Sometimes, usually around August, when the air in Illinois grew thick and the cloying heat sucked all your energy out to evaporate in the sun, we'd hide in the freezer and skate around on the icy concrete if the stock was low enough.

FOOD4U! corporate policy kept the essentials, the merchandise that people actually came for, mostly cheap food, in the farthest corner of the store from the ENTRANCE. That way, customers had to pass through everything else the company was trying to get rid of, invariably picking up something that was never originally on their grocery list. It was just another method of squeezing people just a little tighter, getting a bit more blood from each rock.

Sammy caught my questioning look and shrugged. He hadn't found her either. We pushed through the swinging doors. Back End stretched almost the entire width of the building and contained a loading dock wide enough for two trucks, a hydraulic cardboard press, the garbage compactor connecting the chute to the dumpster outside, pallets of merchandise, a small fleet of rolling pallet jacks to move all the merch around, an eye-wash station that mostly collected dust, the forklift at its charging station, and Oskar the Grouch's workbench.

Oskar hadn't earned his nickname because he looked like the famous green dude on Sesame Street or anything like that. No. He really was a grumpy bastard. Oskar managed Back End like a vile despot, snapping at FOOD4U! employees and terrorizing the truck drivers delivering a load. He was born someplace far, far away, somewhere in whatever they were calling the Soviet Union these days, but had adopted the American West mythos as his own and tended to wear brightly colored snap-buttoned cowboy shirts and black boots with a toe so sharp it could puncture tires, as if his real job was riding the range. It's a shame the snakeskin boots in New Arrivals were undoubtedly too big for him. There was an employee bathroom in Back End, next to his workbench, but Oskar kept it locked and somehow possessed the only key. Dragons hoard gold with less ferocity than Oskar held onto his key. Most employees didn't even know the Receiving bathroom even existed.

He swiveled on his stool, somehow still hunched over the workbench, and glared at us.

I gave Oskar my most dazzling smile right back.

I'm not sure if he knew it for sure or not, but the two of us played a game whenever I was forced to interact with him. The game was simple. Usually, because Oskar kept his radio turned off, claiming the batteries were always dying on him, me or Sammy would get sent all the way back to Receiving with a message, especially if we were dumping a load of garbage from the lot and were headed back there anyway. So even though I was the one supposed to pass a message along, I would try to never speak first. I'd stay mute and delay, mentally timing how long it took Oskar to get impatient and break down and open his mouth.

"What?" he finally snapped.

Only seven Mississippi's that time.

"How's the day been treating you, Oskar?" Unbeknownst to him, the second part of the game had begun. Again, this was simple. How far could I push him before he really crashed out?

He made a sound halfway between a sigh and a growl.

"How's the wife? Kids?" I asked, my voice pure butter and syrup.

"What?" It really did sound like somebody snapping a wet towel.

"Everybody good?"

"What do you want?"

I would have kept going, but he was clearly in an especially foul mood today, and I was always a little worried I might push things too far, and it would backfire in ways I couldn't anticipate. I surrendered. "Have you seen Mrs. Toenails back here? Or at all?"

"Customers not allowed back here," Oskar said.

"Yeah, I get that. Not what I asked. Have you seen her?"

This time, the bastard waited *me* out. In his eyes, he'd already answered my stupid question. He stared at us until I finally gave up and said, "I guess that's a '*no*' then."

Oskar turned back to his computer screen, finished with us. Me and Sammy gave each other a shrug. Sammy rolled his eyes, and I smirked. We pushed through the doors and stepped back into the main floor. We leaned on the bollards on either side of the doorway, thick concrete posts to protect the doorway from any accidental collisions from the forklift and surveyed the rest of the store.

Not much was happening. Employees went about their jobs with the same dull, defiant look in their eyes. Customers milled around, their own eyes empty and emotionless. Most of them seemed to be moving even slower than usual.

Mrs. Toenails didn't pop out and shout "SURPRISE!"

Gloria appeared a few minutes later.

Me and Sammy shook our heads.

"As expected," she said. "Mrs. Merriweather is hard to miss, I suppose." She turned from us to look back at the store as well, taking it all in.

"What do we do now?" Sammy asked.

"It may be time to call the police," Gloria said, weighing each word. She didn't sound happy about it, but I don't think it was because of the situation. It was the way she said "police," like the word tasted rotten. This caught me off guard. It never had occurred to me that Gloria may have reason to view law enforcement with a hint of suspicion or even outright hostility. She was a Sunday school teacher for God's sake. But then again, maybe I was making assumptions. And you know what they say when you assume something...she was South Side after all, so it's not like it was outta nowhere. But it was still kinda jarring.

We followed Gloria straight down the center aisle, back through the registers at Front End. Like I said, sometimes it wasn't the worst thing to have one of the more non-essential positions because it meant if something unexpected happened in the store, you'd get pulled away from your usual boring duties and get to participate in some kind of snipe hunt. For the most part, employees might as well have been sponges, passing the time by moving as little as possible, soaking up pennies from the corporation as the minutes and hours of our lives pile up and slip away. The idea of "killing" time is repulsive. It's like you're killing your own existence, so it was better to have something simple to keep my brain occupied. If it wasn't too physically taxing and it ate up the time, these sojourns were usually welcome. Sometimes, though, it could backfire, involving some awful task that left you filthy and exhausted. Those kinds of days always made the clock slow.

This though? Wandering around, poking into corners, behind boxes, looking for a missing customer? Not so bad. It sure as hell beat peeling wet garbage out of the carts after a thunderstorm.

Along the way, our trio got a few curious looks

from the other employees. Again, anything out of the ordinary, anything that broke the monotony would draw attention, curiosity. We responded to the questioning expressions with microscopic shrugs. Employees can say plenty to each other with just their facial expressions, body language, or simply the eyes. Usually, it was a quick look that conveyed this particular customer was a giant fucking pain in the ass. These interactions had spread to other, still silent gestures. Such as fist bumps with your close buds when you get to work. A nod to associates that you've exchanged more than a few words with. Or a slight raising of the chin to other coworkers you respect but haven't spoken to much. Not to mention how you'd deliberately ignore those you didn't like. By the time we'd gotten to Front End and slipped through the row of cash registers, most every employee on the clock that day knew something was up.

The administrative end of things lay just beyond Front End. The long Customer Service counter was straight ahead, the employee break room and the main restroom down to the left. The main office was off to the right. Kyle was just slinking out of there, no doubt looking to hide out in liquor, but Gloria spotted him and nailed him in place with her gaze.

"I'm afraid we could not locate Mrs. Merriweather," she told him. "It looks to be time to involve the authorities."

Kyle flinched as the unpleasant possibility of cops thoroughly checking out the store crawled through his head. If the police got involved, there was undoubtedly some corporate form or another that he'd have to fill out, admitting law enforcement had been summoned to the premises, and then he'd have the pleasure of personally handing that burning paper bag of dogshit to the head office. That would invite all kinds of unwanted questions from his bosses. And a corporate walk was scheduled for tomorrow. I didn't think this store had ever lost a customer before, and I could see Kyle was weighing the consequences against other horrifying scenarios where he might be found responsible, like a Salmonella outbreak or a crib that kills a kid.

Forget dirty registers. If the cops found a health hazard or some kind of illegal storage of something or other with corporate coming tomorrow, Kyle would well and truly be fucked, like a porn actress who suddenly and off contract finds herself in the middle of a spit roast.

It was obvious to all of us that Kyle wanted desperately to pawn this particular task off on Gloria, someone else, anyone else. His mind raced through the possibilities. Problem was, Kyle was never an idea kind of guy. To him, thinking outside the box was damn near a fireable offense. He was a useful idiot for corporate, someone who was used to letting everyone else figure out solutions and actually do the work while he took credit for anything that went right. Planning ahead was rarely used as any kind of strategy. So his mind ran around like a spider trapped in a bathtub.

Gloria coldly waited him out, using her silence as starvation in a siege.

Kyle ultimately found and seized on one tried-and-true tactic to justify almost anything, a manager's classic first and last strategy: delay, delay, delay. "The basement," he sputtered.

Gloria blinked. "The basement," she repeated with the same robotic voice she used with Boris.

Sammy and I gave each other a sidelong glance. The *basement*? The basement was strictly off-limits. Like the bathroom back in Receiving, a lot of employees didn't know the basement of this particular FOOD4U! even existed. As far as I knew, nobody used it anymore, not for anything. Not even storage of seasonal shit. I'd never been down there. I don't know anybody had. Even the employees that knew the store had an actual basement never used it for anything illicit, mostly because you couldn't get down there.

There were only two entrances. Inside, down a short hall off the break room, lined with maintenance and storage closets, two large, locked steel doors waited across from a FIRE EXIT. I think common belief was that it was just another storage room management didn't use anymore, and nobody paid any attention.

The second entrance was outside, at the back of the building, just off the loading dock, with wide, steel cellar-type doors that had rusted shut over the years. Management covered these up by piling broken plastic pallets over the doors. I didn't know they were even there until me and Sammy killed half an hour watching a colony of mice dart in and out of cracks where the rusted steel met crumbling asphalt. Sammy and I ultimately decided that mobsters were staging illegal races in the basement, where trained mice were piloting their own remote-controlled 4X4s in fantastical racetracks like something out of Speed Racer and the whole thing was broadcast on the dark web. FOOD4U! was getting paid to keep things quiet.

Sometimes you need to entertain yourself and anybody else around to fill in the hours.

I was genuinely curious to check out the basement, even beyond that particular satisfaction of getting to participate in a wild goose chase that wasted time at work while getting paid. Like I said, nobody I knew had ever been down there, so if nothing else, I was looking forward to a dark, cool break from the searing heat of the parking lot.

"Yeah...yeah, until we check everywhere, we shouldn't bother the cops," Kyle said.

"You truly believe Mrs. Merriweather up and decided all on her own self to go check out the basement?" Now that I was paying attention, I could hear a bit of the caustic South Side edge slipping through the cracks of her generally calm, measured tone when she was irritated. Gloria's head tilted ever so slightly. Kyle was oblivious; that's 'cause he's the GM. For us hourly folks, it's like I said, those of us in the trenches can *read* each other. We're stuck there, day after day. We spend more time with coworkers than family. If you had any I suppose. To me, Gloria's body language was a giant neon flashing warning light. Kyle didn't realize he was treading on very thin ice here. If Gloria's head tilt proceeded with a full neck roll, followed with her gray eyes locking in on Kyle's befuddled expression, then he was in serious trouble. Danger, even.

He kept blustering, "If we have to call the authorities, they will undoubtedly need to look everywhere. I'd rather we make sure there's nothing for them to find, whether it's a customer we've missed or, or anything else, whatever that might be."

Gloria regarded him for a moment. Her head slowly

straightened. The danger had passed for the moment, like a shark leaving a surfer to look for fatter seals. But you never knew when it might be back. "All right," she said. "Therefore, I trust you will keep an eye on the Front End while we investigate the basement?"

Kyle forced a smile like he was pretending he was really enjoying his wife's tuna and macaroni casserole and said, "Of course."

While Gloria went into the office to track down the basement keys, Sammy and me meandered into the break room. I suspected it might take a while, since Gloria had to find two different sets of keys, one being for the floor and ceiling dead bolts, and a separate one for the actual door handles. It was beyond ridiculous that Kyle thought it was possible Mrs. Toenails had somehow slipped into the basement without anybody noticing. So, I wondered if I had time to grab an energy drink from the vending machine. I ultimately realized I really just wanted something halfway sweet and didn't actually need any help keeping awake. It wasn't worth seeing Gloria's disapproval, the slight thinning of her lips, lowering of her eyebrows, whenever she caught me enjoying something full of tons of empty calories.

I really wished I didn't care what Gloria thought.

Like Kyle. I truly couldn't give two shits about his opinion on anything.

But for some reason, I didn't like how it felt if I even suspected I'd let Gloria down in some way. It drove me up the fucking wall because I couldn't figure out what was wrong with me. It was just easier to avoid her, to stay as far away as possible.

I should have grabbed a drink. Gloria was in the office for a long time. Sometimes the break room can be so crowded there's not even an empty chair left. Today, though, there were only a couple employees since the morning merch boys had clocked out and gone home, so Sammy and I had our choice of tables. Thank God. There's not a whole lot in most of our lives that is more awkward than sitting three inches from somebody you don't especially like while you both eat or scroll through your phone and pretend the other doesn't exist because you gotta work side by side for eight goddamn hours. Every day.

Today, the only other employees were Kiko, a nineteen-year-old the size of a jockey with purple hair and black, glittery lipstick that matched her nails. I'd heard she'd either dropped out of or wanted to go to art school. She seemed to spend most of her time at work drawing intricate patterns all over her hands. I'm guessing she might have been part of the team that was responsible for textiles, clothing I guess, since that's where I mostly saw her. But I don't know as she ever did any actual physical labor for the store, far as I could tell. She simply lurked in the aisles like a tiny wraith and vanished if you looked at her directly for too long. She could burn hours off the clock with the best slackers of all time. So, my hat was off to her. Today she was playing with a Game Boy older than me.

Then there was Wanda on the other end of the age range, a boomer enjoying her homemade soup and reading an honest-to-god newspaper, instead of looking at her phone. She was somewhere in her late sixties and would wander outside for a break whenever she felt like it. She was the very definition of old school. She went outside and smoked actual menthol cigarettes instead of vaping in the restroom like everyone else. She was the store's HR coordinator, and we were damn lucky to have her. The main reason being she wasn't a corporate tool. She never had a problem fudging dates and figures in your favor if you ran out of sick time or something stupid like that. Gouging corporate, even a little, tickled the hell out of her.

Me and Sammy found our seats. ESPN was on the TV, but it wasn't some dumbass game, it was one of the hundreds of shows where grown men shouted out at each other between beer and SUV commercials. I couldn't decide if that was better or worse than the usual other channel the employees watched regularly, some paternity test and/or divorce thing. At least it wasn't one of the fucking lunatic news channels, favorited by some of the louder white morning merch boys. That made me want to chew the inside of my cheeks until they bled. The best was *futball*, favorite of all the brown morning merch boys, because it was usually in Spanish, and I could tune it out easier.

Most of the employees didn't really pay much attention to the TV. Their phones were more important. At any given time, you'd hear about five or six different languages, all competing with the TV that nobody dared ever turn off for some reason. The battery in my own phone was a delicate, fickle beast that I'd learned was better not to actually turn on or do anything outside of getting it to play music, so I kept it in my pocket and pretended whatever had the guys on the TV so agitated was somehow important. Sammy watched his animal videos. Odd couples were his favorite, where say, a goat might become a tiger's BFF, instead of, you know, lunch.

It was a very normal, very boring fifteen, twenty minutes, the kind you have every day at that kind of job. Those moments that can't really be called fun but aren't awful exactly. And now that I'm thinking about it, it was the last tedium I ever felt at that job, the last time anything was halfway normal.

At all.

Eventually, Gloria emerged from the office, glaring at a ring of dusty keys and muttering to herself. Turned out, those keys opened the door handles but not the dead bolts. So, it was back to the office. She was growing more irritated by the minute, but it was more than fine with me. Me 'n Sammy were getting paid to sit on our asses, and I wasn't going to complain, even if I was getting seriously bored with whatever the guys were yelling about on TV.

Eventually, though, she found the right set of keys. Gloria slid the dead bolts open first with raspy, scratching sounds like ripping off scabs. Dust or rust sprinkled down. The door handles on this side were levers, each one rotating downward. Gloria twisted the handle on the left door. The handle swung into place with a solid *thunk*. She pulled. The door didn't move. She tried the other door, the right side. Same thing. She put both hands on this handle, and as she yanked, she emitted a little grunt, then looked embarrassed.

The door still didn't move.

Sammy said, "Maybe Mrs. Toenails is holding onto it, you know, on the other side."

"Don't be ridiculous," Gloria said.

Still, we all gave the door a fresh appraisal.

"Perhaps this could use someone with a bit more meat on the bone," Gloria said. "Samuel, why don't you try?" Then, under her breath, "If our GM wants us to check the basement, then we will check the basement."

Sammy curled his thick fist around the handle and pulled, leaning back, putting his weight into it. We heard a dry, ripping sound, and the door moved half an inch. I squatted, locating the source of the tearing sound. It was an ancient rubber bottom seal. I guess the doors had been closed so long the rubber had fused to the threshold. Sammy pulled harder.

A sliver of inky darkness appeared between the door frame and the door. I managed to slip a few fingers into the gap. The door felt warm on the inside for some reason. I remember thinking that was weird. You'd think a dark basement would be at least a little cool. But the basement was weirdly toasty. I hooked four fingers around the door and tugged along with Sammy. The tearing grew louder, filling the hallway, as the rubber ripped away from itself. Tepid, stale air hushed out as we dragged the door open.

Grim concrete stairs descended into absolute darkness.

"Wonderful," Gloria said.

I looked back down the hall to the break room. Kiko and Wanda, drawn by the sound of tearing rubber, were both standing in the entrance to the hallway and watching us.

Gloria shuffled close to the edge of the top step but made no other move to go downstairs. Now that the door was open, her anger had dissipated. Sammy and I flanked her. The stairwell was wide enough that the three of us could walk down side-by-side without brushing against each other. By now, my eyes were adjusting to the dim light. The fluorescents from the hallway spilled down the steps far enough to reach what I thought was the basement floor. I squatted down and squinted into the darkness and was disappointed to see that it was only a landing. Just halfway.

I pictured myself descending these stairs, actually walking down those steps into the dark basement, and the ball of crippling dread that had been building ever since I touched the warm door enveloped my mind in a thick cloud of terror. Look, I've had more than my fair share of panic attacks thanks to a really *fun* childhood, but this was different. It was like every cell in my body wanted to shrink away, as if they knew something I didn't. Thinking on it now, maybe it was some kind of primal warning, some sixth sense that my subconscious understood and was screaming at me to run, to get as far away as possible. The thing is, I don't know if it would have made any difference. Maybe it would be better not to know what was coming. I'm not sure.

Would you want to know your life was going to be over soon, far sooner than you ever expected, and there wasn't a damn thing you could do about it?

"I don't see any light switches. Maybe I should go

get a flashlight," I suggested. My fear had me mimicking Kyle's managerial style: delay, delay, delay. If nothing else, you gotta understand this. This sensation or whatever you want to call it, it was like nothing I'd ever experienced. I couldn't tell if it was only in my head, strictly a mental thing, or if it was instead a physical reaction. It felt like both. I couldn't point my finger at something that actually existed inside of me. It was a phantom, everywhere and nowhere at once.

"They are most likely at the bottom," Gloria said. "I can't remember. The lights were already on during my one brief excursion."

"What's down there?" Sammy asked. He looked like I felt, like he'd eaten a dozen or so too many chili dogs.

Gloria gave a slight shrug. "Some kind of manufacturing plant. Built during the war, converted afterward. I don't remember. It closed in the seventies." She cleared her throat and swallowed. She exhaled through her nose, fingers fluttering. I wondered if I wasn't the only one feeling strange and sick. She inhaled deeply once again, held it, then took the first step down. A few more. A pause. Another. Sammy and I watched her like she was using her own weight to test a rotting bridge.

"Huh," Sammy said. "Check it out." He pointed down.

Gloria twisted to see what he meant and followed his finger to the steps behind her. "Well now." She turned fully, clasping her fingers at her waist. "I'm no Sherlock Holmes, but I'd be willing to bet my annual salary that no one, especially Mrs. Merriweather, has been down these steps for a long, long time."

Her footprints, and only hers, were clearly visible in the fine gray dust that coated the stairs, the concrete steps, the safety rails, everything. I wondered what it was doing to my lungs and was about to suggest that along with a flashlight I could also grab a few of the COVID masks kept in a box at the Customer Service desk when Gloria announced, "I've seen enough. If Kyle feels the need to check himself, he's more than welcome. She's not down there."

Gloria gave a nod that sealed her decision with the force of a thunderclap and then came back up the stairs in a sudden hurry, shooing us out of the way. She closed the door, damn near slammed it. Then she took great care to relock everything exactly how she'd found it and pocketed the keys.

While she was doing that, I looked back toward the break room and saw that the Professor had joined Kiko and Wanda at the edge of the hallway watching us. I frowned. It pissed me off for several reasons. First off, we didn't know he was a professor at that point. We just knew him as a probably homeless guy, definitely an alcoholic, who'd been living out of his car for the past few summers at the edge of our lot. He never bothered anybody and always cleaned up after himself, so none of the employees cared one way or another. He wandered into the store once in a while, bought a couple things, disappeared occasionally, but everybody considered him harmless.

Until I saw him in the break room. Customers weren't allowed in the break room, and that raised my hackles, got me mean. Maybe it was some territorial thing. And I wasn't feeling right. I'm not proud about it. I was gonna say something, but Gloria beat me to it.

She said, "I'm sorry, sir, but this is the employee break room. Customers are free to use the facilities provided."

The Professor acted like he hadn't heard. Or didn't care. He fixed us with a direct stare. "Did you go to the basement?"

Gloria tilted her head. "I'm sorry, but again, sir, the break room is for employees only, I'm afraid." Her voice was surprisingly clear and easy to hear. Despite the sports guys yelling at each other on the TV, I realized that Front End was quieter than usual.

I suppose the Professor did look a little like his namesake from Gilligan's Island. Faded blue button-up business shirt with the sleeves rolled up to the elbows, tan chinos. But where the TV version was surprisingly clean for living on a deserted island, it was pretty clear that this Professor was living out of his car. He wasn't wearing socks, just crusty Teva sandals. His fingernails were long, tips black with grime. A rumpled and frayed knapsack was strapped to his back. It had been a while since he'd shaved, and it looked like he cut his own hair. His eyes were red and too wide as he stared at Gloria. He asked again, "Did you go down there?"

Gloria kept her face expressionless, but I could tell the Professor had her genuinely confused. Three quick claps weren't going to work with this customer. She reconsidered her approach. "Can I ask why you are so interested in our basement?"

Self-awareness caught up to the Professor, and he blinked around at the rest of us, like he'd found himself in a dream where he'd just realized he was naked in public. "I uh, well, that's a reasonable question I suppose." He forced a genial chuckle, a clear invitation for the rest of us to join him. He waited, but when no one made a sound, he said, "I apologize. I can only imagine what you all must be thinking. I must appear a madman. Perhaps we can sit and talk. Please understand this. You need to hear what I have to say."

Gloria frowned. "Sir, this is a place of business. I'm afraid—"

"You should be afraid. All of you. I am. Because this is important. Please. It very well could be a matter of life and death. I'm not exaggerating. You must listen to me."

"Is this a bomb threat?" Kiko's voice was full of hope, like a kid hoping for a snow day.

"I don't—" Gloria started, but a yipping bark erupted just outside the break room. She sighed, said under her breath, "Wonderful. Why rain when it can pour, oh Lord?"

"Please," the Professor said. He'd pulled off his knapsack and now turned it over and over in his hands.

The barking stopped. Gloria tried again. "Sir, I can appreciate your obvious passion, but as I've said, this is a place of business. Perhaps we can work out a time to meet, schedule an appointment?"

The Professor was already shaking his head. "I don't—I don't think we have the time."

"It *is* a bomb threat!" Kiko squealed.

"Hush," Gloria told her, then turned back to the Professor. "Look, sir, I'm doing my best to be accommodating here, but I don't understand the rush. Where's the emergency?"

The dog started yipping again, a furious declaration of some kind of deep dissatisfaction.

The Professor nodded, scratching at the back of his hands. He took a shaky breath, looked like he might burst out sobbing any second. "You're right, of course. I...I've been anticipating this exact moment for a long time. I've practiced it over and over in my mind...and now that it is here...it's nothing like I thought."

"I know the feeling, dude," Sammy said. "Nothing ever turns out like I think it will."

"Yes. Well," Gloria said, trying to get things back on track. "Life is unpredictable, Lord knows."

The barking stopped.

The Professor gave it another shot, exhaling through his nose, then said, with some formality, "I am Professor Jay Schultz. My...colleague, Benjamin Shiftlett, and I devoted our entire careers, our lives really, to studying the idea that this universe...is not the only one." The name Benjamin Shiflett rang a bell, but I couldn't remember why. The Professor didn't wait for any kind of response or acknowledgment and plunged ahead in full lecture mode. "Unlike those poor deluded fools who subscribe to string theory and their ilk. I'm talking of course about the quantum foam theory. I'm sure at the very least, you must be familiar with d'Albe and Wheeler's work..." At this he did look at us, checking for any recognition. Finding absolutely none, he continued. "Well, they, and many others, they theorized that this, our world, our universe, was not alone, that in fact, there were many, so many they may as well be infinite, and that—"

"Dude! The multiverse! Sure!" Sammy boomed. "Spider-Man!"

The Professor paused, the outburst derailing his speech. "Uh, I, uh, sure, that is, I guess, in some ways. But not really, no. Look, that isn't the important thing. The important thing, the most important thing, that I want you to understand, is that our world, it may be finished." He looked at us, eyes lit with panic and more than a little sadness. "I don't—I don't know if there's anything we can do about it. I hope. I hope." He seemed to be pleading with us for something, but none of us had any idea what he needed so badly.

Gloria's back had gotten stiffer and straighter as the Professor had gone on about the quantum physics view of reality, and I knew this atheist blasphemy was butting up against her Baptist point of view so hard it was throwing up sparks. So I was expecting her to let him have it, to cast this demon out of the break room, but instead she answered diplomatically, even if the tone was a bit dry. "I suppose there are plenty of ideas about how the universe works."

"Not just *the* universe. *A* universe. *Our* universe, yes. One of many, many."

"Whichever." Gloria tilted her head the other way. "It still doesn't explain your emergency."

"That's why we need to talk. Right away."

"Sir, I wish I could accommodate your request. I do. But I'm afraid I am in the middle of an audit, along with a mountain of shifts to schedule, and we can't have you barging into an employees-only area of the store with some preposterous story." She let out an exasperated sigh and glanced upward for moral support. Without thinking, she added, mostly to herself, "And with a missing customer, we don't need—"

"Someone's missing?" the Professor asked. "When? How long? Now?"

"Okay, that's enough. One, it's none of your business. Two, you need to leave."

"You must listen to what I have to say."

"No, no I don't. I've decided that whatever you have to say is important to you, and you alone. We are too busy for this nonsense. Wanda, when you are finished with your break, would you please call the police and let them know that while Mrs. Merriweather's Jeep is in our parking lot, we have been unable to track Mrs. Merriweather herself down. She is missing."

The Professor raised his voice. "Please. You don't understand. The police can't help. We don't have much time."

The TV froze for a moment, pixels stuttering, before it resumed as normal.

"That is precisely true," Gloria said. She nodded at Wanda, underlining the request to contact the police. Wanda caught the meaning and left the break room, heading for the office. "We do not have enough time. Which is why you need to leave so the rest of us can get back to our responsibilities."

The Professor's open mouth snapped shut. It flattened into a grim slash. He glared at Gloria. When he spoke, an edge of anger shoved the panic aside. "You say there's someone missing. That is one very large sign that it may already be too late."

Gloria matched his anger. "What? Hmmm? What 'may be too late?'"

The Professor took a step forward, shaking his

head. "You must understand this one unequivocal fact. We. Are. Not. Alone."

"No, we're not," Kiko said, looking back at the break room doorway. The dog in the hot-pink service harness had trotted a few feet inside the break room and now stood shivering, watching us with pop-eyed wildness. We all stared at it for a full second without saying anything. It barked again, like it was trying to tell us something important. The piercing yap echoed around the cheap tables and buzzing fluorescents.

Gloria rolled her eyes in disgust. The day was getting out of control, and it wasn't even noon yet. "Enough. Enough. Either you leave now, or we'll have the authorities escort you out. Your choice."

The TV froze again.

The Professor kept shaking his head as he said, "No. There is no choice. Not anymore." He opened the knapsack, thrust his hand inside, and when he withdrew it, he held a small semi-automatic pistol in a trembling hand. He had just enough time to say, "I'm sorry. Don't make me—" when Gloria exploded in sudden motion. I don't know if the fact that he had a firearm had even registered in my brain before Gloria shot her right arm out, some small dark cylinder in her own hand, while at the exact same time, she smashed the wrist of his gun hand with her left forearm, knocking the barrel away. It happened so fast I barely followed the stuttering, choppy movement, as if random frames had been cut out of a filmstrip. Thinking back, it's clear Gloria had taken more than her fair share of self-defense classes. The motion was practiced, instinctive. She'd performed that particular move a thousand times.

I'm pretty sure the Professor had not.

Poor guy was not prepared for what came next.

Gloria hit that big orange trigger and blasted him with some kind of especially vicious pepper spray from six inches away, straight into his open, unsuspecting face. Who the hell knows where she got it, or even if it was technically legal. All I know is that she turned most of the canister loose on the Professor. The reddish spray exploded across his face, blasting into his open mouth, barreling up his nose, soaking into the sensitive upper nasal passages, shellacking his unprotected eyeballs and burrowing under his eyelids. He immediately dropped the pistol and staggered back into the wall, hard enough to crack the glass cases where schedules were posted.

A fine cloud of the stuff billowed back and had the rest of us squeezing our eyes shut and pulling our shirts over our mouths. The dog gave a shocked bark and retreated to the safety of Front End, where it continued to scold everyone in earshot. Only Gloria seemed immune to the spray. I got the feeling this wasn't her first rodeo. She kicked the pistol away and kept the nozzle trained on the Professor even after she'd released the trigger, in case the first long blast wasn't enough.

It was more than enough.

The Professor bounced off the glass cases, hit a chair, and went down, gagging, thrashing, dying. He landed on his back, mindless and blind from pain and shock. He spasmed, and a bubble of greenish vomit popped over his mouth and nose. Most of it was sucked immediately back inside into his airway. Legs flopped on the break room floor. He clawed at the air above him, primal brain suddenly screaming in desperation for only one thing. Oxygen.

"You dumb moth..." Gloria began to say, catching herself when she remembered the other employees in the break room. She shook her head in anger, disbelief. "Why'd you have to go and pull a piece? What is wrong with you?" She kneeled next to him, turning the convulsing Professor onto his side, using a few fingers to scoop as much of the puke out of his mouth as she could. "Samuel, I need your help. I'm afraid this gentleman needs CPR. Kiko, make sure Wanda is calling 9-1-1. I may have overestimated the threat level here." She pounded on his back.

The dog kept barking.

Gloria's eyes found me. "Joseph. Find Kyle. At the very least, he should know what's going on." The Professor spasmed again, struggling to breathe through pea soup. Gloria looked back down at him and frowned, scraped more vomit out of his mouth. "Don't you dare die on me, dumbass. That's all I need this morning."

Kyle wasn't anywhere I could see in Front End like he'd promised.

Like the rest of the store today, Front End was surprisingly peaceful. For once. Almost all the customers seemed to be either looking straight ahead, lost in that classic consumer trance, or staring at their phones with the same mindless apathy.

Every department in the store had its own issues. The chicken room had the crippling smell and general sanitation issues with shocking amounts of congealed industry-farmed chicken fat. Hell, take a look at Exhibit A, the gummed-up rotisserie machine. Receiving could get insanely chaotic if too many deliveries showed up at the same time, severely irritating its fascist overlord with his endless procedures and red tape. And I could spin endless stories about the insanity of the parking lot. Fistfights, drunk drivers, extreme weather. Not to mention how customers would destroy an astonishing quantity of merch throughout the store that needed to be fixed. All day, every day.

Yet, out of all of the departments, Front End was special. No other department had such a huge variety of unexpected issues. Front End was where the rubber really met the road. Front End was where waves of consumers crashed against the cold rocks of economic realities, want and need versus sacrifice, and the subsequent storms generated out of that frothing sea of people. I mean, when we were truly busy, *loud* doesn't begin to convey the chaos and seething roar. Screaming kids, cashiers shouting for a supervisor to override something or other, indignant customers arguing the price on the sign was lower than what was rung up, and c'mon, let's face it, they were usually right, mostly thanks to wrong instructions and/or my favorite, basic employee incompetence. Or demanding a steep discount because the package was damaged, often caused by the very same customer on the way to the registers, and it was the least the store could do. Or if FOOD4U! ever ran out of something, the customer was entitled to a large discount on whatever they had to select instead. Or something was the wrong color.

Or it was on sale last month, so why not now? Or a good old-fashioned shouting match between a long-married couple when their mutual seething hatred exploded. Being in public made no difference. Bonus points if you couldn't understand the language. Or a thousand other complaints, meltdowns, an honest-to-god scream once in a while, and sometimes even laughter.

When FOOD4U! was busy, the masses of people didn't exactly ebb and flow like water, instead customers seemed to pop into existence here and there only to fade away a moment later, like slow-motion fireworks. You'd blink, and people appeared and disappeared at the whims of a bored supernatural toddler. If you had to get through the storm of people, you moved with a spatial awareness those sportsball guys would have been proud of. See, customers never paid any attention to where they shoved their carts. They were more concerned with their receipts or phones, so you learned to walk with your arms up and ready. All of this was yet another reason I disliked being inside. Especially when we were busy.

The black conveyor belts were reliably filthy, and I tried not to put anything on them as they were only cleaned and sanitized if corporate might be sniffing around. When I think about it, I guess I tried to buy as little as possible from the store. Most of my calories came from the fast-food places on every corner in the world. Look, I know exactly what those places are and what eating that stuff all the time will do to me. I'm not stupid. It's all poison, and I hate those corporations with a passion, along with most every other corporation I guess, but yeah, I'm ashamed to admit that I still fork over my wages for the convenience, the taste, and something else I can't put my finger on. Call it what you want. All I know is that fast food ticks nearly every box regarding addiction for me. I'm not exactly ready to give somebody a blow job for a Big Mac, but occasionally shoplifting deodorant from Walmart or Target so I can afford Taco Bell on the way home? Well, I'm not here to judge anybody.

Except when it comes to illegally parking in a handicapped spot.

Then I'll judge the hell out of you.

Fact is, if you parked in a handicapped spot and didn't need it, you'd be lucky if all we did was shove stray carts at your car, played pinball with it.

I wasn't the only one who sized up customers and made capricious evaluations. The cashiers, for the most part, were a sullen bunch, just trying to get through the day balancing actual customer service while simultaneously ignoring said customer. God help you if they made sustained eye contact at any point in the transaction. If they stared right at you, it meant you'd fucked up your role as a customer, and now they had to deal with your sorry dumb ass. I think this skill was a trick they learned from Gloria. The cashiers generally kept their eyes on the product, interacting with the customer as little as possible, only mumbling a greeting and a total. If they did look up, it was usually in any direction except the person in front of them, like at the clock above the office door. They knew damn well never to check their phones. This was something that Gloria had drilled into all employees, especially those in the Front End. She couldn't force anybody to be friendly and cheerful, but she considered checking your phone, even just the time, in front of the customers was one of the worst forms of rudeness, up there with spitting in someone's face.

Sure, some of the cashiers were friendly enough to the customers. For whatever reason, they seemed to genuinely enjoy interacting with their fellow man. This made me suspicious as hell. They greeted folks warmly, asked questions and seemed actually invested in the answers, even asking follow-up questions. Their smiles made it all the way to their eyes.

These people were rare.

Today there was only one. Shelley. She was, without a doubt, the sweetest employee in the whole store. Shelley's personality was light and fluffy, like an overripe dandelion. And yeah, she did kind of come across as about as smart as a dandelion too, since she'd often space out, and you'd have to repeat yourself a few times before she could focus and latch onto the meaning behind your words. She was always patient and never snitched on anybody, so that was pretty much all that mattered to me.

Once a customer, some mean old lady who snarled at everyone, called Shelley a "bitch cow," for not automatically deducting fifty percent because some box was slightly worn or the plastic was a bit torn. I'm not sure what a bitch cow is exactly, maybe a dog that turns into a cow on full moons, or *vice-versa* for that matter, but it didn't faze Shelley. She just smiled sadly as she held out the receipt and said, "I hope your day gets better, hon." The mean lady took the receipt and huffed away without saying anything else. This small interaction fed employee conversations for a few days until some guy lost his mind and started shouting at Razeih, another cashier, and the employees had a new story to dissect and exaggerate.

Opinions regarding the *hows* and *whys* varied, but most employees more or less settled into two camps. Shelley's supporters said her response proved that she really was just a sweet and gentle soul. Haters said it was only because she was a walking pharmacy and was blitzed out of her mind, all day, every day. Of course, Shelley was happy to see anyone and everyone. When you're living in a cartoon world, wouldn't you be?

I thought about that a lot, about how both might be true, and it was ultimately the simple act of egoless kindness that mattered, not Shelley's intention or state of mind, or even the customer's baffled reaction. Then I'd always follow that thought up by wondering if I just wanted an excuse to take a whole shitload of inappropriate medication.

The lights flickered. I don't know why, but fluorescent light feels slower than sunlight, and so it didn't feel so much that the lights were blinking on and off with a strobe effect, but rather the intermittent, artificial greenish fluorescent rays blended with the weak sunlight that spilled from the building's skylights, and for a few surreal moments, the light took on an ominous quality, as if it would infect you with a horrible sickness if it reached your eyeballs, touched your bare skin.

Front End didn't feel right. It wasn't just the tainted light, the very air was disorienting, and nothing felt normal. Something was off. I just couldn't put my finger on what.

Shelley had been assigned the second register closest to the EXIT, smiling as usual and blissfully unaware she was carrying most of the conversation with a customer in a white top who looked familiar. I realized it was the lady with the dog, but the dog wasn't in sight.

Our FOOD4U! Front End had around a dozen registers. Of those, only about six or seven worked at any given time. Five were open today. Shelley was on my left. Near the middle was Tim. Tim was one of the quietest people in the store and would mostly just stand there blinking at you, unless that is, you happen to mention anything about sports. It made no difference what kind. He knew everything. Period. Everything. His head was full of so many statistics I figured at some point he had to have been making things up. Like I'd know anyway. I suppose I could have looked it all up online, but it was easier to take his word for it.

Next down the line was Carmalita. You could gauge her level of irritation by how hard and fast she cracked her omnipresent gum. I think it was a kind of witchcraft. Somehow, she'd create tiny pockets of air in the gum, which she then took great delight in popping, a process she'd repeat thousands and thousands of times all day long. It didn't matter that chewing gum on the clock was a clear violation of company policy. It was kind of like me and listening to music out on the lot. You can only push people so far, take so much away before they draw a line, no matter how arbitrary or petty. Her gum was just a little something that management learned to ignore. Besides that, nobody wanted to get on her bad side. Carmalita's skill with sarcasm was razor sharp. The victim rarely even knew they'd been sliced wide open until much later.

At the far end was Razieh. Mouth breathing White guys always seemed to choose her line mostly so they could ask why she still wore her hijab in America. Didn't she know she was in a free country now? Didn't need to wear that shit here? It didn't matter that it wasn't more than a thin scarf loosely wrapped around her head and shoulders. What I think *did* matter, however, was that Razeih was a stunningly beautiful woman in her late 20s. These guys seemed to take it personally that she hadn't abandoned her heritage for no clear reason only because she lived in Illinois. If any of the bullshit ever got under her skin, I never saw it. She'd just give these chuckleheads a thin smile that would make Gloria proud and move to the next with an almost supernatural level of patience.

No dickheads today, though. But as I liked to say, be patient, it's still early. At the moment, everything around the registers was more of a placid pond than raging whitewater. Even if things were moving more on the slow side, the transactions were peaceful. People stood quietly, waiting their turn, surprisingly tolerant for once. Maybe that's what had me feeling like I'd put my hand in a spider's nest. It most likely wouldn't kill me, but that didn't mean I was comfortable.

Except for the barking dog, nothing was obviously wrong out here.

Nothing obvious, but it still felt very, very *wrong*.

I couldn't see Kyle anywhere. I figured I'd hit the office first, since it was closer. If he wasn't in there, the liquor department was the next obvious place to look. That was halfway across the store, though, down by the freezers.

The lights started flickering again.

"Need a sup over here!" Carmelita yelled. "My register ain't working. Where's Yann?"

"Mine is down as well," Razieh called out.

Shelley held the change out to the lady with the dog, perpetual smile in place. "Here ya go, hon."

The other lady didn't react, didn't reach out, didn't move to take the bills and coins.

"Ma'am? Here ya go." Shelley's hand stretched out farther.

The lady blinked and flinched, clearly shocked to find herself at a register with a waiting cashier. "Oh. Oh my. I'm sorry. I, uh...I don't know what..." She tried to swallow. "Brain fog?" She reached up and clasped Shelley's hand. "Thank you."

"Thank you." Shelley went to draw back, but the lady wouldn't let go. "Thank you?" Shelley tried to pull away again, not too concerned. Mildly perplexed.

The lady held on, her own expression just as confused. "I...I..."

"Ma'am?" Shelley asked, lifting her wrist, pulling the lady's arm along. "Wait. What are you...what are, hey, hey, hey!" Instead of being angry, Shelley began to giggle. "That tickles."

The coins fell from the lady's hand to the counter, spilling onto the floor. One of the bills spun away. The second bill seemed stuck to their palms. The lady still hadn't let go of Shelley's hand. If anything, she seemed to be holding it tighter. Weirder still, Shelley wasn't trying to pull away anymore. They looked at each other, and their expressions were unreadable in the unreliable light.

I heard a sudden crash from somewhere back near Receiving, a reverberating BANG that echoed throughout the store. It may have been followed by a yelp or shout, but I couldn't be sure. I angled my head, straining to hear anything else. There was nothing. The silence continued to stretch, offering no other clues. I decided it wasn't an immediate emergency.

The dog appeared, trotting around the last register down toward the exit end of the register line. It fixed a bitter stare at Shelley and its owner and barked so ferociously both of its front legs bounced clear off the concrete. This barking, it wasn't looking for treats or attention. This dog was fucking pissed.

Shelley and the lady kept holding hands with no further movement. Their arms had sagged down to rest on the little raised check-writing counter, but that was all. They faced each other, seemingly staring into each other's eyes, but it didn't look like they really saw each other at all. Their expressions were caught somewhere between considering a move in chess and about to sneeze.

I hadn't moved either. I found that I couldn't, incapacitated by indecision. Should I find Kyle, or should I try and figure out what was happening between Shelley and her customer, or should I go after the damn barking dog? If I tried to chase the dog, it would simply run away, and then I'd be the fat guy stumbling after a little dog and trying not to fall down in the security video where everybody gathers around the monitors and laughs their asses off while capturing it with their phone to post later on Reddit. I couldn't think straight, couldn't push through my hesitation.

I knelt and set about retying my shoelaces for a quiet moment to breathe.

Over my right shoulder, I heard, "Hello? Hello? Why you playin'?" Carmelita demanded of her customer. Now, I ain't gonna lie. Carmelita's accent could sometimes get a little out of control. Sometimes she sounded like someone shouting cooking instructions at you from a few feet underwater. But if the customer was an asshole, especially a regular who happened to be an asshole like Boris, I understood how easy it was to lose your patience, and I didn't blame her.

Customers never did understand that corporate was monitoring the registers, keeping a close eye on each cashier's speed, efficiency, and accuracy. And once they were at the register, they'd immediately forget what it was like to impatiently wait like everybody else and plumb ignore the people behind them. All of sudden, they wanted to go slow, take their time, and dictate the pace of the transaction according to their own needs.

Today, though, none of the customers paid any attention to the delay between Shelley and the lady. Nobody seemed to be in a hurry.

Carmelita said, "Hello?"

Carmelita's customer didn't say anything.

I automatically tugged three times on the shoelaces, the final step of the process, and stood. The panicky urge to do something physical, anything, broke through the surface of my mind.

I started for the office. Where the fuck was Kyle?

Then the power went out.

The artificial lights vanished first. The fluorescents and sodium vapors sputtered and died out completely, leaving the store engulfed in the dull gray haze of weak sunlight seeping through skylights that hadn't been cleaned in years. Maybe over a decade. When the lights were working as normal, you were forever surrounded by six or seven constantly shifting shadows of yourself. Now, in the absence of artificial light, bathed only in the diffused, colorless sunlight instead, shadows disappeared completely.

It made me feel like a ghost.

Front End was now so quiet I could hear power leaving the various components of the store. The scratching hum of the lights faded away first, followed by the disappearing rumbles of the air conditioning units across the roof as they slowly spun to stop, the loud, confident voices from the TV in the break room died mid-sentence, and finally a hush as the steady growl and hiss of the freezer and cooler in the back of the store died. The electricity that had pulsed throughout the store slipped away and was gone.

Even the damn dog was quiet for once.

Once you stepped through the office doorway, on your immediate left you'd find the door to what was optimistically named Customer Service. It had a long counter open to Front End, and customers could theoretically return merchandise in exchange for actual cash. Per corporate's instructions, Kyle had maintenance post large signs on every pillar and open wall space that promised all items sold by FOOD4U! were "100% GUARANTEED!" in giant baby blue letters, same hue as the company logo. It was all too easy to miss the faint asterisk, buried way up high in the seemingly innocent background pattern. Of course there was an asterisk. If your eyes were good enough, you might be able to read the few vague legal statements at the bottom, including everyone's favorite, "Certain restrictions apply." I'd heard from a dude who'd been stuck at the Customer Service desk for over a year until he quit in disgust that there were literally *hundreds* of certain restrictions. In ten years, I don't know as I'd personally seen a successful return of anything. "Certain restrictions apply," held the same vague, encompassing menace as the phrase stamped all over the employee handbook, "Needs of the business."

Wanda and Kiko stood over a couple of phones at the HR desk. Wanda had the receiver up to her ear, but it didn't look like it was working. Kiko was on the second phone with the same result, repeatedly pressing various buttons. The ceiling in here was much lower than the rest of the store. You could almost reach up and touch the racks of dead fluorescents overhead. Without electricity or a skylight, the office was gloomy and vague, ominous shadows lurked in the corners. Tables and shelves lined the walls, covered with piles of paperwork interrupted only by a few CRT displays and adjoining towers. There were also internal mailboxes for the supervisors and management, a creaking printer and copier the size of a child's coffin, and a first-aid box on the far wall that had might have been refilled sometime during the Clinton administration.

“Where’s Kyle?” I asked.

“His office. He was in there when I got here. Pretty sure anyway,” Wanda said and cocked her head at the doorway, still focused on the phone. Kyle’s office waited on the opposite wall from Customer Service, between a row of file cabinets and the printer. The doorway and file cabinets were shrouded in darkness.

“What happened to the electricity?” Kiko asked.

I shrugged. The door to Kyle’s office was open.

Deep shadows inside made me hesitate.

“Kyle?” I gave the door two quick raps, then held my breath, peeked inside. His office was small and cheerless. The doorway allowed just enough of the flat gray light to spill inside to make out most of the room. He’d thumb-tacked a bunch of motivational posters to three of the walls. Most of ’em seemed to feature rowing teams at sunset. I don’t know exactly what that had to do with running a big-box retail store, but then again, maybe that’s why I pushed carts. “Teamwork is the secret that makes common people achieve uncommon results,” and “Mindset is everything!” and “1% Better Every Day.” The last wall, the one behind his desk, was plastered with his own signs, 81/2X11s that he’d designed and printed throughout the years, advertising Memorial Day employee BBQs, safety meetings, birthdays and employment milestones, reminders to turn the clocks back or forward an hour, and plenty more.

Kyle himself sat motionless at his desk in the far corner, submerged in deep shadows, looking down at either the keyboard or the dozen or so photos of his family, most in frames built by children. My guess was that he was thinking about typing something because his hands looked to be on the keyboard.

"Kyle?" I said to him again.

He did not respond. He didn't even move. Same as Shelley and the lady with the dog. I couldn't even tell if he was breathing or not in the near-total darkness. I momentarily forgot the power was gone and went to flip the light switch a few times out of muscle memory. Kyle didn't look up at the clicking noises. Something told me not to go inside, not to even cross the threshold. I turned back to the office, dug around in the catch-all cabinets under the computers until I found a flashlight.

I tested it, stupidly aiming it right into my eyes. The harsh, powerful beam blew out any eyesight for a while, so I stood there, blinking furiously and shaking my head like some cartoon animal, chewing myself out. I'd be the kind of soldier that would confidently pull the pin on a grenade and toss it uphill, then turn away with my fingers in my ears while the damn thing rolled right back down to me.

I went back to Kyle's doorway and held my breath again. I clicked the flashlight and in the sudden glare that revealed details in startling clarity, I was very glad I hadn't gone into the office.

Black hair connected Kyle and the desk. My first thought was that guy from the movie where he washes up on some island full of these tiny people, and they try to tie the giant down. I looked closer and saw the threads weren't tying Kyle down. They had seemingly grown out of the desk and computer and *into* him. These filaments or hairs or whatever they were, looked like they had wormed into his skin, leaving small bumps around the puncture sites. Dozens upon dozens of the black threads stretched out to his bare arms and neck and disappeared inside his flesh. Some had even gone up his sleeves. A whole bunch poured off the desk, and I wondered if they had gone up his shirt. Or down his khakis.

The light quivered. I couldn't stop my hand from shaking.

His eyes were open and that made it all so much worse.

"Tell Kyle the phones aren't working," Wanda said.

I took one last look at Kyle and clicked off the flashlight, tucked it into the side pocket of my cargo shorts. Don't let anybody tell you cargo shorts aren't cool *and* practical. After a moment's consideration, I pulled Kyle's office door shut.

Wanda and Kiko watched me.

"I don't think Kyle's feeling well," I said and pulled out my phone. The screen came to brief life, stuttered, and then the towering image of Howlin' Wolf faded away for good. I hit every button I could find. Nothing happened. It was a brick. I showed Wanda and Kiko. "It's dead. Keep trying to call 9-1-1, okay? Do you have a cell phone on you?" Wanda shook her head, and Kiko made a face like it might be a trick question.

I headed out the door. "I'm gonna get Gloria."

I was halfway across Front End, between Customer Service and the break room, when I saw something was happening with Shelley. Her mouth dropped open, and as she grunted in stunned surprise, her body started trembling, shaking all over. I wondered if she was being shocked, you know, electrocuted somehow from her register or belt, but with the power out it didn't make sense. A wet stain appeared in the crotch of Shelley's jeans and spread to her inner thighs as her bladder let go.

I froze. The limited training I did get at the store did not prepare me for anything like this. And I was fairly positive I wouldn't find anything that could point me in any kind of helpful direction in the employee handbook either.

The lady with the dog never changed her own blank expression.

Kiko materialized at my side. Her sudden appearance made me flinch. I didn't even know she was there until she said, "My phone isn't working either. Something's wrong with this place."

I looked at Shelley and the lady. "Can't argue."

Kiko asked, "What's wrong with Shelley?"

Shelley was still shivering, but it was slowing down, like the spell or attack was fading.

"We gotta let Gloria know," I said, unsure if I should leave Shelley or send Kiko.

I don't think Kiko heard me. She was staring at the two women. "It's both of them. They're both...what's wrong with them?"

"Gas leak, maybe?" I shrugged.

"Tim! Hey Tim?" Carmelita yelled. "Is your register still working?"

No response.

"Tim?" she called again.

I didn't especially want to look back over my shoulder at Tim's lane, but glancing over there anyway not only confirmed one of my growing fears, that his customer was standing very, very still with the same blank, dead expression, but it also gave me a new one. The customer was Boris the Rattail. Both of his eyes were open. I don't think he blinked the whole time I watched him.

If there was a gas leak or something, and we did have to evacuate the store, where first responders would have to save these people with the same blank, dead stare, I didn't want to think about Boris and his crankiness when he awoke. I didn't envy anybody who had to deal with him, how much of a temper tantrum he'd throw once the paramedics pumped oxygen into him and brought him 'round, but I suppose they couldn't let him rot in that vegetative state. They were obligated to take care of everyone.

Then I got closer and saw how he and Tim were holding hands. Tim had the same dead look as Boris and even though they faced each other, they didn't act merely blind, they seemed totally unaware of the other's presence. They might have been a couple of plants growing side by side. It was almost like Shelley and the lady with the dog, but Tim wasn't shivering or shaking like he was being shocked. He just stood there, still.

I told Kiko, "Go get Gloria. Pretty sure we gotta evacuate the store."

The dog wouldn't shut up. The fear had used up most of my adrenaline, so it curdled into anger like it usually does. I suddenly understood why Yann would occasionally lose his shit, how horribly easy it was to crash out when there was just one too many things going on, screaming for your attention at the same time. Every damn thing just served to magnify every other damn thing until I found myself so blindly furious, I would've enthusiastically punted that fucking dog all the way across Front End if I could only get close enough.

A small voice, down deep, spoke up. If I was ready to kick a poor dog, then I couldn't trust myself to make any kind of solid decision until I got a better hold of my brain again. I also knew now without a shadow of a doubt I would have made a truly awful supervisor and tried to give myself an *attaboy*, even if it was strained, for at least having the foresight to try and avoid all of this unpleasantness.

Of course, at the time this realization was buried too deeply under burning fury for me to stop or alter my behavior in any way. I couldn't pull out of the nosedive. I'm ashamed to say I took a couple steps toward the goddamn dog and snapped at Kiko, "Go get Gloria!"

"Yeah, but..."

"What?" I shot back, ready to smash something.

"I dunno, dude."

"What?" I practically screamed it this time.

"Look." She pointed to the rest of the customers, the typical clusters of people in the lines. "Look. All of them. They're quiet." I'd been so focused on the damn dog, the strangeness of Shelley and the lady, then Tim and Boris, and frankly I was so used to simply ignoring the customers that I'd completely missed how unusually hushed the whole Front End had gotten. As I said, normally, if there's any kind of holdup at the register, like with Shelley and the lady, it doesn't take long for the customers waiting in line to voice their discontent. Most customers weren't shy letting everyone in the vicinity know they were irritated. There weren't many customers today, no, but that didn't explain just how quiet everything had become. I looked beyond Shelley and the lady, beyond Tim and Boris, and when I saw all the slack faces waiting in the lines, I saw what Kiko saw. Whatever it was, they were all affected. They stood there like a bunch of mannequins.

Razieh had the same problem as Carmelita. Their customers had fallen silent and still, same as the rest in their lines. It was impossible to tell what they were looking at. Everyone faced more or less in different directions, but more important than that, their eyes had lost whatever light consciousness gave them. Leaving your register in the middle of a transaction was an automatic write-up, especially if the register malfunctioned, an offense that went in your permanent file, but Carmelita and Razieh abandoned their mute customers and joined Kiko back near the office door.

The dog's barking grew even more frantic, as if it were trying to tear bites out of the very air itself.

The lady holding on to Shelley made a squeezed, huffing noise. I don't know what to call it. I don't think it was something that vocal cords could create. Not even the Mongolian throat singers or extreme death metal growlers could manage something like that. It wasn't a burp, and while that was closer, the lady hadn't moved her mouth. This sound was clearly some kind of gas escaping from an orifice. I don't wanna be gross here, but I am gonna be honest. It sounded like an especially chunky, moist fart. But this wasn't from the lady's butt. It came from somewhere up near her armpit.

"Whoa," Kiko said in an awed tone.

At first, when I saw movement from the lady, I thought it was the sporadic lights. Sure enough though, the lady with the dog had started moving her head. Small twitches at first, followed by more and more wobbling, until it looked like she was trying to shake water out of her ear. Her free arm shuddered, somehow separate and apart, all on its own. A moment later, the agitation spread to the rest of her body, and she began to tremble all over like Shelley had. The whole thing had given me the distinct impression that the lady with the dog had sent an electric eel over into Shelley's body, and for whatever reason, Shelley's taste didn't suit the eel, and so it'd come slithering back through the woman's arms and was now shocking the hell out of the lady in the expensive white sweater in retaliation.

I was still close to Shelley's register and during gaps in the barking, I not only heard those wet farting sounds, I smelled something new as well, something that left scars. All I can say is that this was beyond the worst stench you've ever encountered. Trust me when I tell you that I've been to more than my share of gnarly vinyl conventions where I've barely survived some of the most extreme body odor, flatulence, and general biological toxicity known to man. And after a couple days at each convention, it's quite possible I may have contributed to the overall awfulness. This, though, this was nothing like I'd ever endured. There was the sulfuric element lurking deep within, sure, but this odor also had something more chemical, something so sharp it might prick the tender skin inside your nose, make you bleed if you weren't careful.

The dog stopped barking.

The farting noises burst into life again, this time with a vengeance, sometimes two or three in unwanted stereo, and not only could I hear and smell just how *wrong* it all was, I could see the fabric of the lady's designer sweater flutter and rustle as something puffed out from underneath. This movement was up and down the lady's back, all over her stomach, her slacks. I held my breath, yet again afraid to move.

The lady let go of Shelley's hand and reached up to scratch at the crown of her head.

Shelley's arm drifted down to the buttons on her register, apparently more a result of gravity than any conscious thought. Her palm was nothing more than a giant, dripping wound, a huge hole revealing the bones inside as if something had eaten away the skin and tissue and intricate muscles. There was surprisingly little blood. If it was painful or caused her any concern or worry, you wouldn't know it, gauging from her blank expression. It hadn't changed since the trembling and spastic shuddering had abated.

The lady with the dog kept scratching at her head until she casually peeled half her scalp away like an itchy wig. Bloody bone glistened, even in the dull light. Her mouth fell open, but there was no scream. Except for the farting, she didn't make a sound the entire time. No one did. The left side of her jawbone became unhooked or something, almost like how a snake can distend their lower jaw, then the other side came loose. The entire lower jaw wobbled, completely detached from the rest of the skull, and sank into the swing of meat that made up the lady's chins and jowls. At first, it gave her face a long, solemn expression, but as the jawbone kept sinking and the face stretched even more, the expression became more and more unnatural and painful and awful.

There was a muffled crack from the top of her head where a piece of jagged bone roughly the size and shape of a Dorito popped out from the exposed skull and swung free, clinging tenaciously with one corner. From within, there was another of those wet farts where something gaseous burst free. This time, I could see the moist droplets spray into the air above Shelley's line, like a slow motion sneeze caught in the flat gray light.

One of the cashiers gasped and screamed.

The customers were quiet. None reacted in any way. I don't know if they were even aware of anything that was happening at Shelley's register.

More cracks appeared, crisscrossing over the bloody skull like a shattered Easter egg.

Unnatural movement came from within the rest of the body, like some inner scaffolding beginning to collapse, slowly at first, but gathering steam and violence as whatever structures were truly holding the body together gave way like falling dominoes. I thought her left arm was growing longer as it seemingly reached closer and closer to the floor but then realized the entire arm had somehow detached itself from the shoulder socket and was actually falling through the sleeve of the sweater. It reminded me of when Abid froze a batch of already roasted chickens to save money. Each department head would get a bonus if they came in each quarter under budget. The more money saved, the bigger the bonus. When Abid stuck the precooked, frozen chickens in the rotisserie for a second round, all of the meat slipped easily from the bones, falling apart so utterly he couldn't even pour the dripping carcasses into the plastic containers.

The lady's arm fell completely free and hit the concrete with a tight slap. Blood, strings of meat, and a whole lot of green glop trailed from the upper end. It wasn't cut or ripped out. This was more of a wet putrefaction, a liquid rotting of the muscles and fat into mush, like hydrochloric acid poured over raw hamburger.

The lady started to drop. Her knees didn't so much bend in the typical way as they deteriorated from the weight of her torso. She went straight down, a building being expertly demolished, until one side of her hips snagged on her left knee, and her torso toppled over like a heavy tree in a clear-cutting operation. When her head hit the floor, the entire skull cracked and burst apart as if it had been eagerly waiting on just such an invitation all day, sending dozens of pieces scattering across the concrete.

The impact reminded me of a hairy jawbreaker hitting the sidewalk, but once I saw inside, it didn't fit. I figured I'd see the usual blood and brains inside the skull, but along with the expected gore, there was also this wild assortment of colors and textures. The bits of the brain matter still clinging to the insides of the skull fragments were more like some kind of hipster blended ice cream. So sure, there were the typical bloody red bits, your pomegranate or strawberry, then there were parts that were darker and chunkier and might have been Rocky Road, with maybe even some pink bubblegum flavor peeking out here and there, and woven throughout were smooth, soft stripes of green tea. Some of the green stuff looked to be already melting while the rest stayed more or less solid.

Someone gagged behind me. At some point I'd stopped moving or breathing, frozen, until all at once it all came back in a rush again as the chunks of the lady's brains and skull tumbled uncomfortably close to my shoes like so much soggy confetti.

I jumped back. Looked wildly at Kiko and the cashiers. They stared right back with wide eyes. We all turned to the silent, unmoving customers, waiting in their inert lines that weren't going anywhere. None of them paid the slightest attention to the goopy corpse nuggets. Not even Shelley.

The dog took a few tentative steps toward the dollops of its rapidly decaying owner and sniffed carefully. Then it started to bark again.

And that was when I made the executive decision that this shit was above my pay grade.

2

INTERVIEW TRANSCRIPT-SUBJECT:-REDACTED-

Transcribed by: Ofc. -REDACTED-, Berwyn, IL PD

AGENCY: DEPT. HOMELAND SECURITY
DATE: 29 July 2026
LOC: Berwyn Police Department, 6401 W. 31st St, Berwyn, IL 60402
TIME: 4:37 AM
CASE: 47-5190-0043

PRESENT:

Special Agent Fred Jackson—Department of Homeland Security (DHS)

Special Agent Alex de la Iglesia—Department of Homeland Security (DHS)

Joseph Sutter—FOOD4U! Employee

Unnecessary sounds, such as "um" and "ah" have been omitted from the

following statement for the purpose of making this statement easier to read.

DE LA IGLESIA: Hold up. You wanna know what I smell? Huh? You wanna know? BULLSHIT. That's what I smell. Bullshit.
SUTTER: I told ya. I fucking told you, you wouldn't-
JACKSON: Let's take a moment and-
DE LA IGLESIA: Bullshit! It's bull-shit. You know it.
JACKSON: Easy. Both of you, easy.
DE LA IGLESIA: No. I'm not gonna sit here, thumb up my ass, listening to this cocksucker waste everybody's time with made-up bullshit. It's insulting.
SUTTER: Insulting? To *you*? You're kidding. You're wasting *my* time. You didn't listen to a goddamn thing I said before we even started. Told you straight up you wouldn't believe me.
JACKSON: Art, enough, ok? Take a minute. You wanna go grab a coffee? No? Okay, easy then. Now, Joe. Joe, please. We're on your side. We are. Nobody's blaming you for anything. We just want to know what happened. You can understand why that's important, right?
SUTTER: Gee, you think you could be more patronizing? I know you see a fat burnout having some acid flashbacks or

a freakout from bad 'shrooms. But I'm giving you what you want. I'm telling you exactly what happened.

JACKSON: Come on, come on. You have to admit, your account is, uh, a little out of the ordinary, you know?

DE LA IGLESIA: Yeah, it's bullshit.

JACKSON: Art, dammit. Enough. Save it. Joe… A woman falling apart? I mean, what, pieces on the floor? Those colors? Really?

SUTTER: Okay, whatever. You like this better? Here then. A customer, that lady, the lady and the dog, she went crazy. Yup. Killed everybody. With, uh, a machine gun. Yeah, it was one of those mass shootings. Not like this fucking country doesn't have one of those every goddamn day. Yeah, that's what happened all right. Then, then she set the store on fire. The end. Write that down. I'll sign it. Can I go now?

DE LA IGLESIA: Cute. Cute. Tell ya what. You wanna know something, punk? Something doesn't get advertised—not now, just fucking hang on, Fred. This is just for our guest. He needs his attitude adjusted, one way or another. I don't care I'm on camera. There are too many people missing, gone. We need information. I wanna know what's in his head. That's why I'm gonna explain to the esteemed Mr. Sutter here what's gonna happen, he keeps making up this Tales from the Crypt shit, wasting all our time. You. You listen up and listen good. Either you tell the truth, or you're gonna find out the hard way that times like this, we ignore the Constitution. You have no rights. I got no problem throwing you in a goddamn hole long as I feel like. Everybody thinks they're tough, 'til they spend a few days alone in total darkness. Now then. You want to tell us the truth, or are we gonna have to take your ass to a black site?

JACKSON: Okay, okay, that's enough. Christ. Let's all take a moment. Emotions are running high, everybody's saying things they don't mean—

DE LA IGLESIA: I fucking mean it. I'm dead serious.

JACKSON: Fine, fine. Let's just take a breath. Everybody can calm down. This isn't getting us anywhere. Joe. Joe, I don't know what to say here. You say you're just telling us what happened, but come on. It's…it's a little hard to swallow, you know?

SUTTER: No shit. Why do you think I told you this wouldn't work? You guys wouldn't believe anything I said.

DE LA IGLESIA: It's all lies. Why are you covering up something?

SUTTER: Why, if I was lying, why would I go to the trouble of making up something so ridiculous? What's the point? What, you think this is some master heist where I steal what, fucking wind chimes? Seriously?

JACKSON: Again, that's why we're here. To find out what happened.

SUTTER: I'm telling you what happened. You're making a deliberate choice not to believe me. That's your problem, not mine.

JACKSON: I want to believe you. I do. It's just a little tough to swallow. Still…the site itself, the destruction, doesn't have a clear cause, so I don't know. Tell you what. Let's keep going, you tell us what you witnessed, okay?

DE LA IGLESIA: He's just gonna keep lying. I say we toss him in a cell. Let him think about things for a while. Then see if his story changes.

JACKSON: No. We don't have time. And if I'm being fully honest, I don't think Mr. Sutter here has the imagination to make up events like this. No, I suspect he believes he's telling the truth.

SUTTER: I'm telling you exactly what happened. You don't wanna hear it, that's your problem.

JACKSON: Fair enough. Let's continue.

DE LA IGLESIA: `You get your head straight or I promise, I will knock your teeth out.`

Gloria whispered, "What on earth?"

I couldn't manage much of a response beyond a shrug. I don't think she was really asking a question. It was, of course, rhetorical. Still, I felt strangely responsible to try and explain, as if all of the chaos was somehow my fault, but nothing seemed remotely adequate, and even if I could figure out something to say, found some actual words instead of merely gibberish, I didn't entirely trust my voice to actually produce anything audible.

They'd stabilized the Professor, got him breathing on his own at least. I guess he was still blind as a bat. Sammy had him up on one of the break room tables, wiping at his face with wet paper towels. Gloria left the two of them and came out to Front End, taking a few moments to comprehend the tableau. No one moved. Silence stretched throughout the store. Her steps faltered and stopped when she saw the unnatural hues splattered across the floor.

At least the dog had stopped barking, giving up as the pieces of its owner dissolved into different flavors of muck. The putrefaction continued to boil, and some of the more solid chunks tumbled lazily out of the clothing, pieces that still sizzled. A nearly solid, acrid smoke bubbled out of the carnage and clung to the floor like it was heavy. Seeping clumps of what looked like black and green mold bloomed from within the white sweater. For some reason I couldn't figure out, much of the swampy mess had split into several different types of liquid like oil and water and wouldn't mix. Some of it even gave off the sick rainbow iridescent reflection of spilled gasoline. The sight and smell drove Gloria back to the rest of us still huddled by the office.

She kept backing up until she almost bumped into me, unable to tear her attention away from the splattered mess around Shelley's register. I think the flurry of emotions roaring through her head burned out any effort to gather the threads and process the storm. Repulsion and fascination wouldn't coalesce so she could move on, sort of like how the Technicolor liquids on the floor rejected any merge. It went beyond any one single element for her. The scene offended her on a primal level as a human being, trampling over her sensibilities, by the sudden devastation of the orderly, methodical procedures that had taken her years to install and refine. It was a desecration, a defilement of her spirit. Despite the inherent chaos of a cut-rate, decaying big-box retail store, Gloria had Front End functioning so smoothly that a supervisor or manager was only necessary on certain specific occasions. Everyone knew how it all flowed, everyone knew their responsibility, and thanks to the AGM, everyone worked together to ensure the endless transactions clicked right along.

Now nothing in Front End was right. The whole unreal situation was still ongoing and there appeared to be no logical conclusion anywhere in sight. No one was taking credit for a prank, no one was speaking or laughing or screaming, and the sales at the other registers had all ground to a halt. It had to be killing her sense of propriety that not a single person had even bothered to try and call for maintenance to clean up the mess on the floor.

Gloria had two near-identical wigs. I was close enough that I could tell she was wearing her good one. This had finer strands and tighter, more natural curls. Her face was pale. I knew she was going through a hell of a lot, but her eyes had gotten much wider than I was comfortable with, if you want to know the truth. She stood with both hands covering her open mouth, pressing the webbing between her thumb and forefinger of her right hand so tightly against her nostrils I worried something might burst from the internal pressure. I didn't blame her. I wished I'd grabbed some of the COVID masks when I had the chance. Her eyes darted from the wet piles of clothing and chunky, gaudy puddles, up to a motionless Shelley, over to the also unmoving customers, stuttering across Tim and Boris, sliding to the gaggle of tense employees next to her, and back to the bizarre shit on the floor, all in a nanosecond. In the ten years I'd been at the store, I'd never seen Gloria in such a state of terror and disgust and more than anything, confusion.

With the exception of her eyes, she didn't move a muscle. Her eyes though, the way they moved gave her thoughts away, and I realized that wriggling slivers of confusion and near panic were burrowing throughout her insides. This woman was far too disciplined to ever allow any kind of extreme emotion like anger or even ecstatic joy to be visible on her face or body language. She could control all of it, all of it that is, except her eyes. Those, she couldn't stop. They kept lurching from one ghastly image to the next, making her tense as an over-cranked spring. Yet like an anxious cat, able to remain utterly motionless on the surface in the presence of possible prey or predators, Gloria was nonetheless ready to explode in any direction at the merest hint of the slightest noise or movement.

Gloria's behavior was quite different from when my dad would freak out, but it still held the same bitter taste, this crushing feeling of knowing you were powerless, unable to do anything except watch helplessly while someone you cared about endured a vicious internal battle raging over how and what should determine their own thoughts and actions. Her internal struggle reminded me so much of the first time I saw my dad attempt to rebel against his deteriorating mental health, I almost bit my tongue.

Then I witnessed Gloria achieve something I'd never seen my dad manage.

She clawed herself back from the brink of hysteria and seized control of her mind, soul, and body like a parent grabbing a child who'd darted into traffic, angrily and violently, even if the intent had been born out of love. She didn't accomplish this all at once, but little by little, piece by piece, muscle by muscle, organ by organ, cell by cell. If the power'd been on and you could see the security video feeds, you probably couldn't have seen anything happening anyway, just Gloria standing there for a few seconds that felt like years. Next to her, though, I was close enough to watch it happen in real time as she gathered her wits and reclaimed her entire self through the simple God-fearing force of sheer fucking will.

Gloria's eyes slowed their own frantic darting and began listening to directions as she gained command over her mind once again. When she was good and ready, she began the next step by pulling her fingers away from her face and clasping both hands together at her waist. As she took a moment to reappraise the entire Front End, the muscles in her jaw twitched, and her lips tightened to grim, resigned strips. She made minute, precise adjustments to her back, straightening each and every one of her vertebrae, locking each into its designated position one at a time, deliberately slow and methodical, as resolute and determined as a redwood striving for the sun.

Watching Gloria collect herself made me feel better than swallowing a few of my pills at the same time.

I knew this because I'd tried. Can't recommend it. Didn't work. Like Sammy had said, nothing ever ends up like you think it will. Sometimes, especially after a shit day at work, the nights could be tough, so I'd pop four or five pills in a desperate lunge for anything that might break the endlessly ratcheting chain of awful thoughts. These were nights when I would have gladly chopped off a finger or toe for an unhurried chance to properly exhale and find some genuine, soul repairing rest, not clutching at wisps of sleep while thrashing around on the couch all night, fighting gut-smothering guilt or horror or fear. Yeah, sometimes life could be a goddamn nightmare, and I don't think it's gonna surprise anybody that my upbringing, like the stupid employee handbook, really didn't give me a firm foundation on which to build a solid, sensible reaction to any of this awfulness.

Then again, maybe there was no real solid, sensible reaction.

I didn't want to admit it at the time, especially to myself, but knowing what I know about my own screwed-up mind, and if I'm gonna be honest, I might as well go all the way with all of this, hindsight being 20/20 and all that. That truth was that I was too myopic, and it had never crossed my mind that there was nothing on God's green Earth that Gloria couldn't handle, nothing thrown at her where she wouldn't know exactly and immediately how to fix whatever was wrong. I didn't think it was even possible. But staring it in the face no more than three feet away, I couldn't deny that it was more than a possibility, it was happening, and the undeniable reality of Gloria fighting the same level of panic as I had on those long, empty nights filled me with almost as much dread as the basement stairway.

Now, having Gloria truly back in the land of the living replaced most of the fear with...well, I'm not sure exactly. Not hope. That's something else, something deeper, I think. This was more about being blessed that Gloria was on our side. She possessed an undeniable grit that didn't fuck around. She stepped right up and kicked down locked doors, giving us all potential opportunities, revealing pathways I didn't even know existed. And that meant there was maybe still a chance there was something she could figure out, find a solid idea that might make sense of the situation.

With Gloria large and in charge, we had a chance to fix this.

She turned to me. "Kyle?"

"He's in his office. He, uh, I don't think he's gonna be joining us or helping anytime soon." An insistent, absurd intrusive thought made me want to suddenly explain to Gloria that Kyle needed a haircut, and I had to bite the side of my tongue with my back molars to stifle saying it out loud. Instead, I shook my head and handed her the flashlight.

While she was gone, everybody tried their phones. None worked.

Gloria didn't take long. She came out of the office with a careful, neutral expression. If the sight of Kyle and that black hair had shaken her, she didn't let it show. If anything, she appeared even more resolved to tackle this head-on, fists up, elbows out.

She handed the flashlight back to me. "I think your batteries are dead. It worked, only for a moment," she said and met my eyes. "Long enough."

She approached the line of registers, taking care to give the smoking chunks a wide berth. "Shelley? Timothy? Can you hear me?" She paused, then addressed the entire motionless group. "Anyone?"

Silence.

She approached Shelley and called back to us, "She's breathing, at least." She was almost to Shelley's register counter and had her arm outstretched to grab hold of Shelley's bare upper arm when it struck me like a bolt of lightning on a cloudless day that with just one more step Gloria would make physical contact.

I shouted without thinking, "Stop! Wait! Stop! Don't touch her!"

Gloria, to her credit, actually listened to me. I was kinda surprised, since deep down where she's honest and human, I don't think she thought that much of me, that she'd written off any future potential in me as a lost cause. Maybe she had some pity in there. Certainly, there wasn't any genuine respect. Gloria most likely had determined I was about as useless as tits on a hog, but despite this, she froze long enough to consider my warning. She freshly observed Shelley for another few seconds and withdrew her hand.

She looked back at me and asked, "Okay. Why not?"

I couldn't help but notice everyone else had turned and was also watching me, waiting for some kind of explanation, even if it was nothing more than a guess. I never liked being stuck at the center of attention and went out of my way to avoid any kind of spotlight. My heart stuttered. Everything felt a little off. I was most likely in mild shock, but logic was still grimly attempting to make itself known. If this was a carbon monoxide leak or something, then it should have been affecting everyone in the store. That clearly wasn't the case, as all the employees in the Front End, well except for Shelley and Tim and Kyle, everybody else though, they were still moving and talking. And if any of the other employees had been affected in any other way, I couldn't tell. It could have been a gas leak, but I seriously doubted it.

I started babbling, even with absolutely no idea what to say. "Uh, well. You know, I mean just look at her. What if she's, you know, infected or something? Shelley, she uh, was touching the lady before she, well, before. They held hands for a long time. A long time. Least a couple minutes maybe. Shelley, look at her. She's not right."

"How can you tell?" Carmelita asked under her breath, trying to keep a lid on things so she wouldn't erupt in hysterical giggling. Carmelita never made any attempt to deny she outwardly thumbed her nose at Shelley's preference for overutilizing chemical coping methods, flat out dismissing the drug-addled cashier as weak and a useless waste of already limited employee resources.

"What about Tim?" I said. "Look at him too. Him and Boris."

"I see." Gloria took a few prudent steps back, putting some distance between her and Shelley. "You think what, this condition, it could be contagious?"

"Contagious! Yes!" I nearly shouted. The concept made a reassuring kind of sense to me, in that I understood more or less how an infected person could pass along a virus or germ with a touch or sneeze or kiss. Spread something like the flu, or the plague. Or leprosy. I probably couldn't pass a university exam over the exact details, but I could see how the principle worked in broad strokes, or at least I thought I did. Of course, the longer I turned it over in my mind, the more I applied any kind of even the laziest, most lackluster scientific approach, my new theory began to crumble under the glare of logic and causality. I mean, I seriously doubt the customers, all of 'em, somehow made skin-to-skin contact or coughed in each other's faces to spread this condition. And all at more or less the same time? Please.

Something else had gotten to the customers.

"In those training videos we had to watch, the people responding, they use all kinds of stuff to make it safe," Razieh pointed out.

"PPE!" Sammy interjected, beaming with pride.

"Excellent point, Samuel," Gloria said. "Personal Protective Equipment. What is available?"

"The COVID masks at Customer Service." I was the first to point this out as they'd been on my mind. I used to hate being forced to wear them. It was impossible to wear both a mask and glasses because your breath fogged the lenses. Somebody recommended wiping dish soap on the lenses, but it never did seem to work. Now though, I wanted to strap on two or three masks, minimum.

"Good start, Joseph. What else? Some of you use latex gloves. That may help."

Gloves. Of course. How could I have been so stupid? My hands suddenly felt like raw, exposed magnets, and I didn't want to touch anything, not with my skin bare and vulnerable. I'd never bothered worrying about latex gloves before, mostly because I wore snowboarding gloves in the winter, and summer was too hot for anything.

Nobody wanted to come right out and admit that we all snatched fistfuls of the blue latex gloves every damn day and stuffed them in our lockers for work or sometimes put a whole box in our car for whenever we had to unclog the drain in the kitchen sink, scrub the toilet, change the oil in the car, butcher and fillet a freshly caught fish, or perform even the basic act of chopping up an onion.

Carmelita cleared her throat. "Uh, isn't Maintenance supposed to be, uh, supplied, you know, with a fresh, uh, supply? All that stuff. Paper towels and cleaning spray and gloves. In Don's tilt truck."

"Where's the truck?" Gloria asked.

No one answered. Don had called out, and as usual, no one was quite sure where he'd left it.

Gloria said, "Well, for the time being, I would agree with Joseph and would strongly suggest that none of *you* get any closer than necessary to any of *them*. Even if you wish to help them. Under no circumstances should you touch any of them. Or even get close. Not until we know more." Gloria contrasted the scattered, silent customers with the cluster of anxious employees, assessing the Front End with her usual implacable expression. She spoke slowly, choosing her words with care, like she was under oath, probably already formulating how she would have to approach the inevitable corporate report. "Although the customers are exhibiting an undeniable unresponsive condition, I am unable to determine the cause or even hazard a guess at the moment. Most of the employees, however, appear perfectly normal and healthy, with the exception of this customer." Gloria gave a slight, respectful nod at the sizzling chunks of the woman's corpse. "Or the rest of the customers, I can see no visible or immediate threat of physical danger." She faced Shelley and Tim. "Shelley, Timothy, hang on. I hope you can hear me. We will get you help." She turned back to us and asked, "Who here has called 9-1-1?"

Ashamed, everybody except Wanda shook their heads.

"My phone isn't working," I offered as a lame excuse.

Everybody nodded and said the same thing, holding their phones out as evidence.

Gloria never kept her phone with her at work. It was always turned off and stored in her car. She considered most social media to be the modern equivalent of whispering cruel, mostly invented gossip with your neighbor over the back fence. She let the excuses and demonstrations continue for a moment, then held up a finger. Everyone shushed. She nodded to Wanda. "The landline?"

Wanda spread her hands. "I got through, at first, and started telling 'em about Mrs. Merriweather, then it went dead." Then she shook her head. "But even before it cut out, the call got all choppy. Lots of static. It was all messed up."

"So...?"

"So I don't know."

"Are they responding to the call?"

"I don't know."

"Not one phone is working?" Gloria asked. She hit the call button on her walkie-talkie. No one wanted to make it obvious, but we were all watching closely to see what would happen. Nothing did. Gloria's radio was as dead as the cell phones and my flashlight. And even though nobody wanted to come out and state it out loud, everyone was wondering the same thing. The power was out, so it made sense that the landline and registers were down. It didn't explain, though, why all the cell phones and radios and flashlights had stopped working. It was like an EMP had been set off in the middle of textiles.

"None of this leaves us with much choice," Gloria said. Without fanfare, she marched to the wall and used her elbow to break the glass of the fire alarm. That should have triggered a throbbing wail throughout the store. I'd heard it twice, once when it was tested, and a second time when Don bumped into one of the alarms back near the freezer, cracking the glass. When it went off, you couldn't miss it. The electronic howling shook the walls and made your bones quiver.

Now, nothing. More silence. I was getting tired of hearing my own heartbeat.

Gloria nodded at the fire alarm. "That's it. We're leaving."

About goddamn time, I thought. *Let's get the fuck out of here,* you know? I wasn't the only one. Most everybody was leaning toward the EXIT. They were just waiting for Gloria to turn everybody loose.

Gloria made sure she had everyone's undivided attention. "We will be evacuating shortly. Remain calm. Take only what is on your person. Leave everything else." She turned to me. "Joseph, go help Samuel with our unfortunate guest. He is suffering from the effects of pepper spray and does not appear to be related to...this." She indicated Shelley and Tim, the customers. Under her breath, she added, "It would not surprise me if the Professor's issues are simply good old-fashioned alcoholism."

I nodded and didn't waste any time getting to the break room. It didn't feel like I was on the clock anymore. No, I was on my own time now. And it was time to fucking go.

In the break room, I found the Professor sitting up, legs dangling off the table, taking sips of water offered by Sammy.

"Time to go," I said. "Can you walk?"

"What?" the Professor called out, voice hoarse. It hurt to look at him. His eyes were red, swollen shut. His blue shirt was stained with pepper spray, bottled water, and sweat.

"We're getting out of here," I said.

"Cool." Sammy nodded and told the Professor. "Okay, mister. You can hang onto me. I gotcha. Just like sitting up, nice and easy."

"Leaving won't...running away won't help. It won't," the Professor said.

Me and Sammy looked at each other. We both shrugged, keeping quiet so the blind man didn't know how clueless we were.

"I dunno, man," I said. "I just work here, doing what I'm told, you know? And right now, we gotta evacuate the store." I grabbed the Professor's knapsack off the floor, glancing into it to make sure he didn't have any more weapons but found nothing but some old books. Couldn't see the pistol. I hoped Gloria had it.

"I, I don't know," the Professor said. "I can't see anything. I..." He trailed off, mucus sheeting his upper lip. I helped his arms through the knapsack straps.

"I gotcha," Sammy said, turning him and easing him off the table to a standing position. "And tell ya what, my buddy Joe here, he's gonna help you too."

We got on either side of the poor bastard, each of us wrapping his arms around our shoulders, then lifted him up and off the table. He wobbled a bit, but at least he could support most of his own weight. I tried not to be in a hurry as we shuffled sideways through the break room door and rejoined the other employees.

I heard Sammy's breath hitch when he saw the pieces of the lady. I knew there was a chance he might freeze up, but he kept moving. I was proud of him. I figured it was probably for the best that the Professor was still blind. Easier that way.

Gloria nodded at Wanda to lead. "Let's get everyone safely outside. Once everyone is clear, I will come back for any remaining employees and any unaffected customers," Gloria said, gesturing toward the door. "Do not run."

We all started toward the EXIT, clumped together, more or less following Wanda.

The dog watched all of this intently, staying silent.

Gloria turned to Front End and called out in a voice that boomed like a thunderclap all the way to the back of the store, "If you can hear me, the store is being evacuated. Please meet us at the EXIT door." I flinched, feeling soft and defenseless while something had just screamed out in the darkness, alerting every predator for miles. I met the dog's eyes. It was scared shitless, just like me. Despite this sudden seizure of terror, or maybe because of it, Gloria's voice knocked me out. I knew she sang in the choir but god*DAMN*. Her pipes impressed the hell out of me.

That rolling thunder echoed off the ceiling. Gloria continued, "I repeat. We are evacuating this store. Thank you for your cooperation."

I scanned the aisles. Nobody poked their head out in surprise.

Sammy and I eased the Professor along, a slow caboose at the end of a scattered train of employees. I asked the Professor, "You're a customer, sorta. Why aren't you affected? Like them?"

"I'm not a customer."

"Okay. What are you?"

He looked stricken. "I don't know anymore."

I didn't want to push. My irritation was gone. I still thought he was just the crazy alky dude from the parking lot, but I felt bad for him. Couldn't have been fun, getting pepper-sprayed by Gloria. I don't know, as I'd be strong enough to be up and walking for at least a week or two.

Now that we were leaving, everybody started feeling better. I don't think anybody was overly concerned still. Or at least nobody seemed like they were about to freak out like I wanted to at any rate. The death of the lady with the dog was upsetting and nauseating, sure, but at the end of the day, it was a customer. The rest of 'em on the other side of the registers were all only customers. It seemed that most of the employees had coldly chalked up Shelley's condition to her chemical dependencies. It was only natural that something like this was bound to happen sooner or later.

And it was all too easy to forget about Tim and Kyle.

In fact, I'd bet that most of us, all of us, well except

for Gloria of course, were already putting the weirdness behind us because it looked like the rest of our shift was suddenly wide open. It must be what prisoners feel like getting suddenly paroled after resigning themselves to years behind bars.

Carmelita confirmed this by muttering, "Holy crap, I'm ready for a drink." This declaration was met with emphatic agreements and nervous laughter. The sense of relief was almost palpable. Salvation from all the insanity lay just outside the EXIT. All we had to do was simply walk out the door, and maybe it wouldn't be totally finished, but it sure as shit wouldn't be our responsibility anymore.

I should have known better.

John's job was to double-check the receipts at the EXIT door, stopping customers before they reached the vestibule so he could compare the list on the receipt to the actual items in the cart. He was a thin, wiry guy in his late forties with inexhaustible energy who took his duties serious as a heart attack. Believe me, the position at the EXIT door sucked donkey dick. And not in a good way. Nobody wanted to fill in whenever John had to take his break or lunch. If a sup or manager asked me, I'd claim I was wearing my old glasses, and I couldn't read the tiny numbers. See for me, it wasn't a question of *if* I'd end up in some stupid argument or even a physical altercation with a dipshit, but *when*. That's probably because I was too dumb or stubborn or both to merely pretend, like every other employee, happily going through the motions of comparing the receipt and the contents of the cart but never actually counting or even really seeing anything. Don't ask me why I insisted on doing the job. I couldn't tell you. For some inexplicable reason, I actually took the time to check everything, and that pissed off everybody, customers and management alike.

The problem was that no customer wanted to slow down or, god forbid, stop at the EXIT. That curious impulse to rush or slow down at a whim while inside the store, to linger or trample anyone in their way, happened more or less in random spots throughout the store. The urge to hurry though, kicked in with a particularly strong fury in two particular areas, when waiting in line to reach the registers and then as they approached the EXIT. It brought out the worst in people. Almost every customer promptly decided they were suddenly in a giant fucking rush once the transaction had been completed and they had their change. It didn't matter that they'd spent the last hour and a half wandering the aisles like a zombie missing half a brain. If you tried to slow 'em down or hold 'em up in any way once the deal was done and they were finally on their way out of the store, they'd visibly bristle when asked to show proof of payment, naturally assuming the store had singled them out in suspicion of shoplifting.

Nobody likes to be treated like a criminal.

The customer's assumptions, even if logical, weren't exactly true. The reality was that corporate suspected everyone of theft. Especially the employees. It was expected. So, John wasn't checking to see if any customers had slipped something extra into their carts, not really. He was actually making sure the cashiers had done their jobs and rang everything up without missing, say, a package of batteries or something. Behind the registers, stickers had been plastered all over, reminding the cashiers: "Check BOB!" BOB being Bottom of Basket. In other words, John wasn't primarily examining receipts because of possible shoplifting, his role was to keep an eye on the other employees, primarily the cashiers.

He was sincere and solemn about his responsibility. John acted like it was his own money slipping out the door if he allowed anyone to leave without making damn sure everything in the cart was present and accounted for on the receipt. That's undoubtedly why Kyle and Gloria stationed him at the EXIT as the store's last line of defense against shrinkage. *Shrinkage* was yet another euphemism that corporate had decided to call the disappearance of merchandise.

John held dual citizenship both here in the US and in Taiwan, where he'd lived most of his life. From the stories I'd heard, he'd been a wealthy businessman in Taipei when he'd brought his family over to the US. He now owned a couple of all-you-can-eat Chinese buffets in suburban strip malls, so it didn't sound like he needed another form of income. I suppose it was possible he worked at the store for the health insurance. He sure wasn't the only one here strictly for the benefits.

That's the number one reason why I gave up on my goal of running my own record store. The health insurance costs alone would have eaten me alive. I worked in independent, used vinyl stores for years, building my collection but never managing to save any significant amount of actual cash. Eventually, thanks to infected wisdom teeth that leaked rotten pus whenever I bit down, along with a string of ulcers, my dedication to fighting late-stage capitalism eventually decayed like my teeth. I swallowed my dream and applied at the newly opened FOOD4U!

I didn't own my own record store. And probably never would. But if nothing else, the wisdom teeth were gone, and now I had real medicine to keep the ulcers calm. It worked a whole lot better than guzzling Pepto Bismol every few hours. I still don't know if the trade-off was worth it in the end for my soul.

No, I think John derived something else from his position, something beyond a simple paycheck or health benefit, maybe a kind of satisfaction or pride in ensuring the cashiers had properly performed their task. Usually, with somebody like that, the authority would go straight to their head. 'Cause you know damn well that sometimes, too many times, you give somebody the teeniest bit of power, and they go fucking nuts, evolving into a power-mad dictator fast as snapping your fingers, like Oskar in Receiving, until a fellow employee has to put 'em in their place and remind them, "Hey! Act your wage." No, John was fair. I witnessed plenty of customers lose their temper and throw their receipts on the ground as they shoved their carts past him, daring him to do something about it.

I've been told my interpersonal skills weren't the best, and that was another reason they didn't want me at the door. I'd been generally discouraged from talking to customers ever since I asked this entitled asshole who'd parked in front of the fire emergency exits if he was stupid or just lazy. When the asshole spluttered and started yelling at me in a blustering attempt to intimidate and knock me back into my place as just an hourly wage moron, I simply nodded and said, "Figured. Both."

John could handle customers' attitudes and insults. His only reaction was to calmly call on the radio for a manager. If Gloria was on duty at the time, she'd drag the troublemakers back to the office and give 'em a sharp lecture, making it crystal clear that they could either politely show their receipt at the door, and if that was too difficult, they were more than welcome to never come back. Kyle's approach was more apologetic, following the assholes out to the lot like a lost puppy, damn near begging the customer to return and spend more money as soon as possible.

When we got to the door, John wasn't at his usual post, eagerly waiting to examine carts and receipts. Instead of waiting back near the doorway, he'd leap forward and meet the customers halfway. He'd often check everything, counting everything in the cart while walking backward with the customer until he turned them loose with a flourish and bounced to the next in line. He had a hard time standing still.

Until now. John stood motionless a few paces outside the EXIT doorway in the vestibule, which never happened during business hours. His back was to us, head was cocked to one side, looking outward at the windows of the vestibule and the parking lot beyond, not facing inside to keep an eye out for the approaching customers like he always did. He held the walkie-talkie loosely at his hip, not moving at all.

I started worrying whatever had gotten hold of Kyle and Shelley and Tim and the customers had affected John as well. I held my breath again. As it turns out, he was just transfixed by the sight of something in the vestibule. He must have heard us when we reached the EXIT because he turned, face screwed up like he'd just swallowed something he worried might be rancid.

"I only see it now," he said.

I didn't understand what he was talking about.

All I could tell was that the vestibule had gotten darker since Gloria instructed me and Sammy to search the store for Mrs. Toenails. This was pretty normal. It happened all the time, so I didn't think anything about it, not at that moment. I just assumed storm clouds had rolled through the area, swallowing the bright sunshine with grim, flat shadows. Towering thunderstorms soaked the parking lot with a depressing regularity throughout the moist summers, and there was no reason to think otherwise. A cloudburst could roll through, soak you to the bones, and be gone inside of half an hour. I'd learned the hard way to keep a poncho and dry socks in my car.

I was wrong. It wasn't clouds.

Even though I could easily see both ends of the vestibule and take it all in, it still took me several seconds to work out what I was looking at. The reasoning, civilized part of my mind that's in charge for the most part, kept insisting that the issue lay on the other side of the windows, despite the contradictory information being delivered by my own eyes. Maybe the delay in processing the visual data was a survival impulse, a deliberate mistranslation to keep me tranquil while deep in the emergency bunker, my primal core freaked out over whether I should attack or run away. And since what I was seeing had no immediate explanation, I froze again, just like when I was faced with Shelley and her customer.

The windows were dark because of the black hair.

I don't know why I started thinking of it more as hair and not threads or anything else anymore, but it was the same filament stuff that connected Kyle to the desk, no question. Only there was so much, much more. Maybe that's why now I couldn't see all of it any other way. It was hair-like, and like hair, it was *growing*. Thousands, probably millions of the strands stretched across the windows and walls, clinging to the glass and rough stone, choking out the light. I felt like I'd fallen into an abandoned, overgrown aquarium.

John raised his radio to show Gloria. "Not working."

The vestibule had been added as a buffer between the customers and the parking lot and as storage for the shopping carts when the building had been sold, built when the structure originally designed as a factory was transformed into a retail big-box store. The vestibule served as a kind of cap on the southeast corner of the building, protecting the original ENTRANCE and EXIT as a sort of airlock that allowed the store to maintain a comfortable temperature while conserving as much energy as possible. Customers entered either end while the carts themselves were generally pushed through a half door in the middle, stored in long stacks along the walls. The original building's solid cinderblock walls stretched upward of over thirty feet. The outside walls of the vestibule rose to about four feet and then tall windows took over, filling the rest of the distance to the ceiling. On bright days, the vestibule didn't offer much respite from the sun. It was more comfortable to keep your sunglasses on at all times.

Today though, I swear it grew darker and darker the few seconds we stood there, struggling to understand what had taken over the vestibule. Black hair, or whatever the fuck it was, appeared to be growing out of the cracks between the windows and the cinderblock walls, clinging to the glass as it snaked across the windows. It was also starting to creep down the cinderblocks to the concrete floor where it gathered under the stacks of carts. You couldn't actually see it move or grow, no more than you can see grass grow or the minute hand on a watch move, but even if you couldn't witness it didn't mean the stuff wasn't getting longer, expanding. If anything, the hair seemed to be growing faster when you weren't looking at it.

The hair had also enveloped the automated sliding glass doors at both ends of the vestibule. Ordinarily, whenever someone came anywhere near them, approaching from either outside or inside, the movement would trigger the sensors, which would send a signal for the motor to crank the doors apart. When the infrared beams didn't find anything else to bounce off for a while, the glass doors would slowly and tiredly slide back together to rest. The black filaments were so thick I couldn't tell if anybody was outside or not. Either way, the doors stayed shut.

On the far wall, the mass of black strands had reached the floor and was beginning to creep out across the concrete floor.

The Professor couldn't see shit, but he damn well

knew something was wrong. "What is it?" he whispered.

"It's um, something's growing out of the walls," I said.

"Hair," Sammy said. "Black hair."

"Oh god, we're too late," the Professor said. "The remoras are here."

I didn't know what the Professor meant and didn't want to. The EXIT sign still burned in my brain, even if it wasn't lit on the wall. Outside was so close. I told Sammy, "Gimme a minute," and left the Professor with him. I wanted a better look, pulled out the flashlight, hoping Gloria had been wrong. I banged it a few times. It still didn't work.

"What the hell is that?" Carmelita demanded and pointed.

Most of the employees crept out into the vestibule for a better look at the windows and hair. Up close revealed more than I needed to see, if I'm being totally honest. Something else, these whitish blobs that defied any immediate recognition, had emerged from the cracks as well. We saw then that the hair wasn't growing out of the cracks between the glass and cinderblock by itself as first thought. Instead, it was sprouting from these pale lumps not quite the size of baseballs. Jet black hair erupted out of these small, pallid blobs, sprouting in every direction. The surface of each irregular shaped sphere, from what I could see, was ridged or wrinkled, reminding me of rotten pears that had squeezed out from within the cracks every few feet.

"They look like old man balls," Kiko said.

She had a point. And once she'd planted that seed in our minds, it was impossible to see these things as anything other than the sagging, wrinkly testicles of an elderly man, even if each scrotum had swollen to the size of Kiko's fist. I'm pretty sure everyone else agreed with her but nobody said anything out loud, probably because it was too revolting to acknowledge.

The hair on the floor now stretched a foot or so from the wall.

Carmelita asked, "Can't we walk out the stupid door?"

John shook his head, keeping a careful eye on the waves of black hair that kept growing, piling up even as we stood there, spilling out across the glass and cinderblock, curling through the carts, blotting out the sun. "Too much," he said.

"John is right," Gloria said. "Whatever it is, I have reason to believe it is dangerous. Don't get close. Whatever you do, don't touch it."

"The doors are automatic," Carmelita announced and abruptly walked away from the cluster of nervous employees, heading left to the north vestibule doors. "I ain't touching shit."

"I wanna go home too," Razeih said, taking a tentative step in Carmelita's direction and giving Gloria an imploring look. Wanda and John wavered, caught between giving in to the rising urge to flee and obeying their assistant general manager.

"Carmelita," Gloria said quietly. "Do you not

remember?" She gave Carmelita a moment. "Where are the lights?"

We all watched Carmelita jerk to a stop when she realized the automatic doors wouldn't open without power. She practically winced when it hit her. I'd forgotten myself that the electricity was gone of course, soon as I'd caught my first glimpse of all that creeping hair. I doubt I was the only one.

The hair continued to gather in the corners on both ends of the vestibule, swallowing the rodent control containers, metal boxes full of poison in every corner. It slipped under and through the wire mesh of the stacks of carts, curling over itself and spilling out across the floor. A safe path of around a dozen feet of bare concrete stretched between Carmelita and the doors, but that area shrank every time I looked back as the hair inexorably persisted in swallowing the rest of the vestibule. She'd been around five yards from the doors when Gloria had reminded her about the electricity; now she stood in that narrowing bare concrete path, either unwilling or unable to go forward to the doors or return back to the group.

I studied the doors beyond her, trying to count the old man testicles oozing out of the cracks and gaps. I eventually lost track after counting over twenty-five on that doorway alone. I can't prove it, because like I said, I lost count, but I'm pretty sure more of the balls were squeezing through the wall, getting bigger and sprouting even more and more hair all the time. It was impossible not to view them as anything but senior citizens' hairy scrotums, and even though they were wrinkled and sickly looking, I couldn't shake the feeling that these were nevertheless plump and ripe egg sacks, endlessly birthing black filament. The dark strands eagerly spread everywhere, clinging to the rough cinderblocks, the glass, the metal frames, gathering in the gaps. Even if electricity was coursing through the entire store, I knew with numb certainty that the door wouldn't open. The hair had clogged the gears, filling the tiniest of spaces, blocking all movement.

It reminded me of Yann struggling with the rotisserie doors, and I hoped like hell it wasn't something like this.

Carmelita told Gloria, "These doors, they're fucking glass. All we gotta do is throw something through it." Her voice was usually strong enough to pierce the Saturday afternoon pandemonium of Front End when calling for a sup, but out here in the shrouded vestibule it sounded small and vanished far too quickly.

"We could kick a cart into it," Kiko said like she couldn't wait to smash something.

Everybody looked to Gloria, waiting for her permission.

She shook her head. "No. I don't think so. Like John said, there's too much of that, that..."

"Hair," Sammy confirmed.

"Too much," echoed John.

I had an idea. "Hang on. What if me and Sammy use the snow shovels? You know, to hold it up and out of the way?" I nodded to the cart crew home base, a concrete ledge next to the ENTRANCE. Our battered ice chest rested on the ledge, under a bathroom cabinet attached to the cinderblock wall a few feet down from the doorframe. It held a random collection of hand warmers, forgotten sunglasses, half-empty Dunkin' Donuts coffee cups, a few box cutters, various lengths of twine, and an empty first-aid kit. Three cracked and splintered yellow snow shovels hung in the tool rack on the other side of the cabinet.

Eager to do something, anything, Sammy and I left the Professor on the ledge next to the ice chest and grabbed a shovel each before Gloria said anything one way or another. The shovels weren't particularly heavy or very effective against anything but the lightest dusting of snow, but holding something solid soothed my nerves. Sammy couldn't stop twisting the handle, spinning the blade. Despite my desire for action, I found I was in no hurry to rush down the vestibule after Carmelita and find out if my half-assed plan would work in the real world, happy instead to wait for Gloria's decision.

The day had gone so sideways I didn't know quite what to think anymore.

Gloria shook her head again. "Let's not take unnecessary chances unless we have no choice." The ever-growing hair swallowed the strong timbre of her voice as well. Not only were the windows covered completely, the strands now reached over two and three feet across the floor in places. "Here's what we're gonna do." Her voice had an edge. Hearing it, Gloria gave a small cough into her fist and regained composure. "We will go back inside and check the fire exits. If they do not open, we will exit through the loading dock."

No one was happy about this.

Gloria's face softened for a moment as she questioned her decision, then I saw the familiar thinning of her lips as she dismissed any lingering doubts about her choice to seek an alternative exit. "I do not understand what is happening," she admitted. "However, I can promise you this. We will get out of this building. I also promise you once you are all safe, I will help everyone left inside. This black stuff, I'm afraid there's a very good chance it is dangerous. Please, trust me with this."

I noticed she did not bring up Kyle just yet. It hit me like a soft sledgehammer that not only had the hair gotten hold of Kyle, if it had spread all the way from his office to the vestibule, it could be crawling through the walls of the entire store. Falling through the implications of that felt like I'd kicked my own balls a couple times.

"Carmelita, come back. Together, we'll go through New Arrivals to the closest fire exit." She indicated the ENTRANCE doorway. "Any questions?"

I could tell Carmelita's fear still wanted to smash the glass and run like hell, but she eventually decided to give in to Gloria's authority. She reluctantly turned back to the group of employees still gathered between the EXIT and ENTRANCE.

That's when I saw the blue lights on the ceiling.

Thirty feet above us was one of the most staggeringly beautiful things I'd ever encountered. It didn't make a lick of fucking sense, like everything else this morning. The longer I looked up, the more confused I became. The entire ceiling, the support struts, the pipes, every conceivable surface was covered in dazzling, flickering blue sparks as if someone had sprayed all of it down with silent, cold fireworks. No water or sky or iceberg could hold a shade of blue that intense. My eyes couldn't find purchase, and it all became a glittery blue blur.

Everyone followed my slack-jawed gaze.

"What? What is it?" the Professor demanded.

"Blue lights," Sammy said.

"This has been documented," the Professor whispered. An odd note of satisfaction had crept into his voice. "'Blue stars.' The Eisenstein Incident." He caught himself and blurted, "We must get inside. Shut the doors. Now."

Gloria didn't waste time asking questions. She pulled out her keyring and motioned for the employees to get back inside the store, through the ENTRANCE this time. She went instead to the EXIT. Directly inside, on the right side of the doorway, she unlocked the padlock. This held the chain in place that unrolled the security gates, lowering them at the end of each business day. She dropped the padlock, focusing on unhooking the chain from its safety catch. As employees still stared with open mouths up at the twinkling blue lights, Gloria didn't keep a loose hold of the chain like you usually would, slowly easing the security gate's descent until it came to rest gently on the concrete. She simply opened her fist, letting go, and ducked back into the vestibule. The chain went whisking away through the pulleys with a hell of a clatter, and the gate crashed to the floor with the full force of its weight.

The blue lights shivered as if one single organism with the impact.

Some of the lights flickered away from the struts and pipes, floating unsteadily for a second, sparks caught in the unpredictable crosswinds of a volcano. I frankly don't know if they were insects or what. Maybe that's just something my mind seized on as a placeholder, deciding to view them as something recognizable like moths, because the actual image and movement was too unreal to exist. I couldn't tell if they glowed from within, some kind of firefly on steroids, or if their appearance was instead the result of the alien surface of their wings catching and reflecting the sunlight, throwing it back with a hundred times more brilliance, showering the vestibule and black hair in dazzling blue sparkles.

Bright, glittery movement, high and off to the left. Five or six more of the moth things had detached themselves from the rest on the ceiling. The twinkling lights drifted without apparent purpose or direction at first, then grew stronger, bolder, fluttering down, down, flying with purpose. I realized they were heading toward Carmelita like moths zeroing in on a magical source of light.

She was only halfway back to the group.

The blue sparks settled over Carmelita's head like an electric veil.

She uttered a short, surprised yelp, slapping at her head as the lights burrowed into her hair. She went to cry out again. Her breath hitched, caught. More lights flocked to her. An instant later, she found enough breath to give a full, blood-curdling scream that split the vestibule. The lights above shivered. Her head glowed, glittering with blue sparks. She did not stop screaming.

Razieh ran to Carmelita.

And the entire ceiling came down.

The twinkling blue stars fell, dropping without warning, filling the vestibule. People scattered. Sammy and I brought the shovels up to cover the retreat, sweeping the broad curved blades through the air, doing our damnedest to smack the fluttering blue lights. Both us wanted to make 'em pay, fucking spatter these things like a windshield racing through farmland at dusk. It was difficult to make contact though. The lights or insects or whatever didn't seem to have any weight. They must have had some sort of mass though, thank fuck, because if nothing else, they responded to the same rules of physics as the rest of us. Our frantic waving managed to create small winds, short bursts of air currents strong enough to disrupt the moths, like chasing a mosquito away with a tabletop fan, only less fun and a hell of a lot more effort. Each swing of the shovels swept clouds of the blue moth lights swirling, but they were relentless, flying straight back and getting closer each time because of how long it took us to reverse our grip and rip the shovel back the other way.

"Go!" Gloria shouted, her powerful, rich voice fighting to reach us through the deadening blizzard of the blue wings and the hair coating the walls. "Go, GO!"

Everyone tumbled through the ENTRANCE. Wanda and Kiko had grabbed the Professor and helped drag him inside. Sammy and I were the last across the threshold, sweeping clouds of blue moths away. We were last, that is, except for Carmelita and Razieh.

We'd left them behind. I'm not proud of it, but that's the brutal truth.

Carmelita was curled on the concrete and had mostly stopped moving by then. Razieh had gone to her knees next to her and looked about to topple over any second too. Nothing remained of their faces, only flickering blue lights that sparkled and glinted wildly. The screaming had slowed down when the lights got into their mouths. Nobody knew exactly what was happening to Carmelita and Razieh. We only knew it was awful and would happen to us too if we went out there to help, tried to pull them inside. The moths would get everyone.

Poor Razieh was proof. Help and you die.

Gloria twisted the key and ripped the padlock off the ENTRANCE chain. Despite knowing the two women were beyond any kind of help, Gloria may have held that chain, clutching it for a fraction of a second longer than necessary, staring at the two women on the floor of the vestibule, weighing if she could save them, but if she did hesitate at all, it wasn't any longer than a slow blink.

The ENTRANCE gate dropped.

The blast of the gate hitting the floor drove the moths back, spinning them away. It stunned them briefly, then they immediately flew back at the gate. I worried that the security grille wouldn't stop them, that they might be able to squeeze through the gaps, or even pass effortlessly through solid matter like ghostly turquoise shadows. The fact that we'd managed to sweep them away momentarily with gusts of air gave me little comfort. Luckily, the spaces in the grille didn't offer enough room for the sparkling wings, leaving the moths to crawl impotently over the gate on the vestibule side.

For a long time, no one spoke. The only thing you could hear was everyone fighting to breathe.

Gloria grabbed everyone's attention with her clapping trick. I think we were all more than a little shell-shocked after what had happened to Carmelita and Razeih. With Shelley, it was different. Like I said, a lot of the employees dismissed anybody that took any kind of drugs to cope with life. They saw Don the same way, a doddering alcoholic only able to function at work because management made excuses for 'em. A person with those kinds of problems, somebody like that was just inviting trouble. Too many of the employees viewed what had happened to Shelley as more or less the same thing as a DUI into an icy retention pond.

And like I said, nobody paid much attention to Tim and Kyle. In Tim's case, he'd been too quiet, too distant to make anything but surface connections. Kyle was easy to dismiss because he was the bossman, so fuck him. Had I been one of those out in the vestibule, I realized most of these people would treat my memory like Tim, maybe a moment or two of reflecting on the inevitability of the cyclical nature of life and how it's a shame, before moving on and never thinking of them ever again.

With Carmelita and Razieh though, it felt like members of their own family had just been ripped away, leaving nothing but empty spaces, blank voids in the photos on the fridge. I don't wanna say that work in real life felt like a high school popularity contest, but I'd be lying.

"Anybody hurt?" Gloria asked. The clapping had worked. She had everyone's attention. "Any of those things get in here with us?"

We looked high and low. Nothing. The blue moths couldn't get through the gate.

It felt better to be back in the sunlight, even if it was dim and marginalized thanks to the piss-poorly maintained skylights. I'd take that over the sense of creeping darkness as the hair choked out the vestibule windows. Problem was, the things on the other side of the gate poisoned the sunlight, reflecting the tainted light back into New Arrivals, bathing everything that faced the gate in a soft, unearthly blue glow. The corrupted illumination almost had a physical quality, staining my bare skin with something oily.

I had to turn away. Closed my eyes and exhaled, focusing on the sensation of the ridged aluminum tube in my hands. Inhale. Slow. Exhale.

"And you," Gloria addressed the Professor. Wanda and Kiko had propped him on a stack of tires. "The fool who decided to bring a loaded firearm into my place of business."

His head turned to the sound of her voice.

Gloria propped a hand on her hip. "Why are you here?"

"I told you."

"I heard a lot of crying, something or other about atoms and parallel realities and some such nonsense about beer bubbles. I need something I can use. Start with why you are here."

"To stop it."

"Stop what?"

"The end of everything." The Professor coughed. "That's as simple as I can make it."

"Fine. You want to be clear as mud, that's on you. Whatever. You're gonna make me glad I sprayed you. Let's try something different." Gloria was losing patience. "You've been here what, all summer? Living out in your car. Why wait? Why now?"

The Professor nodded. "You're right, of course. I should have come to you sooner. But how? How could I possibly get you to take me seriously? You already think I'm insane. You'd have the authorities force me to relocate, and I wouldn't be able to continue surveillance. This has been the third consecutive summer that we've been watching and waiting. Hoping it was all just conjecture." He stopped for a pained, wheezing breath. "Ben knew. He could have explained it," he said. "Ben understood it all better than I ever could. You would have believed him. We tried to, well..." Something heavy and invisible pushed down on him with tremendous pressure, hunching his back as if he was twenty years older and near collapse if he didn't find a cane soon.

"The vandalism," Gloria said with a neutral tone. "That was you, wasn't it?"

"Vandalism?" the Professor asked like he couldn't fathom the meaning.

"All that chalk on the floor. All the nonsense circles and symbols and whatnot."

"It was most certainly not nonsense. It was...an attempted surgery, if you will."

"I call it vandalism."

"Ben and I—it was only to help. Help you. Help all

of you. To try and stop it." He lapsed back into memories and didn't say anything else, fingers clutching at each other for moral support. He paused so long I thought he had finished speaking. "And in the end, it was in vain and foolish and accomplished nothing. But you must believe me, it was done, all of it, in a deeply sincere effort to stop it. To save us. All of us."

"That's all fine and good, but it doesn't do much for us at the moment," Gloria said.

"'Remoras?'" I asked. "You said 'the remoras are here.'"

"Remoras?" Gloria asked.

"Sharks," Kiko said.

"Not, no, no," the Professor said. "Remoras are a type of fish that exist within a symbiotic relationship with larger sharks. Their life cycle depends utterly on the movements and eating patterns of a larger beast. These, these manifestations, these flocks of cryptids, this cancerous growth, they are heralds of a much, much larger beast."

"So, the hair's a fish?" Sammy asked. He had me genuinely confused.

"It's more of an analogy, son," the Professor said patiently. He had already warmed to Sammy, like everyone did sooner or later. "That is why Ben and I called them remoras, at any rate. The important point to understand, though, is that the process has begun. If they are here, then there will undoubtedly be more."

"More," Gloria said without expression. "Wonderful." She took a final look at the security gate, then back at the Professor. "Can you walk?"

"I think so, yes. I cannot see very well, however."

"Shoulda thought've that 'fore you pulled a piece."

"I warned you. I told you. I—"

"You said there would be more of these, these remoras, as you call them?"

"Most certainly."

"Then we will continue this later when we have the luxury of more time. Wanda, will you assist him? The rest of you, follow close." She turned and was off, cutting through the displays and down the New Arrival aisles, angling off to the west wall of the store. Kiko and John followed her. Wanda was next, holding the Professor's elbow.

I was almost back to feeling like I had some semblance of control over my thoughts and actions until I looked back to double-check none of the moth things had gotten through the grille and saw that, while none of the blue lights were inside with us, the black hair had already started to grow under and through the security gate.

Sammy saw it too and made an angry noise, deep in his throat. It sounded about as threatening as an especially fierce kitten, but that wasn't important. I was glad to hear it. I'd been worried about him. He'd been keeping pretty quiet, doing his best trying to follow and connect events that appeared to be real and matter-of-fact, all while the incidents themselves defied an easy, logical explanation. I knew it couldn't have been easy for him, making sense of the chaos. All of it, Shelley and the lady, Tim, the smell that clung to you like a cursed wet tissue, the comatose customers, everything, it had to have been eating at him worse than his frequent nightmares.

Like I said, I was proud of him. He was doing well, considering.

Sammy...well, Sammy wouldn't want me telling you any of this.

See, he was awfully sensitive. But he didn't want anybody to know. He hated horror movies and the news and tried to avoid bad stuff, but of course, every once in a while he'd accidentally come across something online, a terrorist attack, a heinous true crime, images or a scenario that would haunt him for weeks. He didn't have enough self-control to dilute his reaction, and if anybody noticed his shock or maybe even tears, he'd laugh it off, make fun of himself, treat it like a big joke, but that was all for show, an act for everybody. He was Sammy the Samoan, and his whole identity was wrapped up in being a positive, happy dude. Everybody saw him as a gentle giant.

I was just as big, but I never heard anybody call me gentle. I mostly got, "That cranky asshole," instead.

I knew Sammy inside and out, better than a brother, and he was a lot like me. A scared little kid hiding inside a big body. I didn't want him focusing on our dead coworkers or all the silent, hypnotized customers. I mean, there were times that just normal, regular life stuff could pile up on him. If he'd been feeling tense for a while, then almost anything could spark a breakdown. One time it was merely the sight of a single child's glove out in the parking lot, frozen and abandoned in the salt and ice.

It broke him.

When that happened, he'd hide it until he could quietly go off on his own, and once he was out of sight of everyone, tucked behind a minivan or big SUV, he'd fold into himself and go to pieces. He'd crouch, wrap his arms as far around his shoulders as possible, clutching at his back, holding himself together so he wouldn't fly apart, all while continually rocking back and forth on the balls of his feet, whispering endless rapid questions to himself.

If I saw his endurance running thin, I tried to run interference, as Tim liked to say. I'd goad him into really *working*, actually sweating and panting as we hit the lot like a wrecking ball and swept it clean. He'd do the same for me when he saw that I was getting snappier and even more toxic than usual. I don't want to come out and claim that physical activity felt good or anything like that or eventually helped make you feel better. I'm not gonna go that far and state that exercise is good for you or anything fucking ridiculous like that. But put a gun to my head, and yeah, I'll reluctantly admit that sweating and panting did tend to help us feel better.

Sometimes, Sammy would just get a little confused about what he should be doing. Once I figured out the situation, I could translate whatever was needed. I'd describe a loose collection of sequential images, almost like telling somebody about a comic strip, and that gave Sammy the tools to build each moment in his head, where he could then comprehend the steps and truly decipher the process.

And once he knew what was necessary, he was off to the fucking races, formulating a goddam genuine *action plan*, another more or less nonsense phrase that was just dumb and nebulous enough to gain instant popularity in the corporate lexicon. Anything could be an action plan. Structuring and navigating the negotiations of a multi-million-dollar merger could be defined as an action plan. Dashing down the street to grab a

Philly cheesesteak and fries during your last break, fifteen of the fastest minutes you'll ever blink and miss, was just as much an action plan as anything else. This term, this so-called *"action plan,"* meant everything and nothing at the same time, so of course the company loved to shove it down our throats, jamming it into every part of the corporate culture, trotting it out any and every time they got the chance.

So, knowing that Sammy was ready and willing to fight gave me a kick in the ass I badly needed and didn't know it.

He was right.

Fuck that hair.

I retightened my shoelaces and said, "Let's go."

"OSHA would not be pleased with this," Gloria said through gritted teeth, pushing hard on the FIRE EXIT crash bar. Legally, these two doors were never locked. They swung open outward, only needing the slightest pressure to engage the broad bar that stretched across each door. The ridged bar would depress with a reassuring chunk, simultaneously releasing the lock while triggering a fire alarm. I don't think the alarm needed the store's power. It ran off a different system.

This particular FIRE EXIT was a hundred feet from the ENTRANCE along the western wall, the first of two sets of exits. Getting here, Gloria had retraced much of the route I'd used looking for Mrs. Toenails. Sammy and I brought up the rear with our snow shovels. Along the way, we passed the kid with the plastic bag of forks, frozen, still holding them in front of himself like he was stuck trying to comprehend the directions. Nothing much looked different. I wondered if he had already been under the influence of whatever had gotten to the customers when I'd seen him earlier.

Neither door would budge. No alarm either. Gloria started to take the door's refusal to open as a personal insult. I'm guessing it reminded her of the basement door, and that made her angry. She gave Sammy a thin smile. "Will you do me the pleasure of giving this door a swift kick or two, Samuel?"

"Amen," Wanda said.

"Hang on," I told Sammy as he squared up to the door.

I hoped like hell that what I was looking at was spider eggs at the bottom of the door, but we weren't that lucky. Three scrotums, currently the size of peanut shells, had emerged from the tight gap between the steel doors and the threshold. Then everyone saw the black hair filling the cracks along the doorframe; the more you looked, the more you saw.

"Wonderful. Let's try the next one," Gloria said, trying to sound hopeful and failing.

The second and last FIRE EXIT on the western was another hundred feet down. We had to skirt the mountain of wind chimes to get to it. The badass vet in the black hat was gone. In fact, I didn't see anybody. The rest of the aisles were empty. Everything was quiet. The only movement I caught was a flash of neon pink down by the ottomans as I looked back toward the ENTRANCE.

The damn dog was following us.

Gloria didn't touch the second FIRE EXIT door

once Kiko pointed out more of the wrinkled, hairy testicles already infesting the gaps.

Everybody avoided looking at each other. Nobody wanted to see echoes of their own rising panic. We'd been offered a big shiny lollipop only to have jerked away at the last possible second. That blissful release, that sudden weightlessness, getting unexpected permission, encouragement even, to go spend your day at a bar instead of work, all that joy had vanished, leaving only a deep lingering dread. If we couldn't get out through the back of the store, we'd be stuck inside with god only fucking knew until someone came to get us out.

"So be it. The loading dock," Gloria said.

We found Abid sprawled face down in a large puddle of blood on the floor in front of his chicken room. I'm no doctor, but I'm guessing there was far too much blood for there to be any kind of reassuring news for Abid. Spatters of it had reached all the way onto the racks of vinyl house slippers.

We'd turned down the big back aisle that ran from the west wall to the east. The doors to Back End were halfway down the aisle, where the main center aisle that ran from Front End to the back of the store where it met in a T-junction. To get there along the back aisle, we'd have to pass directly in front of the chicken room.

Dozens of raw rotisserie chickens lay scattered around Abid, some even resting on his back, as if there'd been some kind of explosion from the chicken room, sending them all flying. I couldn't see anything to back up that theory, though. No fire. No smoke. Apparently, the problem with the rotisserie machine had been fixed at some point because now the doors stood wide open. I still couldn't guess how all the corpses, both man and chicken, had come to be spread out like that across the aisle.

I decided it was pointless to worry about particular *hows* and *whys* anymore and vowed to do my best not to get sidetracked. After all the hair and blue moths in the vestibule, not to mention Shelley and the lady, Tim and Kyle, that line of inquiry just got in the way.

Weird shit was going down at the FOOD4U!, and all that really mattered was getting out.

"Anybody sees any of them blue moth things, holler out," Gloria said, taking a few tentative steps closer to Abid for a better look at his corpse. Yet another dead employee had brought out the thick and unapologetic South Side in her voice. Without thinking too much about it, me and Sammy flanked her, shovels up, and the three of us crept closer, sticking to the center of the wide back aisle. Gloria halted about ten feet away.

Abid was covered in a wide variety of holes, as if he'd been splashed by something corrosive. Both clothes and skin were deeply pockmarked. Gouged, really. Globs of thin yellow slime clung to the edges of each hole and wound. Much of it was thick and crusty. The rest was something that looked wet because it gleamed in the dim light. I sure as hell wasn't gonna be the one who said it looked like snot.

"Lord, I'm looking to you now," Gloria said, mostly to herself, before making a few seriously disapproving, "Nnhnnn-uhhnnnn" grunts that made her opinion quite clear. "Oh, Lord, oh, Lord." She sucked at her teeth for a few seconds before calling out to the group. "Hey, Professor. Can you see this?"

"Not…not exactly," he called back.

"Well, that don't *exactly* help," Gloria said and kicked the closest rotisserie chicken in frustration. It slid over to the chicken room counter and had nearly come to a rest when five or six stubby, segmented spider legs unfolded from under the wing flaps. It scrabbled at the concrete slick with fresh blood. One of Abid's beard nets was caught up on a hairy leg. The raw chicken spun around like a wobbly, homemade radio-controlled Halloween decoration a couple of times.

I think we all screamed. I know Gloria did. I sure as hell did.

The fat spider legs or whatever the fuck caught a groove in the concrete, giving it enough leverage to launch itself across the floor toward Gloria. It scurried through the blood, fast enough to leave a wake, and had crossed the distance to us before Sammy could blurt out, "Oh shit."

I was on Gloria's left and followed the natural impulse to drop the shovel blade to the floor while driving forward with my right arm, scooping the chicken up and swinging it away. Thank Christ I didn't stop to think about it. Years of shoveling snow gave me the skills to capture the momentum of the original scraping movement, slinging the blade around and flicking the contents off to the side. In this case, I flung the chicken over a few aisles toward Front End where it landed with an unsatisfyingly soft splat somewhere deep in Shoes.

More of the chickens began to move.

"That's it," Gloria said. "Back up."

At least a dozen chickens had revealed previously hidden stocky insect legs and now crawled drunkenly around Abid's corpse, with more waking all the time. At the sound of Gloria's voice, they all whirled and scuttled in our direction. Like that first one, they had a tough time finding any grip on the slick floor. Once free of the main pool, though, they moved fast, faster than a puppy with the zoomies, leaving smears and droplets of blood behind in horrific snail trails. Even the ones on top of Abid rose on unsteady legs and tumbled off his body. One landed on its back, scissoring its useless appendages frantically as it rolled around like a turtle on its shell.

Me and Sammy covered Gloria's retreat. Sammy mostly. He'd scoop the tottering carcasses up with a quick, effortless jerk, followed by a sweet snapping motion that sent the damn things forty or fifty feet into the air. Frankly, I was a little jealous. I caught a few and sent them sailing, but I was strictly an amateur next to Sammy. Together, we stopped dozens of chickens cold, firing them into Clothing and Shoes, sometimes farther.

Not gonna lie here, though I want to. It felt fucking awesome to fling that sonofabitch as far as I fucking could. I mean, somewhere deep down where I don't have much control, this visceral surge of adrenaline erupted inside of me, fuel-injected by an undeniable thirst for revenge. I loved it. All I can say is that I laughed out loud when Sammy bounced one of those goddamn chickens at least seventy, eighty feet, all the way off the freezer.

I'm ashamed to say that we even high-fived.

You'd think I would have learned.

See, it was my fault. Not Sammy's. Somebody should have been thinking ahead. And that's not Sammy's job. Yeah, sure it was damn good fun to send those spider chicken carcasses flying and all, but nobody thought about how we probably weren't hurting 'em a whole lot seeing that they seemed to be built mostly out of raw chicken. We should have known that all we really accomplished was to toss motion-sensing grenades into random hiding spots throughout Clothing and Shoes, where they could lurk and wait for fresh prey.

So yeah, that's on me.

We'd retreated all the way back to the wind chimes before Gloria set off for the opposite wall, aiming to take a left when we hit the main center aisle that split the store in half from the front to the back. She arranged everybody in a single file, Sammy and his shovel up front, with Gloria a close second, then Wanda and Kiko and John helping the Professor, with me and my own shovel bringing up the rear.

Out of everybody, I don't know why John stopped to point out the chicken. He was third or so through that spot in Intimates, and I don't know why the thing didn't attack immediately. Maybe it was because the first few employees kept moving, and John stopped right in front of it. All I really know is that I heard John call out to Gloria, "Hey, hey, a chicken—"

And then there was this weird wet hiss.

That's about as accurate as I can get. I don't know how else to describe it. Wet. Like, you know how surf guitars have that dripping, *wet* sound? It was kind of like that, some kind of electric reverb liquid hiss.

John began to shriek in an impossibly high, pleading octave that shredded my eardrums.

It is one of my most fervent hopes that I never have to hear anything like it ever again. I think a large part of me would rather die than listen to anything in that much pain. I know you can't really compare these things, but it was worse than Carmelita or Razieh. Took longer, anyway. I caught flashes of his flailing arms over Wanda and Kiko's shoulders and pushed past the two of them, just to watch as John crashed back through racks of women's underwear on the right. He went down, flailing and howling.

Another wet hiss and this time something squirted through the air.

I whipped my head over to see the chicken carcass on the left side of the aisle, lingering quietly on the top rack where it used its spider legs to wedge itself between two bags of socks. Instead of running forward at us again though, it remained in place while a lumpy, segmented tube now stuck out of the top of the chicken, as if it had pushed itself through the chicken's backbone. The tube or whatever it was had a somewhat different structure and movement than the legs, but they could be kissing cousins all right. This segmented tube contracted, held itself back for a moment, then convulsed with that wet hiss, spurting a glob of sticky yellow snot at John.

I'm not even going to say what it reminded me and everybody else of.

That snot shit ate into him wherever it landed, boiling oil sprayed onto a brittle ice sculpture.

The first blast had caught John's face just off-center. His right temple, right eye, nose, and most of his upper lip were now nothing but a series of meteor strikes, sizzling pits in his skull that wouldn't stop foaming and smoking as the acid melted skin, tissue, and bone, slicing it all away easy as floodwaters on a gravel creek bed. The second and third volleys landed on his chest and groin, gouging massive craters deep into his torso. His arms spasmed, whipping specks of blood into the air above him, mindlessly begging the pain to stop. Legs thrummed the floor.

Two more wet hisses. More smoke, more blood.

I brought the shovel down on the chicken as hard as I could. Again, I wished I'd taken just a half second to think about the consequences of my actions before I moved. Too late. The impact bent both the metal rack and shovel handle, knocking the entire rack sideways. Bags of socks went flying. In the resulting chaos, I lost track of the damn thing. I scrambled backward, keeping low, holding the shovel up, trying to keep my elbows wide to both shield Wanda and Kiko and keep them moving, expecting to hear that wet hiss any second.

The snot finally ate into John's larynx, dissolving his piercing shrieks into gasping wheezes.

Eventually, that too stopped.

In the silence, Gloria half-shouted, half-whispered, "Come *on*! Go around!"

Kiko and Wanda and me kept shuffling backward until we reached the previous intersection. The chicken remained hidden and did not give chase. We turned to our right, moving in the direction of Front End, trying not to run. I stuck to a narrow line down the center of the wide aisle, head on a swivel, eyes stabbing not at just the shadows lurking under the hanging clothing but also up higher, where the chickens could be clinging to the top of stacked merchandise as well, all thanks to me and Sammy. In a lot of ways, keeping an eye out for lurking chickens didn't feel too different than spotting and dodging speeding SUVs on the lot during the final frenzied weeks of shopping before the holidays. That's why I only wanted to use the main aisles. The open space gave me a chance to catch any threats. Cutting through the tight stacks of merchandise risked another ambush. Once we hit the next main intersection, we turned left, aiming again for the east wall, moving parallel to the sock and underwear aisle, giving John and the missing chicken plenty of space.

When we reached the main center aisle we turned left again, to the back of the store. If we followed it straight back for another twenty yards, it would deposit us directly at the T-junction in front of the swinging doors. Gloria and the others were waiting for us in the next intersection, next to Children's Clothing. Sammy was holding up fingers to see how the Professor's eyesight was improving.

It should have filled me with hope.

It did not.

During the short walk, I'd tried to concentrate, focusing only on detecting any chicken carcasses, but the dark thoughts crept through anyway, whittling away my resolve to keep the shock and panic locked down. Insect monsters that sprayed acid like a fly had either somehow grown inside the chickens or ate the carcasses partially from the inside and used the remaining raw pink flesh like a hermit crab shell. And either way, me and Sammy hadn't bothered to stop and consider the consequences when we'd gleefully flung these things all over the goddamn store.

I was directly responsible for a poor man's hideous death.

I couldn't shake how the guilt wanted to tear me apart.

Curious thing about guilt. It needs your help to really work, and if you could, if you had any sense at all, you'd just shut it down, say no thanks, not today. But nope. You open the door, welcome it, only too happy to beg it to come inside. So much of guilt's power comes from its quiet assurance, agreeing with you that this mental anguish is the least you can suffer to prove the depth of your remorse. 'Course, both you and the guilt know damn well you actually deserve far worse. How could I look myself in the eye ever again? Guilt and shame's grubby conjoined fingers poked and prodded at my flimsy reasons and logic, shredding each desperate argument fighting for my innocence, until there was nothing left except to give in and let the torment swallow me whole.

Trembling, I went up to Gloria. "I—" I couldn't finish the sentence. The shadow thoughts had already welled up, spinning around in my skull like a hurricane full of wasps, and I started to gasp. Tears clung to my eyelids. Full sobbing was next. A part of me knew only too well that if I started to cry, I wouldn't stop. I'd been caught up like this a few times in my life, but as bad and awful as the other situations had been, I'd never had a death on my conscience. That meant that if I slipped any farther, I'd be washed off a cliff, and there'd be no coming back. It would consume me totally, reducing me into a shivering pile of blubbering and tears.

Gloria knew this, too, knew I'd be useless.

She gave me a tender slap, holding back but still making sure I felt a slight sting. Then she roughly cupped my left jaw, squeezing my pierced earlobe between her thumb and forefinger, somehow grabbing hold of my conscious thoughts as well, halting the panic in its tracks. I can see now that Gloria somehow understood exactly what was required to snap me out of my haze of self-pity and shock, but I'll be damned if I can figure out *how* she knew. It's astonishing. *I* didn't even know.

It must have been a hell of a fine line. See, if she'd acted motherly, full of unconditional love, embracing me or something emotional like that, the dam inside would have crumbled. I'd collapse in her arms, unable to resist clutching at her like a drowning victim clawing at their rescuer. Same thing if she'd gone too far the other direction and really slapped the shit out of me, knocking some sense into my dumb ass. That might stun me for about ten, fifteen seconds, stopping everything momentarily sure, but that approach would not only simply delay the inevitable, it'd ultimately make everything worse. The more you struggle to push a beach ball underwater, the harder it'll shoot back at your face.

Gloria instinctively knew how to puncture the beach ball.

She tugged on my ear and cupped the back of my skull, pulling my head over and down, until our foreheads nearly touched. She locked her eyes on to mine, speaking in a voice so low only I could hear. "They'll be plenty of time to chew on all this once we outta here. That's later. We gonna get loose here first. You just gotta stick with us, got it? Easy. Put one foot in front of the other, keep a sharp eye for any more them birds, and we outta here just fine. You dig?"

"Yup," I managed and meant it.

We found one more chicken, the one Sammy'd bounced off the freezer. It looked like the impact had broken a couple of its legs, and it hadn't gotten far, I noted with grim satisfaction. Now it seemed only capable of crawling around in a ragged circle. I would've been more than happy to break more of its legs but didn't want to get any closer. Neither did anyone else. Not after what happened with John.

"What is it?" the Professor asked. "I can't make out details."

"Something got into the rotisserie chickens," Gloria said. "More of your remoras?"

"I cannot say for certain. What exactly did you say happened?"

Gloria hesitated, looking for the right words.

Kiko helped out. "Chicken bugs," she said.

Nobody had anything to add. That seemed to say it all, really.

"...that shoot acid?" the Professor asked. "Is that correct, what I've heard?"

"Yes," Kiko said.

"There's nothing...no description in any of the texts fits this phenomenon."

"Wonderful," Gloria said. "Joseph, Samuel. Let us strategize a moment."

After a quick huddle with Gloria, me and Sammy approached the freezer, moving almost as slow as the hair. Beyond the freezer and cooler was the main back aisle, the one we'd been trying to get down in the first place until we ran into Abid and couldn't get past him. The chicken room was left of Receiving's doors, down far enough that we could only see Abid's boots and splashes of blood on the floor.

Since we were between Children's Clothes and Textiles, Gloria had found a package of the thickest, most expensive towels in the store, shook them out, and exchanged them with me for my shovel. We knew damn well the snot would eat right through the cotton, but if the chicken sprayed anything, the towels might be just enough of a shield to interrupt the acid's flight, halt it in midair, and at least slow it down for a second or two, stop it from hitting either of us. As we crept closer, I held the towels up and as far out in front as I could manage, pinching the very edges, prepared to drop them the moment they caught any flying snot before it had a chance to burn through. Sammy had his shovel up as well, keeping a loose grip, ready to switch his hands in an instant.

I don't think the chicken bug had eyes. At least I couldn't see any, but somehow it knew we were there. It crawled faster, skittering around in tight loops, reacting to our proximity. Maybe it knew it was being hunted. It strained with its good legs on one side, dragging the broken legs on the other, a rowboat with only one oar. It collided with the concrete base of the freezer and immediately changed course, hugging the gray base as the good legs shoved its carcass along away from us, using the foundation to keep it moving in a straight line.

When we got within five or six feet, it stopped and quivered in place.

Me and Sammy froze.

The chicken carcass moved like it was trying to shrug its headless shoulders. The tube thing squirmed up through the backbone and strained to get out, stretching the mottled skin at least an inch before it split. The Professor later explained this thing was most likely a proboscis. It rose like a baby cobra and whatever you wanted to call it, I knew damn well the contraction was coming, followed by the inevitable spurt of snot.

The plan wasn't complicated. My job was to toss both towels over the chicken, covering the damn thing so with any luck, the thick fabric would be enough to dampen the spray of acid long enough for Sammy to smash it a few times with his shovel. Soon as I threw the towels, I was supposed to grab something heavy and help Sammy bash the shit out of the chicken. I couldn't see anything that would work, just jeans and coats across the aisle from the freezer. Maybe there was a big box of American cheese or something in the cooler next to the freezer.

I didn't have time to worry about it because we were right on top of the thing.

The proboscis began its contraction.

"Here it comes," I said, my voice sounding high and tight.

"Do it," Sammy said.

I threw the towels at the chicken.

And missed.

They fell short.

Too late, I realized I should have gathered fistfuls of the heavy towels in order to send the bulk of the thick material far enough to reach the chicken. Instead, I was pinching the edges like I said, holding it up in front of my face because I was terrified of the snot hitting my skin. So, when I threw it, the action was pathetic and weak. The towels landed harmlessly a full foot from the chicken.

Sammy and I flinched.

The movement of the towels fluttering down was enough to send the chicken scrabbling back along the freezer, pausing the contraction. I wondered if it couldn't move and spray acid at the same time and decided to risk it. I'd fucked up the towel toss and wanted another chance. I darted forward, snatched a corner of one of the towels, and jumped back.

I was wrong.

A wet hiss.

Thank fuck for reflexes that still work every once in a while. Part of me must have known I'd never get the towel up and unfurled in time, so I whipped the closest freezer door open. Snot splashed against frozen glass, sizzling and popping. Cracks split the door, but it held, stopping the forward trajectory of the snot long enough for me to get out of the way.

Sammy used the shovel blade to scoop up the towel I'd left behind and lofted it at the chicken bug before it could squirt more at us again. This time, the plan worked beautifully. For a moment, you could almost believe there was nothing more than a cat moving under the towel, helping with the laundry.

At least Sammy and I had enough sense not to high-five this time.

The second wet hiss was muffled. Smoking holes appeared in the towel immediately, but the range had been temporarily limited. Severely temporarily. The towel melted in front of us like a single-ply square of toilet paper trying to hold back industrial-strength drain cleaner. In two seconds, the proboscis was back searching for us again.

Gloria yelled, "Split up!" She was crouched about twenty feet back down the aisle, with everyone else huddled behind her.

I went left, diving for the slim shelter of one of the bollards that flanked the swinging doors. Sammy went to the right, opening another freezer door. He leaped inside, crashing into the thin shelves and smashing boxes of fish sticks and tater tots. I hit the concrete and rolled, losing sight of him and the chicken bug.

A hesitation. Then, another wet hiss.

I flinched, instinctively curling into a fetal position.

No pain. I cracked an eye open and felt guilty relief. It had gone after Sammy instead, maybe because he was closer. The snot spattered across the freezer, blowing through the damaged first door in a flurry of glass shards and acid, crashing right through it into Sammy's door. It bore the full brunt of that blast and wouldn't withstand another. He kicked and ripped at the shelves inside, trying to twist through them into the middle of the freezer, where the overstock was stored on six or seven pallets. I knew he wouldn't make it past the shelves though. He was too big.

The proboscis was already contracting again.

Another blast would hit Sammy's skin.

Jolted by desperate inspiration, I lunged across the aisle while upending the thirty-gallon trash can that had been living next to the bollards at the Back End doors before I'd even been hired. I slammed the can over the chicken carcass. Half-empty water bottles, disposable coffee cups, empty candy wrappers, and the rest of the garbage spilled everywhere. It didn't matter. I just prayed the thick black plastic would last longer than the fluffy towel.

The can shivered as the chicken struggled against the inside. If the snot had been unleashed, I couldn't tell. Nothing came bubbling through the plastic immediately, and that gave us a few seconds at the very least. I worried the chicken bug might be strong enough to lift the deceptively light can, enough to slip out anyway, so I kept my hand flat on top, pushing down, and called to Sammy. "I need something heavy. Quick!"

He looked out through the cracked, dissolving glass, saw what I'd done with the trash can, then disentangled himself from the shelves while grabbing the heaviest merchandise he could find. Ice cream. He piled the gallon boxes onto the can, one after another. After he'd stacked at least ten gallons of ice cream, I pulled my hand away. The upended can didn't move. Sammy added a few more boxes just for the hell of it.

I waved at Gloria and the rest. She was already up and moving, the others hurrying along behind her. The dog had joined the group at some point. I had no idea when, but it was now following along at Wanda's heels, smart enough to be quiet.

They joined me and Sammy at the doors to Back End. These were double-wide traffic doors which meant they could swing in both directions. Each had a decent-sized rectangular window, so you didn't crash into anybody on the other side. I peered in. Back End only had two skylights and was dark as hell. I could make out enough to see that nothing was moving. Dim, but normal.

When I went to push through, Gloria put her hand on my arm.

"Lord knows what's waiting in there," Gloria said. "I'm tired of jumping from one frying pan into another fire every time we make a move here. We don't need to end up like Abid, rest his soul." We all looked at him in the pool of blood. She turned to the Professor. "So, what else do you and your books say we got to look forward to?"

"I, I really have no basis to predict anything. The reports do mention the blue stars, yes, but that phenomenon was only observed at a fair distance. You can imagine, there were no survivors, you understand, close enough to...there was no mention of, of hair or chicken carcasses. Or bugs."

"Or there were no survivors left to mention it," Kiko said.

"What does it mention?" Gloria asked. "I'm tired of being unprepared."

"Well, bear in mind that these reports are only a

collection of, of fragments really, mostly from an incident in 1886 in this very location. Primarily, it mentions a...congregation, I suppose. You may call it a cult. Both would be true. Also, of course, the blue stars."

"And?" Gloria pushed.

"Giant rats."

Gloria snorted, doing her best to abort a barking, mocking laugh. "Tell me something I don't know. I live in Chicago. What else ya got?"

The Professor looked like he didn't want to answer. Finally, he said, "Tentacles. Lots of tentacles."

"Giant rats I can believe. But tentacles? I dunno. Like, octopus tentacles? Calamari? In Illinois?"

"Ben and I assumed it to be an exaggeration, a myth. Now, I am not so sure."

"There's no water here," Wanda pointed out.

"Up here, no. But down there." The Professor pointed at the concrete in front of him.

I couldn't help but think of the basement and shuddered.

"That's fine," Gloria said. "I have no intention of going downstairs. We are leaving through the loading docks. If we're lucky, Oskar is unloading a delivery, and one or both docks will be open."

Gloria handed me my shovel and held the door open with her foot while me and Sammy crept through.

I noted that Oskar's bench, straight ahead, was empty. Before we'd even cleared the door, I was checking out the ceiling, looking for any of the blue moths. I only saw thick, deep shadows among the struts and pipes. No lights, blue or otherwise.

I should have been scouring the floor.

I was on Sammy's left, our shoulders touching. Soon as the door swung shut on anxious faces, we pivoted, back-to-back, shovels up. Sammy faced east, toward the loading docks, the stacks of pallets, another FIRE EXIT, a line of pallet jacks. I faced west, scanning the bathroom door next to Oskar's bench, the garbage chute to the dumpster, and the hydraulic press for all the cardboard boxes.

I thought I heard some sort of whisper but immediately forgot about it when I spotted another goddamn chicken bug, lurking near the bathroom door.

It was almost too late.

That wet fucking hiss.

Thankfully, the snot fell short, bubbling into the concrete, six inches from my toes.

The chicken bug scurried at us.

I kicked a cart half full of damaged merch at the thing and got lucky. The front wheels passed harmlessly around it but one of the back wheels caught the sucker, grinding it into the floor. I jumped forward, scooped the wounded chicken bug up and tossed it into the cardboard compactor. I slammed the gate, hit the green button and tried not to smile as hydraulics drove the massive slab of solid steel down, crushing the boxes and with any luck, the bug.

As the machine hissed and rumbled, I quickly scanned my half of Back End to make sure there weren't more of the chicken bugs back here. Apart from a pile of boxes that would ordinarily earn a stern rebuke from Gloria and a couple carts full of garbage since the garbage chute was locked, per OSHA regulations, this half of the long room was empty. I wondered how the chicken bug had gotten through the swinging doors. I didn't think it had enough strength to push them open but didn't have a chance to follow that thought far because I heard Sammy sucked in a ragged breath.

Down at the far end of the dock where the trucks unloaded, the slowly twisting body of a man was somehow suspended two feet off the ground at the open mouth of the back of a semi-trailer. It was the hair. The guy, a truck driver I figured, was caught up in a few dozen of the strands. The rest of the doorway was wide open, inviting even. Then I saw the pulsing scrotum egg sacs all around the doorframe, sprouting between the steel and the stone cinderblocks.

At first glance, apart from the truck driver, the far end of the loading dock looked dark without power. The other rolling door was closed.

It wasn't only shadows.

The walls and ceiling were *infested* with hair.

On the floor, the hair clung to the shadows like moss, avoiding the brightest spots in the center of the dock as if it didn't like the sunlight.

Every ten or so seconds, the truck driver would gasp and struggle for a moment. He was a rebellious puppet, but the strings didn't act like they were working together. When he'd jerk against the hair, each individual strand acted as its own entity, pulling with varying degrees of strength and urgency, twisting him higher, contorting him in unnatural positions, as if ivy was pulling a skeleton slowly up a wall through the decades.

"We gotta help him," Sammy said. "He's still alive."

So was Carmelita. For a minute anyway. It sounded like a terrible idea, and I wanted to say so. But this was Sammy. I said, "Okay."

"The floor is lava."

"The floor is lava."

We eyeballed the bare spots in the concrete where the sun came through the strongest, where we'd have to jump, gauged what path would be safest to the truck driver. I snapped my fingers when an idea hit. The pallet jacks. Instead of leaping from spot to spot like using rocks to cross a stream, we could ride the pallet jacks. These nifty gadgets were basically two forklift blades attached to a hydraulic handle rather than a big machine that you drove around. A single employee could move a thousand-pound pallet of merchandise with relative ease. And the store didn't need to indulge in any more expensive training to certify any extra employees as forklift operators.

I rolled the closest pallet jack off the line, snicked the lever on the left side of the handle down to engage the hydraulics, then used both hands to swing the entire handle up and down, like operating a pump handcar on railroad tracks. This lifted the twin blades half an inch off the concrete with each swing. Then I saw a problem. If we rode them like scooters, it wouldn't take long for the wheels to become ensnared, and if we stopped in the midst of all that hair, we'd be trapped. Instead, once I had a few inches of clearance, I sent the jack sailing by itself across the loading dock, straight through lines and pools of shadowy hair. It didn't take long for the darkness to get caught up in the three-inch-wide polyurethane wheels. Snarls of black filament gathered, clogging the axles, slowing the pallet jack's momentum. It came to a shuddering stop five, maybe four, feet away from the truck driver.

Sammy liked this game. He was already cranking his own pallet jack higher before mine stopped for good. He took a wide stance, rolled the jack back and forth a few times to gather steam, then with a tremendous grunt, hurled that sucker across the loading dock like it was an Olympic sport. It hit that hair like an over-cranked lawn mower, spitting fragments of hair into the air. Sammy's jack curled wide and crashed into the far wall. The driver jerked with the impact. Filaments started curling over and around the pallet jack immediately, but I had another one ready to launch by then.

We sent all ten pallet jacks across the floor and in the end, we cleared a more or less continuous straight path to the driver, with varying lengths of black hair littering the bare concrete like a lazy bartender's shop. Sammy solved that by trading his shovel for Oskar's push broom. He swept the remaining pieces along in front of us and occasionally off to the side, shoving away bigger clumps if they were too close.

I thought we could use the shovel to jab at the hair, cutting each strand individually. It might not be the gentlest way to get the guy down, but I didn't see any other choice. I stopped two feet away, unwilling to get any closer. I didn't like how the hair above the rolled-up door box was clumped up there precariously, apt to spill with any vibration. Deciding to try and test things with an isolated strand, I chose one farthest from the rest, connected to the guy's ankle. The way it disappeared under the jeans, over the tops of the boots, didn't give me a clue as to how the hair was hanging onto him, only that I couldn't shake the feeling it had searched out bare skin.

I gave it a tentative jab about six inches up or so.

The shovel blade did not break the strand of hair.

But it knew something had attacked it.

It reacted by drawing the ankle higher, contracting into itself somehow. The rest of the filaments sensed this sudden movement and responded in kind, pulling at the guy until he groaned.

We needed something sharper. "I really wish we sold chainsaws," I told Sammy.

"Or weed whackers."

"Or machetes."

Sammy's eyes widened. "Do we still have those knife sets? The butcher knives!"

"Man, I dunno. Even if we have 'em, they'd be all the way down in House Shit. There's still a lotta chickens out there."

Sammy looked at me. "We gotta try, man."

Again, I didn't want to but said, "Okay."

Sammy said loudly, "Sir, sir, we're gonna get you help, so don't die, okay?" He gave the guy a gentle, what he thought was a reassuring tap with his broom. "We're gonna—"

The guy jerked and screamed. His eyes shot open. They were almost completely black. I thought something was really wrong with his pupils. They were way too large as if he was on some heavy tranquilizers or something. Then I realized that hair had nearly completely grown over them from the inside.

Me and Sammy recoiled as he thrashed in his sparse web. Great waves of hair rolled off the top of the rolled-up door box and strands drifted down at us, impossibly long, unfurling eyelashes. We screamed and scrambled back to the relative safety near Oskar's workbench. Hair now hung like a dense curtain across the mouth of the trailer. More and more swallowed the driver until there was nothing left but a vague cocoon that looked like a photographic negative of some spider's meal, an ebony mummy. The hair decided it didn't care about the sunlight anymore and started creeping across the bare floor left in the pallet jacks' wake.

We heard a muffled, "Get off me, goddamn it," and the bathroom door burst open.

It was the vet, brandishing a fire axe. He'd taken the one from Receiving next to the FIRE EXIT. The glass was broken, and the rectangular box was empty. Of course nobody'd heard anything, no more than when Gloria had broken the fire alarm in Front End. Oskar had hold of his jacket, trying to hold him back. The vet was trying to shake him off. Obviously, they'd had some sort of argument.

Behind them, in the murky bathroom, I saw Yann slumped in shadows, next to the sink, under the automatic paper towel dispenser. Most of his right arm was gone. A belt had been tied around his upper bicep, but the tourniquet didn't look like it had been enough. His eyes, half closed, had rolled up, and now showed nothing but white.

The vet shook off Oskar's desperate clutches and stalked forward, his axe up and ready, like we held our shovels. The fire axe was a hell of a lot more badass than a stupid snow shovel. I wish the store had more of 'em, but there'd been none next to either FIRE EXIT along the western wall. The vet's eyes darted about, no doubt looking for the chicken bug.

Oskar stumbled to a stop behind him, just a few steps out of the bathroom, freezing when he saw me and Sammy. "No! No! You'll let more in." He looked terrified to be out in the open.

"Where's that fucking chicken?" the vet asked.

I nodded at the compactor. It had just completed its cycle. The gate unlocked itself and rolled up. I hoped like hell the chicken wasn't in any shape to climb the walls or jump out.

"What happened to Yann?" Sammy asked.

Oskar interrupted him, staring at the loading dock. He pointed, baring his teeth. "Look. Look! More. It's longer. There's so much more."

Gloria must have been watching through the swinging door windows because the next thing I knew, everyone was crowding into Back End behind me and Sammy. Wanda carried the dog. The space in front of Oskar's workbench got crowded.

"What happened to Yann?" Sammy asked again.

"That chicken got him," the vet said. "Chased us back here. This guy,"—he tilted his head at Oskar—"had us hide in the bathroom."

"No choice!" Oskar shouted.

"Thank you," Gloria said, ignoring Oskar. "For helping Yann."

The vet shook his head. "He didn't make it."

Everyone stared into the dim bathroom in silence.

"So now, lemme guess." The vet broke the stillness. "You folks can't get out up front, so you're back here."

"Unfortunately, you are correct," Gloria said. She studied how the hair had spread throughout the loading dock, creeping along the walls, across the floor. "Perhaps a silly question, but have you checked the fire exit back here?"

"First thing," the vet said. "Won't open."

Gloria nodded long and slow, thinking hard. "Then from what I gather, we have to assume the large doors and every emergency exit are all blocked."

"What does that mean?" Oskar demanded. "You have checked? All doors?"

"Most, yes."

"Most!"

"The only doors left are the fire exits on the east wall. You're welcome to check them, but I'd bet dollars to doughnuts they won't open. No more than the others," Gloria said.

"So, what do we do?" Wanda asked. "It doesn't make any sense. It can't be true, that we cannot leave. That simply can't happen. It can't." She seemed to be trying to convince herself along with everyone else.

"Then…how do we get out?" Kiko asked.

Gloria shrugged. "I don't know. I don't. We may not be able to."

"No!" Wanda said, voice quavering. "That's ridiculous. All we have to do is walk outside. It's right there!"

"I know it doesn't make sense, Wanda dear," Gloria said softly. "I'm sorry. I don't know what else to do in the meantime except wait for help. We need more information. Professor?"

"What?"

"Your remoras, or whatever you want to call them. This hair, the blue lights, the bugs in the chickens, whatever is happening with the customers. You called them harbingers. Why are they here? Why are they in my store?"

"They are here to prepare the way, to clear a path. I believe this is why they have sealed the building." He started reciting something from memory. "For they are the precursors of oblivion, those who herald—"

"Fine, whatever," Gloria cut him off. "Right now, I just want to know how long we've got."

The Professor rolled his palms up in surrender. "It could be minutes. Perhaps hours. I cannot say for certain without entering the basement. I doubt we have days. Not with the remoras already here."

"I'm not so good at waiting for help," the vet said. I didn't doubt it. "Longer we sit around, longer we give this shit to take over."

Gloria glared at the loading dock and said, "I see what you mean. We may not still be around by the time help arrives." She put her hands on her hips, kept her gaze roving throughout Back End. "We may not have a choice. I don't know." She sighed. "I'm fresh out of ideas. Anyone? Professor?"

"It may not even matter anymore," he said to no one in particular.

"Well, I'm not ready to lie down and die yet. As I

see it, I'm still responsible for the employees of this store," Gloria said. "Anybody else?"

I held up my shovel. "This isn't sharp enough for the hair."

The vet hefted his axe. "And I don't think this'll get through enough of it. Not as fast as we'd need anyway."

"Let's burn it!" Oskar shouted without warning. You could tell the idea had just hit him because he started pacing around, working it out. "We get a fire going, make, we make torches! Yes! We make torches and burn our way out."

Gloria said, "Okay, but I'm not so sure I want to be stuck inside this store, if that fire gets out of control. Those fire doors. They. Do. Not. Open. You follow? We'd be stuck. Burned alive or choking to death on smoke."

"We test it!" Oskar insisted. "We test a small part on the concrete."

I tried like hell to think of possible complications. I sure as shit didn't want to do something stupid again, such as tossing fucking deadly chickens around the store. But I couldn't think of much, and that made me worried I was simply too dumb to see anything beyond the obvious.

Gloria finally said, "Okay then. Unless anybody's got a better idea, then we'll see what fire'll do to it. But we must be careful. We need to get a small sample away from the rest. If this stuff is truly flammable, I'd rather not have to add a raging wall of fire to our list of concerns."

While Gloria and Oskar searched his workbench for something with which to build a torch of some kind, Sammy and me and the vet ventured down the loading dock to the edge of the creeping hair.

The vet gripped the axe from the bottom of the handle, held the whole damn thing straight out, pointing at a conspicuous clump, farther out than the rest. I was so busy marveling at the dude's astonishing strength, how he effortlessly held over ten pounds straight out, keeping it steady the whole time, I almost missed it when he said, "See if you can't slide it out over here a little. Give me a better angle."

Sammy lifted his push broom over the clump of hair, gently lowered it, and then delicately pulled it back, rolling the twisted strands closer. The hair, well it reacted, I guess. We all watched as it *moved*. It was slow, but you could definitely see the strands squirm in slow motion. The very air in Back End transformed, as if the currents of massive waves of static electricity suddenly shifted direction, pummeling us with unseen tides. Every strand of hair in the entire room altered course and headed straight at us. It was no longer like watching grass grow or paint dry. This was more like keeping a wary eye on hungry snails gliding toward you over wet rocks.

We had a window of time, but it was closing.

The vet sensed this as well and didn't hesitate any longer. He stepped close, lifting the axe with one hand again, and didn't even bother to swing it. He simply allowed gravity to take over, letting the dead weight of the thick axe head fall to the concrete. It sliced through the black strands easily, staining the blade's edge with a black slime.

Sammy swiftly used his broom to gather the loose strands, separating the clump from the rest in the loading dock, and pulled it over. Everyone gathered in a loose half circle around the lock of hair near Oskar's workbench. The hair kept slithering apart, the strands spreading out to wriggle toward the employees, and Sammy had to continually use his broom to gather the filaments, keeping them halfway contained.

Oskar tightened the teeth of a fairly large crescent wrench over a broken clothes hanger and sealed it with duct tape while Gloria went into the bathroom. She reappeared with an industrial-sized roll of toilet paper. The stuff was so close to cardboard it wasn't even uniformly bleached white and felt more like aluminum foil or parchment paper if you were lucky. Nevertheless, as the old saying went, "A wise man shits on company time." Gloria softly closed the door behind her, cutting off the sight of Yann.

While Oskar held the crescent wrench steady, Gloria quickly wrapped a wad of toilet paper around the end of the hanger, then turned to Wanda.

"I'll need your lighter," she said.

Wanda readjusted the dog in her arms and shook her head. "It's in my locker."

"Wonderful," Gloria said. "Man's been master of fire for four hundred thousand years, and here we are without a simple spark."

Kiko said, "Nah. I got it," and pulled out a silver Zippo lighter.

Gloria narrowed her eyes. "I didn't think you smoked."

"I don't." Kiko didn't elaborate, just popped the

lighter open. She flicked the little wheel and a flickering flame appeared.

"All right. Everyone get ready," Gloria said. "I don't know what will happen. We might have to run."

Everybody tensed, stepped back, ready to bolt.

Oskar held the torch at the halfway point, where the wrench was clamped around the hanger, and offered the handle to Gloria. She looked down at the torch but made no move to take it. She looked back at Oskar. "Your idea," she said.

His mouth opened and closed a few times as he tried to find the words. "This is not the job anymore. You're not the boss. You can't tell me what to do."

"I'm not."

"Then take it!"

"No. Your idea, your obligation."

"What is this, obligation?"

"Human decency," Gloria said.

"Oh goddamn it," the vet said and took the makeshift torch. We later found out his name was Hank. Hank held his axe in one hand like it was a hatchet and the torch in the other. Before he touched the toilet paper to Kiko's flaming Zippo, he regarded the slowly writhing hairs on the concrete. "Back up," he told everybody. "Like Gloria said, no telling how this shit'll react."

Everybody respectfully went as far back as they could, near the swinging doors and compactor. Wanda used her hips to nudge a few of the garbage-filled carts to the far wall and against the garbage chute to make more room.

Hank touched the scratchy toilet paper to Kiko's flame. The wad burst into flames, releasing a tangible, inky smoke, more like pollution from a smelting plant than mere toilet paper. Keeping the axe ready, he lowered the flaming end of the torch to the squirming hairs. Nothing obvious happened. Hank pulled the flames away and checked the hair. They hadn't caught fire and continued to slowly move same as before a wad of burning toilet paper had touched them. Hank tried once again before the paper burned away completely, this time setting the whole torch on the concrete, letting the flames rest directly on the hair. The fire went out almost immediately.

This enraged Oskar. He was backed up against his workbench and grabbed the closest heavy thing at hand. This happened to be his computer monitor. He ripped it away from the workbench and hurled it across the loading dock at the wall of hair, trailing stray electronic cords. It sank into the hair with an eerie lack of sound.

"Feel better?" Gloria said.

"If not heat," Sammy said, "what about cold?" He handed me his broom and unclipped the fire extinguisher from the wall.

"You might have yourself an action plan there," I said.

Gloria shrugged and said, "Why not." It wasn't a question.

Sammy twisted the red canister and read the instructions. He always felt better, more confident, if the instructions had pictures. "Says to stand back six feet."

"Careful where you point it," Hank said. "Stand over here, so the spray'll scatter those pieces back at the rest."

"Gotcha," Sammy said. He settled into a spot around five or six feet from the lock of hair. Holding the extinguisher in his left hand, he pulled the pin out with his right and squeezed the lever. White foam sprayed out of the nozzle, easily shooting across the six-foot distance, blasting the short lengths of hair back to the growing mass. It even pushed the tip of the torch out of the way. Sammy kept up the attack, moving forward, sweeping the nozzle from side to side, coating the leading edge of hair in the frothy chemicals.

The extinguisher sputtered, hissed, and ran dry.

No one said anything as we kept a close eye on the white foam. I don't know as anyone even breathed. I had to fight a childish urge to cross my fingers. Less than thirty seconds later, we had our answer. Black tips emerged, like a beard through shaving cream. Thirty more seconds and the foam began to noticeably dissolve and evaporate as ever-growing hair wiggled through it. Five more minutes, and you'd never know it had ever been there.

"Anybody else?" Gloria asked.

Silence.

"Wonderful."

"Lemme see if I have what you're saying straight," Hank said. "These remoras, they're like special forces clearing an LZ."

"I would think so, yes. The emergence is reported to be a delicate act, requiring a certain precision, and the...forces, they have arrived first. To establish a beachhead, you might say."

"So the goal here is to get out of this building before this other, bigger whatever, before it shows up?"

"For you, yes, most certainly. As for myself, I can see better now." The Professor almost chuckled. "Yes, precisely. Better. I can see better in many ways. I know what needs to be done." He gave a sad smile. "It may indeed be my destiny to join Ben. However, I owe it to him and to this world, all of you, to attempt to end the madness." He drew himself up and squared up to Gloria. "I must go to the basement."

"The basement?" Gloria asked. "We can't get outside, and you want to go where? The basement? And then what?"

"Stop it."

"How? Ask politely?"

"We have records, incomplete to be sure, but obviously, they found a solution in 1886. Otherwise, let me assure you, we would not be having this conversation. We would not exist."

I don't exactly know what else they said for a while. I'd started disassociating back when Gloria had theorized the hair had welded all the doors to the cinderblock walls, and we had no clear way of evacuating the store, so by now I was mostly gone, deep in my own head, trapped in a room without doors. This kind of thing tended to happen when I'd stayed up all night or at the least, at the end of a very long, stressful day. I'd feel the panic start to well up, and my exhausted brain would kick into survival mode and shut everything down. I'd go icy numb, feeling like everything was happening from a great distance away. I could hear folks talking, but it was like they were in another room, and whatever they were discussing didn't involve me.

Every once in a special while, though, if the fear had enough fuel, it would override the automatic shut-down switch, flooding me with a horror so intense and utterly complete, all I could manage was not to lose total control of my knees and most of the lower half of my GI system. That's where I was when Gloria and the Professor started arguing about the basement, wondering if I should apologize profusely to everybody and duck into the bathroom to relieve myself on the toilet next to Yann's one-armed corpse or just shit my pants out here in front of everyone.

"We need to focus on getting out of the building," Gloria was saying.

I keep at least a couple of my emergency pills in a sandwich baggie in the change pocket of my shorts or jeans every day. Just in case. I'm no stranger to panic attacks. As casually as possible, I turned and slipped one into my mouth, hoping no one was watching. While waiting for it to work, I tried to get through the crawling seconds by exhaling long and slow, focusing on my tried-and-true go-to method for slowing down my racing mind, box breathing. Once I had a handle on that, even if it was a bit shaky, I started, through physical sensations, grounding myself in the dreary reality of Back End. I'd been taught to start with taste, followed by smell, but the smoke of that yellow snot still clung to my clothes, threatening to make me vomit even before my bowels went totally liquid, so I skipped the first two sensations and tried to simply listen, to follow three separate sounds in the room.

It didn't work so well. All I could hear was Gloria and the Professor. And I didn't want to think about what they had to say.

"Yes. Please go," the Professor said. "Find a way out. Go. Get these people out. If I fail, if it truly is the end, maybe you all can find peace out there, for whatever time is left. Leave me the keys." His bleary, red eyes stared at Gloria. "You know something has to be done."

So then, next down the checklist on the anxiety worksheet was simply listing four things I could see. Again, it wasn't working so well. I didn't know where to look. The entire loading dock was out. Everyone surrounding me was beginning to look like I felt, scared down to the marrow. As usual, it was safest to go straight down. I stared at the concrete at my feet, focused on the torn bits of cardboard. A scrap of plastic wrap. A splinter from a wooden pallet. My own distressed hiking shoes.

"My responsibility is for the safety of this store's employees and customers."

The Professor was getting animated and indignant. He should've remembered what the pepper spray had done. Obsessed with what he clearly viewed as his life's mission, ignoring any lingering effects of the spray, he went about making his point like he was still in the classroom. "Okay. I get it. You think you're doing your job. Understandable." Here he was, talking about the end of the world or something, and he couldn't believe he was being controlled by nothing more than a lowly assistant general manager from a neglected retail branch in some godforsaken wilderness. He shook his head. "Don't make this any harder than it needs to be. Don't you get it? Get out while you can. That's the best you can ask for if I fail."

"Perhaps I did not make myself clear."

"What? You worried I might steal something? You should know that's the last thing on my mind."

I kept the box breathing going waiting for the pill. Four seconds inhale, hold for four, exhale for four, and hold for another four. Don't stop.

"My responsibility is for the safety of this store's employees and customers," she repeated in the same robotic customer service voice.

"Like to see you try," he added, with a touch of unnecessary sneer.

I couldn't blame him much. Fear turns us all into assholes sometimes.

"If you are suggesting I might find it difficult to remove you from the premises," Gloria's smile grew sharp enough to slice tomatoes. "You have a short memory."

"No. I certainly remember." The Professor's voice was steady, but we all heard the thick slab of tension swimming in the undercurrent when he asked Gloria, "What about your memory? Did you not hear me when I told you what was happening here?"

"Oh, I heard you," Gloria said, her back still straight as an ironing board. She was around five foot three or four, and the Professor had to be over six feet, but somehow she looked down at him. "Understand this, sir. *Hearing* you and *believing* you are two different animals. You claim to know what is happening here, and we need to listen to you, yet nothing you have given me has been useful. Or even true. In the break room, one of the few things I understood is that you claimed employees would be the first affected. We've been exposed the longest, you said." She opened her palms to him. "Looks to me though, like something is wrong with the customers, not the employees. If something like you say is happening, why not everyone?"

The Professor waved that away. "It was a theory, our best guess. This isn't what...we were wrong, no question. I don't know why. You must admit though, while we have some of the details wrong, something seriously abnormal is most definitely happening here." A splinter of hysteria had crept into his tone. "Or would you like to go for a walk down there?" He pointed at the loading dock. The truck driver, utterly cocooned, hadn't moved in a long time. Hair now covered the entire end of the long room, with only about fifteen, twenty yards until it reached us.

Panic clawed at my mind with insane, fresh strength.

I kneeled and began to retie my shoelaces, nailing my gaze to the concrete. I heard Hank say in a tired voice, "None of this matters if we don't find a way out of the building." That stark reminder of our situation should have set off another explosion of terror in my guts but instead, I found myself oddly fascinated by the scraps of garbage on the floor. I wondered if my pill was finally working, and if so, man, it had kicked in with a vengeance, thank fuck. But after a few seconds, I knew that wasn't it. It didn't feel right. This wasn't the pill. This was something else that I couldn't understand.

Until I realized the answer to getting out of the building might be right in front of me.

"Gloria!" I blurted, interrupting a debate over the merits of checking the FIRE EXITS along the eastern wall. "Do you have your keys?"

Of course she did. Her retractable security keyring was just as important part of her uniform as her employee name badge.

I thrust my chin at the carts full of trash and the locked door about four feet up the wall. "The garbage chute."

Everyone took a moment to work it out. The garbage chute led to an inescapable trash compactor, true. However, it was well known throughout the store that nine times out of ten, Don forgot to relatch the gate at the far end of the compactor. So all Gloria had to do was unlock the door, exposing a square metal chute, four feet high by four feet wide, that extended out from the building at a slight downward angle, until it opened up into FOOD4U!'s second compactor. This one worked sideways, compressing the garbage from right to left, shoving it down to one end. If the hair hadn't gotten in there, and Don hadn't locked the far gate, there was a damn good chance we could crawl through and get out.

Either the pill kicked in or the possibility of escape gave me the chance to get my head above the ocean of fear and breathe for a minute. Probably both. Whatever it was, peace settled in me, calming my bowels, easing the constricting terror. I found I could more or less function again.

Me and Sammy shoved carts full of garbage out of the way to clear a path for Gloria. She flipped through her keys and found the right one. I grabbed my snow shovel. Sammy got his push broom. Hank joined us with his fire axe. Nobody else wanted to get too close. No telling what might come out of the garbage chute.

Gloria unlocked the handle. The CLICK was awfully loud. If something was on the other side, it would have not only heard the lock spring open but felt it through the door as well. She gently turned the handle, then gave us a look, telling us to be ready.

She stepped off to the side, out of the door's path, and whipped it open. As it swung past her, Gloria flattened herself, hugging the wall, making herself as small of a target as possible.

The chute was empty. No hair anyway.

Everyone exhaled together. Gloria leaned over, and we both peeked inside.

The rancid smell was enough to make a raccoon puke. I don't think either of us minded, because we could see a sliver of sunlight. Don hadn't locked the compactor.

We had a way out.

"For once. Mmmm-mmmm. Thank you, Jesus." She looked to the rest of us. "Okay then. Form a line."

"Let me stay," the Professor said. "I beg of you."

"Sir," Gloria snapped. "You know damn well what I'mma say." She forced herself to take a few breaths through her nose and settle down before she answered. "Whatever is happening here, the authorities will no doubt be better equipped to deal with these aberrations than us."

The Professor said, "You're making a mistake."

"That is certainly a possibility. I am but human," Gloria said. "My decision is final." She turned to me. "Your idea," she said and nodded at the open chute.

I examined our escape route. The metal chute was more rust than actually sheet metal, covered in the slime from tons of rotting fruit, moldy frozen tater tots, grease from a million chickens, and spilled ice cream, and even though I'd have to go crawling down through all of that disgusting sludge on my hands and knees, I didn't give a shit.

Sweet normal real life waited a few dozen feet away.

"PLEASE!" the Professor screamed, making everyone jump. "You must listen to me. Why can't you just listen?" He focused on Gloria. "You have everything to lose. Everything! Leave me behind. I can do it. I assure you. I do not need help. I am stronger than I look."

"You must be," Gloria said, gentle now, her anger under control. "Got pepper-sprayed, right in the face, and look at you now. Yessir. You're tougher 'n leather, all right. But we need to be real here. I really think this is something for the authorities to deal with." With that, she turned back to the garbage chute and gave her head a little tilt, motioning for me to get moving.

I hefted myself onto the ledge, and as I went to lift my knee up and leverage the rest of my bulk into the chute, I thought I heard something at the bottom of the chute. A fresh shiver scrabbled back up through my guts, something inside telling me to slow the fuck down. I froze, eyes and ears totally alert in full prey mode.

"Besides," Gloria said. "The vanda—well, you know. When you and your partner tried that thing with the chalk on the floor. That was...unsuccessful? I know you tried, but...maybe now you can let go, let someone else take care of things."

"I've told you, the police, the authorities, the so-called 'experts,' they can do nothing. Even if it wasn't too late, they would never understand. Their minds are like yours. Closed. Or empty. Our attempt was doomed from the start. We had misinformation that caused a fatal mistake."

This time I did hear something, some sort of rustling, almost a whisper of running water. Then it was gone. It was enough though, more than enough to bring the uneasiness up to a slow simmer. I eased off the edge of the chute, lowered myself back to the floor, staring into the darkness, listening with every fiber of my being.

I couldn't hear anything else, so I turned around. Wanda and Kiko were next in line, watching me with quizzical expressions. Behind them, Oskar was getting impatient. "Let's go. Come on."

The Professor was still hanging back by the workbench, reluctant to join the small group at the chute. Sammy and Hank flanked him. "We gave everything to save you." The Professor took a hitching breath, trying not to cry. "It accomplished nothing but cost me everything."

"Let's go!" Oskar urged me.

The Professor said through shaky gasps, "It got inside Ben, and so he, he—" He choked, unable to continue. He closed his eyes. Tears streamed down his face.

Gloria's own eyes zigzagged, and her eyebrows flickered up in shock and recognition for a quick second, then settled and relaxed. Her voice radiated understanding and sympathy. "Ben was the poor soul who shot himself two weeks ago out front, isn't that right?"

The Professor kept his eyes shut. "It got inside him," he said. "Got in, and we, we couldn't get it out."

Gloria spent Thursday evenings and Saturday mornings volunteering at the outreach program organized and funded by her church. I didn't catch her truly compassionate side very often, at least not here at FOOD4U! anyway, so even if she kept that side of herself hidden or, at least on the back burner, while she was at work, it was very much an involved and active part of the rest of her life. Even with the church's support, sometimes she knew that all she could offer was a sympathetic and understanding face for folks scraping along, surviving on the streets, eking out the best living they could while their own sense of reality didn't always jibe with what everybody else agreed was real. She turned this empathy to the Professor.

"Ben. Benjamin Shifflett, is that right?"

The Professor nodded. "*Professor Emeritus* Benjamin Schmidt. Rest in peace."

"He was important. Special to you." Gloria had a skill in phrasing something where it could pass as either a question or a confirmation. People tended to take it however they needed or wanted to hear, gave 'em confidence. It made you trust her.

"He was my partner. My love. My whole life. We met in grad school all the way back in the seventies. Jesus Christ." More tears appeared, slid down. Both eyes this time. He swallowed. "Yeah. Yeah. He was special. Yeah."

"But something, something got into him," Gloria said carefully.

Another nod. "Yeah. It got inside him." He looked fully into Gloria's face. "But don't ever think that it pulled the trigger. No. Oh no. That was him. Ben. That was my man. That was all him." He saw Gloria's questioning look and said, "Nothing made him do it. He made that decision by himself. Maybe he was worried about what might happen later. Maybe he didn't think we could really stop it. Maybe. I don't know. I don't want to think about that, can't think about it. The only thing that is important is that it was an act of bravery. Not cowardice! No. Not cowardice. Defiance!" Spittle flew as words exploded out of him. "Yes, it was inside him, and we couldn't get it out. So Ben, Ben decided. He made the decision on his own. He couldn't stop it, inside him, you see, not..." His hands flailed around to indicate us for some reason I didn't understand. "It was growing in him, and it was getting worse, it was just a matter of time before, before..." He searched our faces, confirming that we understood this one important point. "He did the only thing he could do. The only path forward left available to him. If he'd waited, if he'd let it continue consuming him, there'd be nothing left and therefore, well, the only option was to remove himself from the battle and deny his opponent its full victory."

His gaze dropped. "So. He is dead, yes. Gone. I am, however, consoled by one undeniable fact. It did not consume him. Not all of him." He slumped against the workbench, spent.

Gloria nodded as if she understood. "I am sorry. Truly. But it is time to go."

"Yes!" Oskar shouted at me. "Time to go." He flung his arms out. "Go! What is problem?"

Everyone looked at me, which made everything worse. I tried to find the words. "Uh, something's wrong."

"What do you mean, Joseph?" Gloria asked. "More hair? Blue lights?"

"No, it's um, I don't know. Something's off."

"Here," Oskar said, pushing forward. "I go first."

As much as I wanted to say sure, go right on ahead dipshit, be the crash test dummy and find out what's waiting for you in the trash compactor, I held up my hand and lifted a finger, telling Oskar to give me a minute. I couldn't sacrifice someone like that in cold blood, even if he was an asshole.

"What! What is problem!" Oskar demanded.

I sorted through the cart of garbage next to me, found a plastic water bottle, still around three-quarters full. This was one of the most common things discarded around the store every day. I pulled it out and held a finger to my lips. Shhhh. The garbage chute waited, quiet and empty and inviting, everything apparently safe.

I set the water bottle sideways in the center of the chute, let it go. It rolled down, going faster and faster the farther it got. It was nearly bouncing from bottom to cap when it rolled off the end of the chute into the empty black space of the trash compactor.

A heartbeat of silence.

Then what I heard wasn't the water bottle hitting the bottom of the compactor. Not at all. What I heard was something buzzing or burning or scratching. Whatever it was, it was nothing I could recognize. Something fluid shifted in the compactor and made the entire thing lurch. I could only really sense this happened because I heard the metal squeal in protest, and I saw the sliver of sunlight shiver and disappear completely. The end of the chute became dark as a tomb. Somewhere in that inky darkness over the far edge, the water bottle exploded in a violent POP.

"Still wanna go first?" Gloria asked Oskar.

Something glittered down in the darkness, something so tiny I wasn't sure if I was seeing anything or not. I cupped my hands to protect my eyes from a nonexistent glare and peered into the void. Nothing at first. I exhaled, willing my pupils to dilate, soak up all the available light. Then, a minuscule red flash. Another. Then, a smattering of randomly blinking red lights appeared.

They instantly reminded me of the blue lights, and I couldn't move.

I couldn't breathe.

Seconds stretched into years.

A tiny question burst into life at the back of my

consciousness. I tried to ignore it, push it away in childish desperation. But the horrific possibility fought tenaciously to the forefront of my thoughts. It burned through the clinging shadows like a laser. What if this indecision, this startling paralysis that kept creeping into my soul, whatever was going on, what if I was feeling the same thing as all the brain-dead customers?

My goddamn pill wasn't helping near enough. It had pushed the fear under the floorboards, but that almost made things worse. Even if I wasn't acutely feeling the effects, I still knew it was there. Waiting for its chance to escape. Everything was muddy and blurry. I didn't like how my thoughts crawled sluggishly along, like my brain needed to be switched off and on a few times to reboot the damn thing.

More flickering red dots appeared, until a bubbling, uneven line could be discerned down at the far edge of the chute. They weren't like the blue moths. It wasn't simply the lights were a different color, the light itself was less intense, more opaque. And the movement was totally different. This knowledge should have made me feel better, more secure, safer. It did not. More and more gleaming red sprinkles appeared. Then the movement became unmistakable. The lights were creeping closer.

And each light belonged to a pair.

My blood froze when I realized I was looking at dozens of tiny red eyes.

My first thought was mice. Our FOOD4U! had a hell of a pest infestation problem. Images of the rodent control poison traps flashed into my head. These metal boxes that had been tucked into every nook and cranny of the store. The vestibule alone hosted at least one, sometimes two, in every corner. Each was the size of a pretentious hardcover book, and a dozen of these things were supposedly more than enough to eradicate entire colonies. That's what the salesman had claimed, anyway. Kyle, true to form, had gone with the lowball price from a sketchy pest control outfit that dumped thirty or so traps through the store and came back around to pretend to check on 'em every six months or so.

If the poison and traps had any effect, me and Sammy couldn't tell. When it was slow, or we didn't feel like doing much, we'd draw out the clock watching the mice scurry thirty feet up the rough cinderblock walls, never once falling, to hide in cracks in the eaves. The building had such a huge population it even drew predators out of the nearby forest preserves. It wasn't unusual to catch raccoons, foxes, and coyotes lurking around the edges of the lot in the early mornings, watching the building with hungry eyes. Once, a hawk, intent on snatching breakfast, had zeroed in on a mouse scurrying through the open doors and unintentionally swooped into the vestibule. The bird had gotten disoriented, whirling through the tight space, dodging struts and pipes, but it ultimately smacked into the large windows several times before we managed to drop a cardboard box over its stunned body and help it outside. That's a high-five with Sammy I don't regret. After watching the hawk collect itself for a few minutes, it eventually flew up to a light post and rejoined its mate, and you better fucking believe we celebrated.

These things with the red eyes, they were not mice.

If I had to guess, I'd say they were young rats. Not quite infants, because they moved with a speed and agility that gave the impression they'd been feasting on chocolate-covered coffee beans all day. I couldn't tell if they had hair or not because they all had a pale, pinkish hue as they came further into the light. The tails seemed longer than they were supposed to be, almost twice as long as your typical city rats. Maybe I should have been glad, relieved to see something halfway recognizable, not like the chicken bugs. At least these things looked like they might have evolved on this planet, a cousin to naked mole rats or something. But this relatability, this was almost worse, as the recognition of a swarm of rodents unlocked a primal, instinctive squirming horror. The growing legion crept forward in tentative movements, probably wary of anything else that might come rolling down the chute.

Dozens more followed.

Then hundreds.

A flood of adrenaline burst through the dam of my shocked paralysis and sent crackling electricity surging through my nerves and muscles, and I leaped at the door. Everybody in line caught a glimpse of the creeping hordes of rodents before I grabbed the edge of the door with both hands and slammed it shut with a resounding *CLANG* that echoed back and forth Back End a couple times until the hair absorbed the sound, swallowing it whole. The handle locked automatically. Thank you, OSHA. I held my breath.

Nothing happened.

For a good ten seconds, I didn't dare hope.

Silence behind the door.

Another ten seconds where nothing at all moved, and I almost crossed my fingers again.

Then the first baby rat squeezed through the gap between the edge of the chute and the door, a crack barely the width of a pencil. Apparently though, that was more than enough space. Another followed almost immediately. The two baby rat things scrabbled down the smooth wall, nimble and fast.

Oskar pulled me out of the way and lunged at them like it was he'd been nursing a personal grudge against this particular couple of rats for a few years now. He crushed them easily with his cowboy boots. Another squirmed out, and another. Oskar kicked at the wall, smashing the crawling rats against the cinderblock with his thick heels. One of the rat's bodies burst open like a water balloon, squashed organs sticking and sliding down the rough wall, revealing strange white blobs peeking out of bloody tissue.

We didn't have a chance to examine them because more and more, twenty, thirty, forty rats were now squeezing out from behind the door, and I don't know if some signal had been released, but most of 'em didn't bother even trying to scramble down the wall anymore, they just dropped from the edge of the chute, falling straight to the floor. They'd land and squirt away, disappearing behind carts, pallets, slipping into cracks. More kept coming, until the bottom of the door was alive in squirming, pink baby rats. There must have been so many piling up inside the chute because they started emerging from the gaps in the doorframe next to the door handle, skittering horizontally along across the wall and even scurrying upward to the ceiling.

Gloria shouted, “Back! Back to the main floor!”

She was right. It was hopeless. We backed away from the garbage chute. All of us that is, except for Oskar. He wouldn’t quit, panting and stomping on the lightning-fast rats. You’d think he’d bought his boots special for this occasion. The action lit up his face with a childish inner glee. I don’t know, as I’d ever seen him truly this full of joy, where nothing in life, no food or sex or drug, could come close to the pure ecstasy of crushing monster baby rats under his cowboy boots. Despite his enthusiasm, he couldn’t keep up. There were too many. Dozens climbed the walls. Hundreds shot across the floor, surging in all directions.

They swarmed over Oskar’s boots, grabbing hold of the black leather, then darting and pushing under the frayed cuffs of his jeans, scrambling up his bare legs. He punched and kicked at his jeans, growling and cursing in his native tongue. Me and Sammy jumped in to help him. Sammy with his push broom, shoving great tides of the wriggling pink bodies across the floor, like globs of leftover sushi that refused to die. Me with my shovel scooping them up and flinging them into the carts and at the cardboard compactor on the other side.

Too many, streaming everywhere. They swarmed over the broom and shovel. Me and Sammy had to start stamping at the soft bodies. Each little body felt like crushing a cluster of four or five grapes under my hiking shoes.

“Come on!” Gloria shouted at us, holding one of the swinging doors open while Kiko and Wanda and the dog rushed to her. Hank covered their retreat, swinging his fire axe around along the floor in great sweeping arcs, not so much cutting the rats in half as smearing them wholesale into the concrete. The Professor had remained frozen at the workbench, still ensnared in a shroud of shock and grief.

I felt the first bite before Kiko made it out the door.

For maybe the first time in my life, I came close to regretting wearing cargo shorts.

The rat snapped at my ankle, its vicious, oversized front teeth scraping the thin layers of skin off my ankle like peeling an onion. The unmistakable vibration of jagged teeth scraping on bare round bone shot through my nervous system, drilling straight into the center of my mind, threatening to obliterate any conscious thoughts. Three more had already scrambled up my other shoe before I could even cry out, "Gah!" in mindless rage and disgust. Burning explosions climbed up my legs as the rats clambered over each other to sink those razor-thin front teeth into my skin. One chewed into the tender flesh behind my knee, and I nearly went down into the swarm.

The same thing was happening to Sammy. Rats had scrabbled high enough up his body to burrow under his T-shirt, tearing into his torso. He bit down a scream, made that angry kitten sound, and managed to reach out to grab Oskar. We dragged him with us as we staggered back to Hank. Rats had gotten to him as well, slipping past his swinging axe blade and swift, crushing sensible brown shoes. Some clung tenaciously to his socks, biting through the thin material, while others climbed higher inside his slacks, searching for bare skin.

They'd reached the Professor too, nosing their way under his chinos and clawing upward. Their bites shattered his own paralysis and sent him lurching toward the swinging doors. Kiko had already gotten out, so had Wanda and the dog. Gloria slipped through as well and held it open from the other side.

When some of the rats got too close to the hair, I saw the strands quickly wriggle around the baby rats' limbs, dragging them down under the thick waves of unending hair. I guess the remoras maybe weren't working in tandem. They certainly weren't playing nice with each other. The rest of the rats learned their lesson and gave the hair plenty of space.

We hit the doorway and tumbled through. The instant we were clear, Gloria swung the door closed, hanging onto the handle so it wouldn't swing back into Back End and allow more of the rats to escape. Once shut, she held it with her foot. The doors couldn't be locked, but they were ringed in stiff gaskets that created a fairly tight seal when shut together. A rigid strip of rubber was screwed to the bottom of each door. This door sweep was there to help keep out drafts, moisture, and pests. The rubber physically touched the floor, and it didn't seem as if the baby rats were strong enough to squirm under it. Gloria kept one eye on the gaps and the other on us as we thrashed and yelled and kicked and yelped and slapped and stomped on the wriggling baby rats.

Of course, I wasn't paying much attention to what Gloria was doing right then. My legs were consumed in a howling forest fire, but I was more concerned about the five or six Tasmanian devils loose inside my cargo shorts. The thought of those fuckers biting my dick or balls filled me with terror so extreme I thought my heart might burst. I whimpered and frantically slapped at my groin, panic dialed up to eleven. I stuck my hand into my pocket and managed to grab one of the baby rats and squeezed it until it burst. I popped one more open before the others scrabbled free of my boxers and dropped to the smooth floor of the back aisle.

Eventually we killed the rest of the little pink nightmares remaining inside our clothes, stomped on as many that escaped as we could, and when they were all dead or gone, the only sound was harsh gasping for the next several minutes as the initial shock wore off.

Then I had to go and notice something even worse.

I was bent over, my hands on my knees, sucking air in through clenched teeth, desperate to ignore the shrieking agony ricocheting throughout my body. Clutching instead at my usual safety net, I tried to focus on the one-two-punch of box breathing and staring at the floor. This time though, my tried-and-true strategy betrayed me. Because there was a baby rat right down there on the polished concrete between my shoes, still alive. It had only been partially stomped, snapping the backbone in an abrupt right angle, leaving the back legs lifeless. Strangely though, the hairless tail still flicked around like a cat with too much catnip. The pink, fleshy rodent stretched its front legs forward, scrabbling at the cement, trying to drag its inert back legs along. It started coughing, then choking. It spasmed, reminding me of the chicken bug's proboscis, and vomited blood, splattering it in fine droplets across the chipped gray paint.

Blood and something else.

Something small and white, like fine grains of bleached rice.

Sometimes, I wish I didn't wear glasses. Sometimes, I wish I could navigate through my life leaving most everything I had to deal with in an unfocused, blurry smear so I could ignore it easier, leaving only the things I actually wanted to see with any kind of clarity. Sammy and I often invented useless contraptions like this when the clock refused to move. Forget a video camera in a pair of glasses, I'd rather have something like the filters in a video app, something that would recognize customers and digitally transform them into walking pixelated piles of shit with goofy sunglasses. Sammy thought that was halfway funny, but he wanted customers to look like kittens for some reason that kept making him giggle.

I suppose it goes back to the question, would you want to know about bad news when there's absolutely nothing you can do about it? That whole, "ignorance is bliss," thing. Too many scoff at this approach. I don't know as folks give it enough credit as a page in your survival blueprints. All I can say is that I truly wish I hadn't really gotten a good look at what was scattered in that clotted blood the monster baby rat had puked across the polished concrete.

The fine grains of white rice were moving.

I drove my heel into the rat, crushing its head. All that really accomplished was to spatter the blood and spread the white specks even farther. I couldn't draw a breath, while at the same time I was screaming in my head so loud it blew out my eardrums from the inside. I couldn't help flashing back to when a roommate decided to take in a stray cat, and we discovered the same kind of white flecks wriggling around in the cat's severe diarrhea. After a visit with the vet, we discovered the cat had a mature tapeworm and those were discarded segments of itself, each stuffed with eggs.

I stumbled away, feeling my gorge rising, and twisted around to find the closest skylight, something that would give me the most illumination. I chose a large wound on the side of my calf mostly because I could see it somewhat clearly; the bastards had ripped through my AC/DC lightning bolt tattoo. Gritting my teeth against the pain, I squeezed, and blood gushed out of the ripped flesh.

I wiped it away and before I could really stop and think about it, I scooped my index finger deep into the shredded meat, scraping the ragged bottom, not so much ignoring the pain as relishing it. The worse it felt, the better. I held the finger up to the light. Even though it was coated in slick crimson liquid, I could see at least two squirming white blobs caught under my fingernail. I wanted to vomit. Fucking monster baby rats hadn't been enough. No, the monster baby rats had to be infested with parasites. Parasites they'd eagerly passed on to us.

Wonderful, as Gloria would say.

The implications crashed into me like a train hitting a short bus. I didn't need a medical degree to know that it was most likely too late. Those things were going to ground deep within us, and they wouldn't be emerging until their host was dead. Maybe, and it was a long shot, doctors or scientists could find some heavy-duty antibiotics or some kind of exotic medicinal flower to kill whatever was now using our bodies as an all-you-can-eat buffet. Maybe the experts could induce a fever in us or something, enough to cook the little bastards. The possibility of being cured, being healed, felt so far-fetched it read like a bad punchline.

But hey, for the sake of argument, let's say the boys and girls with stethoscopes could fix us. We still had one glaringly obvious problem. Even if some kind of treatment was available, and that was a big goddamn if, we'd all have to be airlifted out and dropped off at the closest hospital, like immediately. The longer we waited for medical treatment, the more of us those things would be able to eat.

These concepts flashed through my head in near-instantaneous bursts, and I understood without a shadow of a doubt that the four of us were doomed. It wasn't complicated. The rest of the people in the store might make it out. Me, Sammy, Hank, and the Professor most certainly would not. We unwillingly carried ravenous seeds that would, sooner than later if not already, take root and sprout.

Surprisingly little emotion arrived with this icy understanding. Given my state of mind with everything that had happened today, I should have been curled up in a fetal position on the floor, weeping uncontrollably. I suppose inevitable tidal waves of fear and regret were on their way. They just hadn't landed yet. Maybe this was more dissociation, more of the mind's self-defense, freezing out the fear while logic and reasoning examined the limited remaining potential outcomes without messy, sticky emotions getting in the way and gumming up the works.

"Don't," I told Gloria, Kiko, and Wanda. I didn't know what else to say.

"What the hell is it now?" Gloria asked, exasperated. She'd been wanting to comfort Oskar, who had far more bites than any of us, all the way up to his neck. His clothes were soaked with blood. I didn't want to think about how many of the fine grains of rice were now pulsing through his body, looking for a warm, cozy spot to call home.

A grim, fatalistic resignation descended over my thoughts, blotting out everything else. It was a relief really, a strange comfort to have the ever-present fear finally throw up its hands in defeat and bow out, willing to concede there was nothing left for it to do once I'd been infected with some kind of unnatural parasite carried by monster baby rats. I mean, what choices are realistically open to you after something like that? What do you fight? Nothing. Absolutely nothing. Bitter peace settled throughout my body. At the very least, I'd calmed down enough that I wasn't as worried I might lose control and give in to the overwhelming urge to claw at my skin, tearing and gouging the flesh, scraping the white flecks out with my bare fingers.

Once I let everybody else know about that particular bit of nasty business, almost all the others eventually found their way around to my point of view, although some took longer than others. The Professor, who'd been primed for this sort of news and half-expected it, took it rather well, stoically even. Hank reacted at first with blinding fury, insisting on returning to Back End to slaughter as many rats as he could manage. He'd ranted for a while, how revenge was good for the soul, but once he'd gotten the initial explosion of anger and despair out of his system he calmed down and saw how kicking the swinging doors and retaliating wouldn't help any of us. Oskar didn't say anything, just closed his eyes.

Sammy was the only one who refused to see the truth. He couldn't stop clinging to whatever chance we had, no matter how slim. I didn't want to hear it. His hope and determination was exhausting, and it started to irritate me. I wanted him to shut up before I said something mean, I had to try and explain to Gloria why her and Kiko and Wanda had to leave the four of us behind and find their own way out.

I realized I'd given up, and I didn't care.

I'm not gonna lie. In some ways, it was easy to surrender, as if I was being warmly welcomed to sink into the sticky, reassuring trap of my own submission. The invitation had been open and extended once that lady's head had burst apart like a wet, overstuffed piñata. So, the idea of giving up had been building in my very bones throughout the day, and a big part of my brain was preparing for the end, shrugging off any possibilities for escape as a pipe dream. Anything we tried would be a blind stab in the dark, a futile, useless gesture. Our lives were nothing but terror and darkness, and none of our struggles mattered in the end. We would all end up like the lady in the white sweater, crumbling into nothing more than multicolored chunks of meat and smoke while our dog scolded us.

But as much as I wanted to tell Sammy to grow the fuck up, his eyes were so wide and terrified, so desperately full of the need for hope and love, I couldn't bring myself to spit out the truth. The truth being that me and him, as well as Hank and Oskar, we were well and truly fucked. And fussing over an illusion of salvation while deliberately ignoring the inevitable only served to prolong the torture.

Again, it was Sammy. I couldn't stop myself telling him what he wanted to hear. "Yeah, okay dude. We can do it. We'll get everyone out and find help."

Gloria knew my words were mostly bullshit, and while she didn't want to pop Sammy's surprisingly resilient balloon of hope, I knew her own conscience wouldn't allow her to abandon anyone either. She claimed our conscience was actually the Holy Spirit, guiding with the Lord's light, revealing the true path. Hope may have been harder to kill in Gloria than Sammy. Perhaps it's true there wasn't much, but what was there was battled-scarred and tough. Gloria's well of hope, small as it may be, would never run dry or die.

She knew damn well people with hope worked harder to survive than those without, so she began to point and issue instructions. "Okay then, first aid and fast. Let's stop the bleeding. Kiko, run to Pharmacy. We need disinfectants, bandages, sports tape, that type of thing. Take an empty trash bin with you and keep an eye out for those chickens. Stick to the main aisles. And don't get too close to any customers either. Meet us in Housewares."

Somehow, I still had hold of my bent snow shovel. I held it out to Kiko. She took it with a reverence that I didn't expect. The handoff became a solemn moment, thick with poignancy, like I was bestowing Excalibur to her from my deathbed. Then she grinned, gave a mock salute, propped the shovel on her shoulder at a jaunty angle, and went skipping away down the aisle toward Front End and Pharmacy.

"Wanda, let's get these boys to the furniture and mattresses, so they can take a load off, get 'em patched up." She went to assist Oskar, freezing with a pinched look on her face. She clearly wanted to take us by the arm, place a motherly hand on our back, ease our suffering as we all limped to House Shit. She'd realized simply touching us might get her infected. Gloria swallowed, battling with herself. The Holy Spirit didn't seem to be favoring one side or the other. In the end, a harsh understanding of this new wrinkle in our predicament became clear. However unfair and cruel it felt, the safety of the three uninfected female employees took priority over her instinctive need to comfort the men, personally tending to their wounds, becoming one of them. In other words, she was torn between being selfish and protecting herself, Kiko, and Wanda, or staying true to her immortal soul, helping fellow humans any way she could, which was how she conducted herself every single day here as the assistant general manager at FOOD4U!.

"Oskar, can you walk?" she asked.

Fresh blood kept seeping through his torn clothing, so much so that he left footprints with each dripping, unsteady step. "I'm fine. Fine," he practically snarled.

While he didn't seem to have any fear of the baby rats, the possibility of more chicken bugs running around made him nervous as hell. "Let's go. Go now," he said, unable to tear his eyes off Abid's corpse.

Wanda was first down the center aisle. In her arms, the dog kept a sharp lookout. I only heard it bark once, and that was to alert Wanda about a chicken bug nearby that had somehow nosed its way into a sweatshirt and couldn't get out. It kept scooting around under a spiral rack of hanging sweaters. I don't even think the bug knew we were there as we all went quietly past, giving it as much space as possible without getting too close to the other side of the aisle, also full of its own dark little hiding places.

I wondered if the dog felt like I did. Quiet. Calm, even. I suppose maybe I was feeling like that because of my pill, but frankly, I doubted any prescription anti-anxiety medicine would have made much of a difference with the day I'd had so far. Maybe if I'd swallowed ten or fifteen. With the dog, I suspected it had relaxed a bit, having gotten all of its terror, disgust, warning, hatred, all of it out, vomiting everything during that never-ending explosion of barking in Front End earlier. Now the dog had eagerly settled into Wanda's care, adapting to its new role as her protector, secure and ready to work. I felt a twinge of shame remembering how I wanted to kick the damn thing when it was terrified and defenseless.

We reached House Shit. Oskar cried out when he collapsed on a queen mattress. He had bites everywhere. The Professor leaned against a dining table, like he was worried if he sat down, he might not be able to get back up. Sammy perched awkwardly on the edge of a Lay-Z-Boy, favoring his left hip. I groaned and winced as I eased onto a sofa.

Hank shook his head. "Strip first," he commanded, already unbuckling his belt and kicking off his brown shoes. Gore clung to the thick soles.

Me and Sammy grumbled and whined as we got back to our feet. Oskar stayed where he was. It hurt like hell to peel off bloody clothing. Some of the blood had already begun to clot, and when I pulled the fabric away, it tore, causing fresh bleeding. Any other day, I would have rather eaten both of my socks after a rainy weekend than get undressed in front of my coworkers, but it didn't seem worth worrying about anymore.

Kiko arrived, pushing a cart full of supplies. She'd plundered Pharmacy with zeal, grabbing bottles of hydrogen peroxide and rubbing alcohol, bandages of various sizes, Extra-Strength Ibuprofen, bags of cotton balls, even rolls of sports tape. She'd also picked up a box of latex gloves and a pair of surgical scissors. Once Gloria had on gloves, she went to work on Oskar like a nurse in the ER, cutting away his clothes.

Down to his underwear, Hank took a bottle of hydrogen peroxide and poured it over himself. We all took our own bottles and followed. I let the peroxide run down both legs. Foam hissed and sizzled at every bite. It stung a bit but wasn't too awful. The process didn't get bad until we followed up with rubbing alcohol.

Yeah. The rubbing alcohol.

Please. Please, please listen to me. I cannot recommend this. I don't care if you've been used as a chew toy for a swarm of baby rat monsters, and even if the same rat monsters have also passed on some kind of horrible parasites that are already worming their way into your bloodstream. Trust me. You'll still want to skip the rubbing alcohol. That shit might as well have been napalm. It burned a thousand times worse than the original bites. I'm fucking serious here. You can thank me later. *Just say no*, kids.

Despite our best efforts at self-control, neither me or Sammy could stop ourselves from yelping and jerking away. It got to the point Hank had to hold on to one of our biceps like a vise so we wouldn't run away while Gloria splashed that vile stuff on our wounds from a few feet away like she was attacking a vampire with holy water. The Professor wasn't much better, hissing in agony and jittering his feet when it burned into the bites on his ankles. Gloria said, "I'm so, so sorry," and emptied a brand-new bottle over the punctures covering Oskar's body. Oskar screamed and thrashed on the mattress.

Meanwhile, Wanda and the dog went off to grab bottles of water, crackers, paper towels, as well as sweats and T-shirts. We wiped the blood and peroxide off as best we could. At least the alcohol dried and evaporated fairly quickly. Kiko used the snow shovel to gather all our filthy clothes into a pile and pushed the blood-soaked laundry well out of the vicinity, leaving them under the golf shirts in New Arrivals.

Hank waved Gloria off despite the protection of her gloves and began to systematically apply bandages to

Oskar's numerous bites. Oskar's face had paled considerably since escaping Back End. Once all the blood had been wiped away, his pallor was closer to cottage cheese. His eyes had sunk into his skull like two hard boiled eggs buried deep in rattlesnake dens. Oskar had been bitten so many times that Hank used most of the bandages on him alone and ran out halfway through patching up the Professor's first leg. Band-Aids were woefully small and wouldn't stick to skin smeared with blood and peroxide anyway. So me and Sammy used cotton balls and sports tape in an effort to at least cover the rest of the bites on us, seal 'em up. Finally, once all the bleeding and flinching was over, we tore off the annoying price tags on the new clothes and gingerly slipped into them.

Gloria had Wanda and Kiko drag over a few of the dining chairs, but not too close. The women sat in those while the guys sank back into the bloodstained recliners, couch, and mattress. Everyone drank bottled water and nibbled on crackers, deliberately refusing to acknowledge the stillness and silence of the vast store that loomed over us, filling our minds with a foul mist, blanketing our thoughts, muffling any reasoning and logic.

I figured if I tried eating anything there was a good chance I'd end up dry-heaving next to the couch and decided it was safer to just sip water. I swallowed five Ibuprofen, and while the medication didn't totally extinguish the pain, at least it got the constant reminder of rat bites out of my direct line of sight for a while so I could manage to focus for a continuous few seconds at a time on anything else.

"Next step?" Hank said, looking pointedly at Gloria.

Gloria shook her head. "I don't know." Her voice was so low I had to strain to hear her. "Been asking myself the same thing ever since we got out of Back End. We only have—"

"Is it getting darker?" the Professor interrupted. "Or is it my eyes?"

We all glanced around, trying to discern if the limited sunlight had decreased. I held my hands out, squinting to see details. Once the power had vanished, the store had gotten fairly dim, mostly thanks to the greasy skylights. Now that I was critically evaluating the level of illumination, I did notice a slight change. It had gotten darker but had been so gradual I hadn't paid any attention. If I hadn't been directly asked, I would have been clueless as usual, totally unaware of the gathering darkness until I finally realized I couldn't see much of anything.

"What time is it?" Sammy asked. "It can't be night yet."

"My watch stopped at quarter past eleven," Wanda said.

"It's nowhere near sundown," Gloria said. "It can't be."

I struggled to my feet, tripping a string of sharp, fresh bursts of pain off through my legs. My muscles had grown stiff while I rested and were reluctant to go back to work. I stumbled a ways to the nearest skylight and looked up. It didn't take long before I wished I wasn't wearing my glasses again. It did not shock me in the slightest to see that hair had started growing across the plastic bubble.

I went back and explained why the light was fading.

"Well, there goes my idea," Hank said. "I'd been trying to figure out a way to build a bunch of platforms, so we could climb up to one of the skylights. Then maybe break out. Least get to the roof." He curled his impressive fists together.

"The knife sets!" Sammy almost shouted, going back to his original idea of trying to cut down the truck driver. "We get a bunch of the big ones, whaddya call 'em?"

"Butcher knives," Kiko said.

"Yeah, the butcher ones. Maybe the bread ones too, the ones with the little teeth. Let's get some of those, use 'em around the fire doors. Cut our way out," Sammy said, trying to keep his tone casual, disguising his desperate hope, as if the listener's awareness of it might taint or curdle the outcome, when little kids fake casually ask their parents' permission for a sleepover. Hope lurked in each word, obvious yet bashful, like a bear hiding behind a tree.

"Fuck that hair," I said, trying to give him support.

"While I appreciate the sentiment," Gloria said, "I'd prefer to move forward without foul language."

"Ah, come on," I said. "Sometimes you need to swear. Doesn't feel right to say, 'Oh yah, it's sure been a heck of a day, all right,'" I said in my absolute best flat, Fargo accent. I swear I saw a hint of a smile from Gloria, but it was gone before I could truly be sure. I shrugged. "Just feels good to say it. Can't explain why, just...FUCK!" I yelled. "You know? Makes you feel better."

"Fuck yeah," Sammy said and giggled.

"Fuck! Fuck! Fuckfuckfuckfuck!" Kiko shouted, marching her feet, stomping with each word.

"Joseph." Gloria fixed her tired eyes straight at me. "I've been using foul language as poetry long before you were born, and daresay I would astound you with the depth and magnitude of my depravity and blasphemy. I know all too well the therapeutic effects of using shocking language." Now she did smile. "Young folks like to think they the first ones ever to break a rule."

That got a grin out of Hank as well.

Gloria continued. "I've since followed the light, best I can. I choose to hold myself to a certain standard and would hope for the same level of respect from those around me. Perhaps it is an old-fashioned idea, the golden rule. 'Do unto others as you would have them do unto you.' Of course, your choice in how you react is entirely that, yours."

Gloria shifted her gaze to all of us. "That said, once in a while, you are correct. Maybe it isn't only healing in itself but necessary for release as well." Her expression was sad, her wig a fraction askew. She took a long breath, then just as long letting it out. "The fucking truth is we put those fucking knives on clearance two fucking weeks ago, and now we're fucking sold out."

"I want to know more about what it is you think we're up against," Hank addressed the Professor, trying to find a position that didn't hurt too much. "You mighta told these fine folks what you think they wanted to hear, but I don't think you told 'em all of it. So, spill. Lay it all out. Don't worry about how it sounds. Let us decide."

"I tried," the Professor said. "I got pepper-sprayed trying to help."

"Shouldn't have pulled a piece." Gloria shrugged.

"What choice did I have?" The Professor raised his voice. "You refused to listen. 'Golden rule.' You dismiss anything that doesn't come out of your precious book of folk tales, anything that doesn't fit into your narrow, religiously commodified view of the world. 'Nonsense,' I think you called it."

"My religion is the reason you're still walking and talking," Gloria said and gave him her most brilliant customer service smile. "You're lucky I didn't think it would be very Christian to watch you choke to death in the break room. Would've been easier. Where I'm from, if 'n you're dumb enough to pull a gun on folks, they'll bury you so deep nobody'll ever find you."

The Professor didn't have a response to that.

"And likewise, my views on our Lord and Savior Jesus Christ have absolutely nothing to do with, shall we say, taking a healthy, skeptical response to the lunacy you were spouting this morning."

"Do you think it's lunacy now?"

"At the time, how could I have known?"

"Look, pal, no offense, I would've thought you were nuts too," Hank said. "But now, things...well, things have changed, haven't they?" He gestured at the silent store. "Been wondering why I didn't end up like them." He pointed to the family who'd been checking out the bunk beds. The kids still knelt on the top bunk as if they'd fallen asleep in front of the TV while the parents faced the bed, not moving either. I didn't want to look at them long, didn't want to know if their eyes were open or not. That felt too intimate.

"Yeah," Gloria said. "That doesn't make any kind of sense to me either."

"I, I don't know. I can't explain it," the Professor said. "Ben and I theorized we would start to see, uh, disturbances around the store first. The Eisenstein Incent lists events, isolated at the beginning, escalating for a period of months. Perhaps this time, with everything happening simultaneously, perhaps it learned or evolved from last time, shortening the time frame. Again. I. Don't. Know."

"So why some people, not others?" Hank reminded him.

"Given the information we'd gathered, Ben and I made the logical deduction that the longer one is in the building, the longer one is under the influence from the other side." He looked at each of us in turn. "Surely you can see the logic in our calculations. I do not understand why none of you succumbed, but you can all *feel* it, can't you?"

Nobody had to answer out loud to confirm his question.

"Therefore," the Professor followed his trail of thoughts. "Time of exposure is not a factor, at least not entirely. It contributes, to be sure, yet..." He trailed off. Without thinking, he crossed his legs and winced when he bumped one of the many bandages. "I don't understand. I don't..."

"I do," Kiko said.

"You do?" Gloria said without a hint of condescension. If she felt otherwise, she was smooth, keeping her tone clean, sounding warm and sincere. “Please,” she invited Kiko.

Kiko interlaced her ink-smeared fingers around her knee and asked, “This building, it wants to eat people, right?”

Everybody looked at the Professor.

“Yes, er, well, not exactly,” he stammered.

“There’s something big in the basement,” Hank said to get him started.

The Professor took a deep breath. “That’s...that’s one way of putting it. Big, big is relative. It’s getting close, yes.”

“This shit right up in our face, the rats and the hair and those goddamn chickens, all that, you called ’em the ‘remoras,’ the advance forces, right? That’s what wants to eat us.”

“It remains to be seen if consumption of our bodies is truly the end goal of the remoras. The sheer number and variety would seem to suggest perhaps another ulterior priority of simple incapacitation.” The Professor caught everybody’s look. “However, if ‘being eaten’ is easier to grasp...”

Attention went back to Kiko. “Whatever. It got into the customers’ minds. Most of ’em anyway, right?”

We all more or less agreed.

She leaned forward. “It’s simple. That’s why customers. It could only get through to the people who *want* to be here.” She gave a sly grin and pointed to each of us. “You all *hate* to be here.”

Everybody chewed it over.

"You assume that I do not enjoy my career," Gloria said, professionalism reflexively kicking into gear.

"Oh please," Kiko said.

"And you?" Gloria persisted. She tilted her head toward me and Sammy. "Their lack of enthusiasm is clearly obvious. Wanda is ready for retirement. I'm not sure if Oskar is capable of finding happiness. But you?"

Kiko smiled brightly. "I daydream every day about bringing a giant machine gun that never runs out of bullets, and I get to shoot people all day long. Sometimes it's a big ass sword. Most days it's a gun."

"Customers or employees?"

"Mostly customers. Mostly."

Gloria reassessed Kiko, probably like most of us. "Okay then. It does make a certain sense, in some ways," she said, though she still sounded doubtful. "It doesn't explain him, for example." She indicated Hank.

"Of course it does," Kiko said. She turned to him. "You can't stand being here, can you? You hate it worse than we do."

Hank was quiet so long I thought he was ignoring the question. Finally, he spoke, sounding achingly tired. "I despise this store, this company, the customers, the employees, everything goddamn thing about this place."

Kiko nodded with satisfaction. "Knew it. Every time I saw you."

"Then why on Earth—" Gloria started, then reframed her question. "What brings you back, week after week?"

Hank sighed. "My wife. She's, well, she was the one who used to shop here. I came with her once, ended up waiting for her in the car. Refused to ever come in here with her ever again. No point. Let her have her fun. Why not." He exhaled, hard and fast. "Used to tease her that she was addicted to this soup you sell, Rosie's. She couldn't get enough of the ham and split pea. Had it for lunch every damn day." He grew quiet again, struggling not to lose himself in the memories. "Well. Anyhow. Now I'm the one who eats the soup. For her. She's gone now, little over a year. And uh, I wish she wasn't uh, and I...all I got these days is time, so I still shop here, much as I can't stand it, for Carol. I get her soup every week, wander through this shithole, to be with her, close as I can."

He cleared his throat and forced a chuckle. "That's why I hate this place."

"My condolences," Gloria said. "If nothing else, at least this establishment has given you a new set of experiences today to remember us by." Hank gave her one of her own brief grins in return, appreciating the dark sentiment. Yet again, Gloria knew how to read people. I don't think she'd try a joke like that with a whole lot of other folks.

"What about Tim? Or Shelley?" Wanda asked. The dog sat on her lap, quietly monitoring the conversation. "Especially Shelley."

"They were touching the customers," Kiko said. "When it happened. I think right then, when it took the customers over, if any of us were too close, they went to touch them, to, to spread it I guess."

"Contagious," I said.

"Fine," Gloria said. "Still doesn't explain what happened to Shelley's customer." She gestured to the nearby family, motionless for so long they might have been mannequins. "None of the rest went to pieces."

"I'm not sure if it is entirely ethical to speculate over the cause of death using store gossip as evidence. They called that presumption in my pre-law class." Kiko scratched the dog behind the ears. It leaned into her touch.

"For the sake of argument..." Gloria prompted.

"Okay," Kiko said. "What if you were gonna take over someone's brain, and when you get there, it's not working the way all the rest of them do. What if, 'for the sake of argument,' you know, it's tripping its balls off?"

Kiko gave us a moment to consider the implications, then followed it up with, "That might cause problems. Might even be contagious in reverse. If Shelley was truly loaded, like people say she was, then it might, um, confuse anybody who isn't prepared for it. They call it a bad trip, I think. Like when we gave an edible to my friend Tonya. She. Freaked. Out." She looked from person to person, a swirling mix of conspiracy and challenge in her eyes.

The dog stretched, went quietly through the group, sniffing at us each in turn. I held out my hand, palm up, giving the dog as long as it needed to check me out. I felt like I owed it. I felt the cold touch of its nose as it pressed into my hand. I stroked its chin, and it jumped into my lap. The name PEACHES has been stitched into the top of the hot-pink fake SERVICE DOG vest.

"Professor?" Gloria asked. "Thoughts?"

"I, I suppose it is possible. As you said, it follows a certain logic," the Professor said. "It does not, however, change our immediate predicament. The fact is, the manifestations we have encountered thus far, they are nothing, nothing compared to what is surely almost upon us." He swept his arm around, indicating the store at large. "These remoras, they are nothing but the condensation that forms on the other side of a solid barrier when a cold ocean waits on the other side. None of it truly matters, not really, not when faced with oblivion. Perhaps it would be a mercy to be pulled into the void first."

I kept petting Peaches and thought about whether it'd be better to die quick.

"I'm sorry," Hank said. "Maybe it's time you tell us exactly what's in the basement. But take it slow. Explain it like we're little kids. My high school graduated me 'cause I was a hell of a football player, not 'cause of my studying."

"I knew it was only a matter of time before we got around to the damn basement," Gloria said.

The Professor nodded solemnly, pressing his hands and splayed fingers together in an exaggerated praying, steeple gesture. He touched his thumbs and forefinger to his nose, gathering his thoughts. He said, "To begin with, plunging into the heart of quantum physics is not for the faint of heart." He paused dramatically, growing more confident now that he was in his element.

But look, I gotta be honest and apologize here. I think I'd been sitting still for too long. All the panic and running, those moments where I believed I would drown in absolute terror, the guilt and all the baby rat bites, all of the awfulness of the day caught up with me with a vengeance, and exhaustion steamrolled over my sincere efforts to pay attention and be present.

I'm afraid that right around when the Professor

started explaining the thing in the basement, what it was, where it came from, why it was on its way, and what would happen when it got here, and all of the rest of it, I just couldn't help myself, I didn't have any fight left inside.

And so yeah, I kinda fell asleep.

3

INTERVIEW TRANSCRIPT-SUBJECT:-REDACTED-
Transcribed by: Ofc. -REDACTED-, Berwyn, IL PD

AGENCY: DEPT. HOMELAND SECURITY
DATE: 29 July 2026
LOC: Berwyn Police Department, 6401 W. 31st St, Berwyn, IL 60402
TIME: 6:12 AM
CASE: 47-5190-0043

PRESENT:

Special Agent Fred Jackson—Department of Homeland Security (DHS)
Special Agent Alex de la Iglesia—Department of Homeland Security (DHS)
Joseph Sutter—FOOD4U! Employee
Unnecessary sounds, such as "um" and "ah" have been omitted from the

following statement for the purpose of making this statement easier to read.

DE LA IGLESIA: Are you fucking kidding me?
SUTTER: Yeah, yeah, I know. I—
DE LA IGLESIA: ARE YOU FUCKING KIDDING ME?
JACKSON: Okay, okay. You need to—
DE LA IGLESIA: I need to knock some sense into this piece of shit.
JACKSON: Just calm down.
DE LA IGLESIA: Calm down? Seriously?
JACKSON: Take a breath.
DE LA IGLESIA: You take a breath. Calm down. Fuck me.
JACKSON: I know, I get it. This is…
DE LA IGLESIA: This is BULLSHIT! You're listening to the same bullshit as me. And what? We're supposed to what, take his word for it? He's fucking laughing at us. How much am I supposed to take? No, seriously. Fucking listen. How much, huh? How much more time are we supposed to waste while sitting here listening to this bullshit, his thumb up our ass? Huh? Come on. Tell me. How much shit are we supposed to swallow while he laughs at us?
JACKSON: I'd appreciate—
DE LA IGLESIA: Don't do this, Art. You know it's bullshit. You know better.

JACKSON: And so do you. I'd appreciate a little professionalism.
DE LA IGLESIA: Professionalism? Oh okay, okay. Sure. You're saying I need to be more professional when it's Storytime with Mother Goose in here? And the one who's gotta be professional? From where I'm standing, I'm the only goddamn professional in the room. No, no, stop. Look at these pictures. Both of you! Look at them! Here, this one. Yeah, see this used to be a real living human being. A person. A woman, in fact. A...Mrs. Carmelita Lopez. This poor lady, she was identified by her husband. Kinda hard, without a face, huh? Wanna know how he knew it was her? Two things. A tattoo on her ankle and her goddamn wedding ring. Uh-huh. I'm supposed to be professional and nod politely I guess while this, this piece of human garbage, sits there with a straight face saying that Mrs. Lopez was killed by fucking butterflies?
SUTTER: No, I said they were more like moths, but—
DE LA IGLESIA: You better shut the fuck up. They checked you out. I don't buy your explanation for those wounds on your legs for an instant. No little bitty parasites either.
JACKSON: No more. Go for a walk. Get

some control over yourself. You should hear yourself, Art.

DE LA IGLESIA: And you should hear yourself, Fred. It's pathetic. Can't fucking believe this shit. I need some air.

DE LA IGLESIA EXITS.

JACKSON: Okay. Let's, um, let's take a moment and uh, catch our breath. Change the subject a minute. You said, um, that an employee, Shelley Erickson, had a significant drug problem, at least according to the other employees.

SUTTER: I don't know if I'd call it a 'problem.' She did her job just fine, got through the day. What do they call it, functioning?

JACKSON: My point is that it was fairly well known that Ms. Erickson regularly ingested a sizable amount of both legal and illegal substances. Would that be fair to say?

SUTTER: That was the word, anyway.

JACKSON: What about drug use with the other employees?

SUTTER: Um, well, I don't know if I know anything about that, you know?

JACKSON: I can assure you can speak freely with me. If necessary, we can redact anything we want before releasing any documents or say, audio or video files.

SUTTER: Like what we're doing here?

JACKSON: Yes. So, the other employees…

SUTTER: Well, like I said, Don was a hell of an alcoholic. Functioning, right?

JACKSON: And the others?

SUTTER: I don't know, man. Not really. I never hung out with 'em, you know?

JACKSON: What about at work? Besides Shelley?

SUTTER: I heard rumors a few people, they'd vape in the restroom. Coulda been cannabis, I guess. Don't know who they were, though.

JACKSON: What about you and Sammy?

SUTTER: What about us?

JACKSON: It's a big lot. Plenty of time to yourself.

SUTTER: And?

JACKSON: And I think you know exactly what I'm getting at.

SUTTER: You sure this won't get back to FOOD4U!?

JACKSON: Absolutely.

SUTTER: I suppose me and Sammy mighta taken a hit once in a while. How else you gonna stay sane with a job like that? I can't really drink anymore. Shit, it made us better employees. I got nice when I was high, for fuck's sake. What does that tell ya?

JACKSON: That you need it to get

through the day. Did you get high at any point yesterday?

SUTTER: I hate to break it to ya, but weed doesn't make you hallucinate like that.

JACKSON: I'm not suggesting it does. I'm trying to get a sense of your mindset.

SUTTER: Look, man. It's legal here now right, so I guess it doesn't matter. I smoke all day, every day. Yesterday, I didn't have much of a chance. Not 'til the Professor's lecture. If you'd told me yesterday morning when I clocked in, I'd end up toking on my vape in front of Gloria, I would've laughed in your face. Come on. But I'm telling you right then, I didn't care anymore. It sounded like we were all so screwed. No hope. No hope at all. I guess I didn't think, just pulled it out. Took a hit, passed it to Sammy. Now here's the really funny thing. I'm not lyin', not trying to get out of trouble or something, like, but I'm telling you Gloria, after Sammy, she grabbed my weed pen from him and took a hit, then passed it right back. Swear to the baby Jesus.

JACKSON: So, it's true to say you did not fall asleep.

SUTTER: Nah, man. I was just kinda high and didn't want to have to try and explain the shit he was telling us. Your partner's not the easiest guy to talk to, you know?

JACKSON: He's upset at the loss of life. So, what did the Professor have to say?

SUTTER: I didn't take notes, like there was gonna be a test on it, you know?

JACKSON: That's okay. Just give me whatever you did manage to grasp.

SUTTER: It's not gonna make sense. I know I spaced out at times, I'm missing stuff. Like, important stuff.

JACKSON: That's fine. Go ahead.

SUTTER: Okay, man. Don't say I didn't warn ya. So… You understand how, when you get down to shit like molecules and atoms, fundamentally, it's all just mostly empty space, right? Like, ninety-nine-point-nine fucking percent. The Professor said people argue over that all the time, but he said that him and Ben, they didn't think it was really empty space at all. He said it was being occupied or used. That's not the right words, but I don't know exactly how he put it. Anyway, that space, that was where the other universes exist, I guess. He really went off for a while, how some of the subatomic properties technically existed in every universe, that all these universes sorta shared some of that stuff. Oh, and he considered the beer foam bubble analogy to be useless. He said they got it all wrong, you'd only see one bubble. It all depended on your position in space and time when you were observing the bubble in relation to the universes themselves.

JACKSON: That's um…

SUTTER: Yeah, it makes my head hurt too. Doesn't even make sense when I'm really fucking high. What can I say. You asked. I'm just repeating what he said, best I remember.

JACKSON: So instead of a bunch of beer bubbles in foam, you're describing something more like Russian nesting dolls?

SUTTER: Those wooden dolls hiding inside each other? Kinda, I guess. Except the way the Professor described it, every doll would be the same size. Each atom in our universe is more or less the same atom in every other universe, but because each universe occupies a slightly different space, I guess you'd say, the atom in each universe is built slightly different, so it became something else. Yet it exists right next to each other universe, you see?

JACKSON: Not really.

SUTTER: Me neither. But that was his theory anyway. And there some kind of force that I really didn't fucking understand that keeps it all separate yet together.

JACKSON: Then what was in the basement?

SUTTER: The Professor said there was an entity that could manipulate that force, whatever was holding all the universes in balance, and it could move independently from universe to universe, consuming all matter within each one before moving on to the next. The Professor said this thing could create a weak spot in the barrier between each universe, then send its remoras through to help it from the other side.

JACKSON: If this thing can move through atoms or whatever the hell it is you're babbling about, why bother with the remoras? It could just pop out anywhere, even midair.

SUTTER: I don't think it worked like that. The Professor made that pretty clear. Once the thing was here, well, it was over, one way or another. He didn't know how long it might take, but it wasn't like, a long time. Like hours. Before that happens though, it uses the remoras. But they can only come through solid matter, not liquid or gas. Something about how solids keep atoms in fixed, stable positions, so the remoras could get a handle on 'em, go to work getting through.

JACKSON: Why here?

SUTTER: Someone called out to it, back in the 1800s. This lunatic robber baron, you know the type, somebody with more money than common sense, he was obsessed with ancient cults and prophecies about the end of the world. Thought he'd become a god. Built what he told the government was a supply depot outside of Chicago, added a ton of railroads all around it. Nothing too suspicious about that, 'cause in the 1870s, nobody had more train tracks than Chicago. The important thing though is in those days, the tracks were made out of iron. So, what he really did was create a giant homing beacon, this huge symbol, a fucking dinner bell he could ring right out there in plain sight. See, when the earth's position is just right, and when the stars are aligned just right, you can supposedly give this thing a phone call. I know, I know. You think I'm full of shit. I don't blame you. But the tracks are still there. Go on Google Earth, you can see it yourself. The Professor showed us a printout. Might as well have been a goddamn target. And what do you think was right in the middle of the symbol?

JACKSON: I can guess.

SUTTER: And you'd be right. The Professor said this cult had built a secret shrine or whatever under the supply depot. The leader believed that when the entity came through to our universe, he and the rest of the true believers would be there to welcome it, and not only would it spare their lives, the robber baron would become immortal.

JACKSON: It's probably for the best that Art is not present to listen to this.

SUTTER: Man, I'm just telling you what the Professor said, at least how I understand it.

JACKSON: Your understanding is… You understand this is all useless, right? What am I supposed to tell my superiors? That a universe-eating monster was at Earth's doorstep, and we're all lucky as hell it only ate a shitty store?

SUTTER: That's up to you. You wanted me to tell you what the Professor said.

JACKSON: So, the robber baron. He sends this thing a signal. Okay, sure. What happened?

SUTTER: It began with the manifestations, I'm guessing just like a lot like the shit we saw. But the Professor said there was this kind of faith-based vigilante group on the robber baron's tail, a mix of priests, rabbis, imams, some African spiritual leaders. Yeah, they were a regular religious United Nations. They'd been investigating the robber baron, tracking him. I guess this wasn't his first attempt to crack open the supernatural. They'd been chasing him through Africa and Europe and followed him out west. Apparently, these guys were genuinely worried he might succeed in bringing about the end of the world. They managed to infiltrate the ritual, assassinated the robber baron, and prevented the entity from entering our universe.
JACKSON: And the Professor knew all this, how?
SUTTER: It all came from the books he had, all these hand-written journals and notes.
JACKSON: Jesus H. Christ. That's the 'evidence?' Don't make me go get Art.
SUTTER: I know, I know. Sounds like a crappy TV show. 'The God Squad!' Tune in and watch a bunch of wacky religious dudes with superpowers solve a supernatural mystery each week!

JACKSON: Okay fine. So, if they already stopped it once, why's it back?
SUTTER: The stars, man. They keep spinning, round and round, and before you know it, we're right back where we started. The stars, they're back in alignment or whatever's needed, and the railroad tracks, they're still there, so…yeah. Sounded like these guys didn't know they'd left the door wide open, and this thing's been waiting for the chance to come back around and try again.
JACKSON: What's it look like? How would I know it if I saw it?
SUTTER: I don't know as it's something you can really *see*, you know. It's more something you'd *feel*. That's what the Professor said anyway.
JACKSON: How'd they manage to stop it in the first place, back in, what was it, 1886?
SUTTER: Gloria had the same question.

"A ritual," the Professor said. "I suppose you might compare it to an exorcism. Certain words, certain phrasings, they have power. Especially if applied with force. The visual representation of runes and sigils. The presence of fire is essential, as the constant transformation of molecules provides a sort of distraction, a force field, if you will."

"It sounds…thin," Gloria said. "Magic words and whatnot."

"The only magic word I know is 'please,'" Hank said.

The rest of us kept quiet and tried to process the Professor's show and tell. It wasn't easy, reminding me of this one time when a couple of chuckleheads tried like hell to cram an 85-inch TV in a Chevy Spark. They wrestled with that sucker forever and never did get it loaded. Had to go borrow a friend's truck. That's what this felt like, slogging through the Professor's explanation. None of it really fit in my head. Wished I could borrow a brain from someone smarter for a while so I maybe could understand at least a little what he was talking about.

The Professor had really tried to get us to fully grasp his concepts and theories, pointing out various graphs and figures from the books and journals in the knapsack, but we were a tough crowd. I mean, I'm pretty sure we'd all been students like Hank. We'd all barely graduated high school. A class or two at Oakton, the local community college, was about the extent of our higher education. Quantum mechanics and subatomic particles and half-forgotten lectures on physics as sophomores flitted through our minds. I knew how Sammy felt when he got confused and couldn't connect the dots.

"You and Ben already tried this," Gloria said, unconvinced. "Didn't work. What makes you think it'll work this time?"

"There may have been several factors, but I now

firmly believe that proximity is our weapon. That is where it is vulnerable," the Professor said. "I'm convinced it was too far away to truly be affected, like..." He paused, thoughtful. "Like trying to pepper spray someone from across the store." He looked pointedly at Gloria. "Instead, we are going to wait and pepper spray it straight in its face."

Gloria looked very tired. She rubbed her eyes, rolled her neck. The rest of us waited for her decision. We were long past following any kind of command chain in the store, and there wasn't any real reason to listen to our AGM anymore. It's not like anybody was worried about getting written up if they weren't performing their job duties. Somehow though, everyone knew Gloria was our best chance of getting out, so it felt natural to look to her to make the serious decisions. She looked heavenward for a long moment, then let her gaze fall on the Professor. "Unless anybody has a better idea, let's do it. What do you need?"

"Light. Fire. I imagine it will be quite dark down there. Do you sell candles? I'll need five, no six, for the ritual. Perhaps some sort of torch so we can see."

"I'm sure we can dig up some candles," Gloria said.

"I'll take care of the torches," Hank said.

"Paint of some sort," the Professor said. "Black, if possible. A large white sheet as a canvas."

"How's this supposed to work, exactly?" Gloria asked.

"Once the shrine has been located, if we aren't too late of course, I mark the floor with the sigils, prepare the sheet, place the candles at the proper angles, and wait for the proper moment."

"When's that?"

"The emergence. The absolute first thing it must encounter in this universe is this sigil." He pointed to some swirly circle sun eye thing in his book. Clearly important, it was large enough to demand its own page. "I must confront it with this."

"A thing that eats universes." Hank said. "And this little picture is what, gonna scare it off?"

"They call it a symbol because it is a representation," the Professor said softly. "Often something so powerful it is only safe to handle the depiction, rather than the power itself. Take the flag on your hat for example. This particular symbol—" He stabbed the picture in the book, "While it may mean nothing to you, it apparently means a great deal to the entity." He gave a slight shrug. "We have collected volumes, dozens of ceremonies, each with their own unique variations and cultural influences. However, the only two consistent elements across the variety of the rituals are the sigil and the prayer. Ben and I believed that...well, it no longer is important." He glared at Hank. "Yes, you are right. It is true that we do not understand it fully, only that this sigil is highly potent and not to be taken lightly. I highly doubt it 'scares' the entity away, or if the entity can even feel fear, or any emotion for that matter, but then again, I cannot rule it out. Two fully independent instances, involving cultures with no knowledge of one another, each hundreds of years apart, yet both describe successful efforts in driving the entity away, primarily using this exact image. It took us twenty years of research to find and verify this information. Twenty years."

"Just curious is all," Hank said. "I come from a different world. Twenty years with the physics of bullets and bombs. Want to understand the rules here, is all."

"We're losing light, fast," Gloria said. "If we're gonna do this, then let's get it on. Hank, you said you could build some sort of torch?" He nodded, grabbed his axe, and headed off toward Foods. "Samuel, will you assist Wanda and grab a set of sheets? Take the large garbage cans. On the way back, swing through Hardware for paint." Our hardware aisle was a joke. It seemed to be mostly items that a truck stop hadn't been able to sell. Stuff like car air-fresheners, screwdrivers, picture hangers. I doubted they'd find paint there. "I cannot remember what all we have in stock." Gloria turned to me and Kiko. "We shipped our scented candles back last week. Corporate couldn't ignore a press release that claimed the main chemical ingredient was carcinogenic. The only thing we have in stock is back in the clearance section, the Chanukah candles." She asked the Professor, "Will those work?"

I gave Peaches one last rubdown and set her on the floor, then tried not to grunt and groan too much as I got to my feet.

"From my experience, they can burn quickly," the Professor said. "However, if we hold off until the last minute to light them, then yes they should be fine. They will fulfill the requirement. As long as we have six candles lit around the symbol on the floor, those inside the borders will be protected. The entity should arise from a prepared altar in the shrine. For this, we have the sheet. But who knows where it may emerge. It is coming through from another universe, after all. So, we mark the floor as well, in case it materializes from the floor, or even the ceiling."

"Makes as much sense as anything else." Gloria nodded at us. "Good luck. Hurry back."

Kiko gave the snow shovel back. She'd found herself something better in Pharmacy, a family-sized aerosol can of hairspray that kinda shocked me was still legal. By itself, the can wasn't all that threatening, unless you were the ozone layer. Or trying to breathe when somebody used it in a tight bathroom. It was only when Kiko brought out her Zippo, flicked it open, and held it ready to go in front of the nozzle that I finally figured out what she had in mind.

Hank had his axe. Now Kiko had a goddamn flamethrower.

My snow shovel felt inadequate. It struck me this must be how the guys who worried about the size of their dicks feel like, the manly men who bought the biggest damn pickup truck they could find and stuck massive patriotic flags all over it. Never mind the fact the trucks were pavement princesses, with tires that would never know the taste of dirt. Sammy had to stop me more than once from going up to these swaggering assholes and asking them if they were familiar with the term 'overcompensation.'

I damn near laughed out loud and got a curious look from Kiko. The emotion surprised me. I'd been mostly calm ever since the Professor had given his lecture, hadn't given in to despair totally, but wasn't gonna jump up and click my heels either. I didn't know where that came from. It was like wanting to tell Gloria that Kyle needed a haircut. Maybe the building, the closeness of the entity, maybe it was getting to me. It struck me that today I'd spent more time inside than I had in months, maybe years.

That particular thought gave me whiplash. Instead of laughing, now I felt like puking. I felt like I might have more control over a kite in a typhoon than my own emotions and thoughts. I wasn't feeling quite as defiant as I'd been when we'd gotten out of Back End, where I truly thought the worst had happened. That was bad, but remember, kids, in life there's always something worse waiting out there. Once I'd crawled out of my hole of self-pity, I remembered I wasn't the only one left in the store. The men had been infected, and I honestly didn't hold out much hope for us. But Gloria, Wanda, and Kiko, they didn't deserve any of this. I might be dying, but that didn't mean they had to as well. So, I promised myself I'd help the Professor and do whatever it took to get Gloria and Kiko and Wanda and even the damn dog out of the building before I gave in to my fate.

Me and Kiko skirted the wind chime display and the same customers stuck in the same places. The clearance section was back near the chicken room. We peeked around the corner. Abid was still face down in the middle of the back aisle. We couldn't see any chickens and moved swiftly to the clearance shelves. They were a mess. When customers thought they might be on the scent of a good deal, they'd paw through everything on these shelves with the methodical intensity of a dog ripping all the polyester fiber out of their favorite stuffed animal. Kiko covered me while I used my shovel to push aside all the mangled packages and last remaining items, finding three boxes of Chanukah candles left on the bottom shelf.

It might have been faster to cut back down the center aisle, but we stuck to our original route. Safer that way. No telling where the rest of the chickens were hiding. Or if the baby rats had squeezed under the doors to Back End and were now spreading through the store. If nothing else, the deepening darkness would make it easier to spot the blue moths if they made it inside.

We should have been worried about what was in front of us the whole time.

The customers.

They'd been standing around like nothing more than mannequins, and it wasn't long before they became just another fixture of the store that you ignored. Trust me, customers were easy enough to ignore when things were normal and FOOD4U! was open for business. Now that they didn't talk or move, we all forgot about them once we got to the vestibule and found the hair and blue moths.

Gloria and the Professor were organizing his books and supplies on the one dining room table on display. Wanda and Sammy brought back a set of sheets and children's finger paint and thick black Sharpies. "Hardware, no. Office Supplies, you betcha," Wanda said.

"Yes," the Professor said. "Yes. The paint can be used on the floor. Better than chalk. And the markers can be used on the sheet. Excellent."

Hank returned with five empty gallon planters,

half-gallon cans of off-brand vegetable shortening, and a handful of dish towels. He set the cans up in a line on the table and peeled off the plastic lids, then the aluminum safety wrap. After generously coating each dish towel with the white goop, he pulled out a serious looking pocketknife and opened it with one hand. Of course he carried a damn knife. He cut an X in the middle of each lid, then fed a twisted dish towel through, jamming most of the towel deep into the can of shortening, then snapped the lid back on top with a few inches of the slimy towel poking through. The can of shortening went inside the empty planter.

I was setting the candles on the table next to Hank's torches when I happened to glance over at the family at the bunk beds. They were staring at us.

"Um, folks," I said, trying to keep my voice even, everything calm and cool. Everyone glanced over at me. I nodded to the family now watching us from about thirty feet away. They hadn't moved away from the bed, but each member of the family, Mom, Dad, both brothers, had either turned their head or even turned completely around so they could see us easier.

"Wonderful," Gloria said.

I looked for more customers to check if they'd woken up as well. Couldn't see any from our position around the dining table in House Shit. The only audience we had at the moment was the family at the bunk bed.

"Interesting," the Professor said.

"No, no it ain't," Gloria said. "We got no more time for dilly-dallying. Let's get to the break room. Kiko, you keep an eye on that family. Professor, you got your pack, everything in there you need? Okay then. Hank, you, me, and Wanda are gonna take everything on the table. Joseph and Samuel, you can assist Oskar."

Oskar groaned. "I don't want to move."

"I'm sure you don't," Gloria said. "But we cannot leave you here." She stole a quick glance at the staring family. "Not now, not anymore. I'm sorry. You can rest on a table, like the Professor."

I was about to suggest me and Sammy go find Don's tilt truck to transport Oskar when I thought I saw something move over by the bunk bed. I whipped my head around, ready to raise the alarm if necessary. The family was still staring at us, but they hadn't moved. At least, I didn't think so. Then, between the parents, I saw one of the boys wobble. He shifted his arm. Leaned forward. The other arm followed.

"Something's happening," I said, not caring that didn't explain anything. It got everybody's attention anyway.

The kid on the top bunk was around five or six but moved like an infant attempting with varying degrees of success to get their unfamiliar limbs to listen and obey. He managed to crawl to the edge of the bed with an unsteady, shaking motion. His right arm reached out, between his parents. They ignored him, focused only on us. The boy's hand clutched at thin air, his center of gravity shifted, and he tumbled off the top bunk, landing flat on his face. All of us back by the dining table grunted involuntarily and flinched. The boy's parents didn't react, didn't break eye contact with us.

The boy's body toppled over, crumpling onto the bottom bunk first, then sliding off and slapping the floor. The parents still wouldn't, or couldn't, look at him. After a second, he started to writhe around, pushing himself up with his left arm. His right forearm hung limp, clearly broken cleanly in half, like a broken stick in a wet sock. He made no sound. But he did start to crawl toward us. It was awkward with the broken, useless arm, and it reminded me of the chicken bug near the freezer. I wondered if it would be cruel if I put a trash can over him like we'd done with the chicken.

His mom took a trembling step toward us.

"This may accelerate our timeline," the Professor said, slinging the knapsack over his shoulder.

"No shit?" Hank said, as if it wasn't glaringly obvious and started gathering his cans of vegetable shortening. Wanda and Gloria helped him, gathered up the finger paints and sheets and markers as well.

"Sorry, Oskar," I said. "Time to go."

"No," Oskar said. He wouldn't look at me. His skin was the color of something that lived under rocks.

Back over by the bunk bed, the mother shakily brought her back foot up and slightly forward in a second shuffling step. The movement left her swaying a moment as if unclear how to find her balance.

"Let's go," Gloria said.

Sammy met my eyes, checking in like usual when he wasn't sure what to do.

I got the feeling Oskar just wanted to be tucked in and kissed good night by his babushka back in Russia or wherever. I said, "I know, but I don't know what to tell ya, man. We gotta go."

The boy slowly wriggled his way across the floor. The mother took another step. The father took his first.

Sammy said, "Yeah, we really gotta go."

Gloria and everyone else waited at the edge of the aisle for us.

I kneeled near him. "Oskar, what you did back in Receiving kicked ass, man. I don't know how many of us would be here if you hadn't done it. I know it took a lot out of you. Right now, though, we gotta move. And here's why. Look over there. That family, the ones at the bunk bed? Yeah, they're on their way to say howdy."

That got his attention. He cracked open an eye. I watched it get wide when he saw I was telling the truth. I couldn't see the boy anymore. The mom and dad hadn't gotten far, only a few feet, but they were most definitely on their way. And Oskar knew it.

"I don't wanna know what they have to say," I said. "And I don't think you do either. So, let's sit you up, and me and Sammy'll help you out from there."

The second boy toppled off the top bunk and smashed to the floor.

Then he started crawling toward us, following the rest of his family.

We couldn't see anybody else from our temporary base in House Shit, so none of us knew if the rest of the customers in the store were waking up like the family at the bunk beds. Or if they'd snapped out of their trance and started to approach us simply because we were nearby, and we'd woken them up, caught their attention somehow. Like every other goddamn thing in the store today, none of us had a clue what was really happening. All we knew was that the only path to the break room available to us was straight through Front End. We couldn't sneak around the way we'd come, out through the vestibule and back in through the EXIT door, because the vestibule was full of the blue moths.

We crept out of House Shit and on our way through the racks of New Arrivals as quietly as possible. Gloria and Hank led the way, followed by the Professor and Kiko with her hairspray. Wanda carried Peaches. Everybody kept low, moving furtively. That was tough with Oskar, as he couldn't really walk. So, like with the Professor, me and Sammy got on either side of him to bring up the rear of the procession. Oskar draped his arms over our shoulders and hung there. He was able to support his own weight by taking a step every now and again, giving Sammy and me a moment to catch our breath, but then his knees would give out, and he'd sag between us. We mostly dragged him. If we didn't have hold of his arms, he would have collapsed. I started to think it might just be easier if he just lay on his back on the floor, while me and Sammy each took an arm and dragged him along the smooth concrete, because at least we could get lower and hide behind all the racks of merch.

Hank stopped at the end of an aisle and held up his fist. I figured that meant to freeze and be silent. Me and Sammy eased Oskar to a sitting position, rather than expecting him to stand on his own. He did his best to keep his pained grunts to a minimum. Once he was settled, I got brave and peeked over the circular rack of children's flammable snowsuits.

Front End was still full of customers.

None of 'em seemed to be waking up like the bunk

bed family at least. They all remained in the exact same spots, same body stance, all clumped along the row of registers like garbage washed up along a beach. The break room was on the other side of the clusters of a few dozen customers, and the only route would be to cut through the disorganized lines. Gaps between register lines were either blocked by motionless customers or loose chains. These were notoriously sticky and difficult to unclasp. It was easier to just go under them.

We huddled at the edge of New Arrivals, careful to keep out of sight of the customers.

Gloria said, "I don't think it's a good idea to get close to any of 'em. But I don't see how we can get to the break room any other way."

"The family, they were slow," Wanda said. "It's like they forgot how to walk."

"I don't think getting through 'em will be a problem," Hank said. "They're still asleep. But what happens if we wake 'em up? The thing that worries me is that there's no door in the break room. What happens if they come after us, like the family back there? Everyone'll follow us right inside." He turned to the Professor. "How much time do you need?"

"It depends how fast we can find the shrine. The ritual itself can vary, but once the emergence begins, it, uh, should be over quickly." The Professor sounded like he was trying to convince himself more than the rest of us.

"If we can get to the basement," Gloria said. "We can pull the doors shut behind us and lock 'em."

"We may stand a better chance if we split up," Hank said. "You and the Professor and everybody else get to the basement. I'll stay up here for a while, keep the customers busy while you complete the ritual. Things get complicated, I'll follow you into the basement, lock the doors behind me."

"I don't like it," Gloria said. "Too much can go wrong, and we have no way of communicating."

"I don't like it either," Hank said. "But we're past the luxury of being able to pick and choose what we'd like to do."

I stole another peek, just to reassure myself that the customers were still hypnotized. Nothing in Front End, as far as I could see, had changed. I knew much of the light had faded away, but I could swear there were shadows on the floor around the customers that I hadn't noticed before, as if the concrete was dirty or something.

Despite my vow to do whatever it took to get the women out of the building, I decided I'd volunteer to stay upstairs on the main floor with Hank. I'd rather take my chances on the rest of the customers waking up than have to face that grim stairwell to the basement. But then again, I didn't want it lying heavy on my conscience that I'd inadvertently volunteered Sammy to accompany the Professor and Gloria into the basement. If the remoras had managed to infiltrate the store up here, then there was no telling what else might be down there, lurking in the absolute darkness.

"One thing at a time. Let's get everybody to the break room first," Gloria said. "We'll see what the customers do. Maybe we'll get lucky, and they won't notice."

I put my palms flat on the concrete and readjusted my aching legs. My knees cracked, and I froze, but the sound didn't carry far. The floor was covered in grit, something that would usually have brought about Gloria's wrath on a normal business day.

"Looks like number ten might be our best bet," Hank said. "The lines at nine and twelve are bad, but there should be enough space to get through."

"You sure?" Gloria asked. "What about the far side? Between registers one and two? What if we were to cut through over there?"

Hank shook his head. "It's tight. If we don't get through fast enough, the rest of them could corner us in Pharmacy," he said.

I rested a moment on my haunches, brushing my palms on my new sweats to wipe off all the crap from the floor that had stuck to my skin. It was time to retie my shoelaces and get ready for the scramble to the break room. I didn't know how we'd carry Oskar that far, but decided we'd figure it out as we went.

The grit on my palms wouldn't wipe away. I turned them over and looked, but couldn't see anything. No dirt, nothing. It still felt like I'd grabbed raw fiberglass or a bunch of stinging nettles. Even my glasses didn't reveal anything. I rubbed my hands briskly together, but the sensation persisted. I'd started considering the possibility that I was having some sort of allergic reaction, or I'd pinched a nerve, automatically assuming the problem was with my own body.

I should have known.

Hair had started growing out of the concrete floor.

At first, strands emerged from tiny cracks or discolored patches every few inches. Then, as I watched in disbelief, more and more filaments began curling out of the floor, until it started to look like a field of weeds poking through the soil's dry crust. I mumbled, "Aw, shit," right about the same time everybody else discovered the hair. Cries of disgust and shock as everyone jumped to their feet. Me and Sammy yanked Oskar off the floor. The seat of his sweats clung to the concrete for a moment, stuck somehow. We pulled harder and the sweatpants tore free. Strands of the hair had started growing into the fabric, grabbing hold and refusing to let go. He leaned against a rack, strong enough now to hold himself upright.

Everyone had jumped to their feet, scrambling away from the hair, slapping any part of their body that had been touching the floor, violently brushing away anything that might still be clinging to their skin or clothing. Then there was this horrible, frozen moment when we looked up and realized that not only was the hair eagerly growing out of the floor across the entire Front End like black grass sprouting in time-lapse photography, but that we'd also inadvertently stumbled out into the open. Now the customers were all staring at us.

In the span of two seconds, our simple plan to slip past the catatonic customers and hide in the break room had fallen apart faster than the lady with the dog.

Something made me check the aisle behind us.

Sure enough, the family from the bunk bed was following, heading straight for us in total silence. They looked like they'd been practicing learning how to walk and move like regular human beings. They'd mastered the learning curve and could now keep their balance while moving at a fairly brisk walk. Even the two boys had managed to find their feet, and all four came for us, arms held out like a stereotypical cartoon zombie. Well, both boys each had a broken arm, and those hung at awkward angles. It would have been almost comical, but something was off about their hands. I caught strange movements from the palm that didn't have any immediate explanation.

Then the mom tripped and fell. She didn't try and stop her fall, to ease the impact in any way, just boom, slammed face first into the concrete. One arm was thrown forward, and that's when I got my first good look at what was up with all of their hands.

A hairless cord of muscle or flesh of some sort, about the diameter and width of a long rat's tail, squirmed out of a small, bloodless slit in the center of her palm, and now writhed around as if sniffing the air. The tip opened and closed like some sort of hungry heavy-metal flower. Petals ringed with sharp-looking thorns fluttered like a fish trapped on the bank gasping for oxygen. The rest of the family kept coming. They all had their arms up and reaching for us, and all had those hairless rat tails stretching out from their palms; the closer the family got to us, the more frantic the wriggling of the prehensile tails became.

Gloria tensed, ready to run. "Do we go for it?"

There was no cover out in the open area here where the customers organized themselves in lines for the registers; we were totally exposed. And they were all watching us. The plan to slip quietly between registers 10 and 11 without detection was off the table. So much for the element of surprise.

One of the closer customers at the end of their line

was the first to take a step in our direction. It didn't take long before more followed. Pretty soon the whole group was starting to shuffle our way.

I looked back. The bunk bed family was only a few yards away.

Something tugged at my left foot.

It was the fucking hair. It was already long enough to curl over the black soles that protected the bottom and sides of my shoes. I swore and jerked my foot away. Problem was the same thing was happening to my other shoe. As I jumped up, jerking both feet off the floor, I saw that the hair was now so thick it was getting difficult to even spot the concrete. In less than two minutes, the bare gray concrete had grown a black lawn in desperate need of mowing. Pretty soon the hair would be too long for even a lawnmower, and you'd need some kind of heavy-duty machine with sharp steel teeth that could chew through the thickest grass and underbrush, even saplings.

We froze, stuck between the customers shuffling from Front End, the field of hair erupting under our feet, and the surprisingly agile family behind us.

I was all for making a run for the break room, dumb enough to think we still had a chance to dodge all the slow customers in Front End, since they hadn't had enough time to get used to how their bodies moved yet. Then I saw how every customer had their arms up, all with their very own snake-like, hairless cord of muscle reaching out the center of every palm. And the more practice they got, the faster they moved.

Peaches growled, warning us about the approaching customers. Wanda had her in her arms again, keeping the dog safe out of the hair.

"Any ideas?" Gloria shouted.

The herd of customers from Front End was twenty feet away and creeping nearer all the time.

The bunk bed family was less than ten feet away and closing fast.

Hair now covered the floor. We had to keep hopping from one foot to another so it couldn't get hold of either shoe.

Nobody had an answer for Gloria.

I brought up my snow shovel and shoved the blade against the father's chest as he reached for me. He grabbed the handle. The rat-tail appendages squirmed from both palms and attacked the grooved aluminum, snapping at it until a green liquid oozed out of the mouths of the flower petals. But right then the two boys went around either side of their father and came straight for me, arms straight out, fleshy tentacle things snapping at the air, vibrating with urgency. They would have gotten me too, if it wasn't for Sammy and his big push broom. He rushed in from the side and pinned both boys against the stacks of tires with the wide broom head.

A blast of fiery chemicals shot past my head, spraying the father dead in the face. Rivulets of harsh chemicals coated his eyes, his nose, his mouth, but he didn't react whatsoever. It might as well have been a light misting of a subtle perfume. I flinched away. It may not have bothered Dad much, but even a tiny wisp was enough to burn my eyes, lungs. A hissing sputter and the pepper spray ran dry. Gloria threw the container at the father's head. It bounced off and went spinning away.

I jabbed Dad with the shovel blade, trying to knock

him off balance. It didn't work, and for some reason, I couldn't bring myself to try again. It felt like trying to kick the dog, I guess. It wasn't this dude's fault. He hadn't done anything to deserve this. I got a firm hold of the handle and braced the shovel against the father's chest again, keeping out of the range of his arms. I yelled something inarticulate as he kept reaching around the shovel, straining to reach me.

Hair grabbed at my feet. I hopped. Again and again.

And here came the mom.

Not for the first time that day, I thought it was over. We were done. I couldn't see any way out. Me and Sammy were holding off the bunk bed family by the skin of our teeth, barely keeping those horrible appendages snapping and straining inches from our flailing arms. No one was left to stop the mom. All she'd have to do was slip around her husband and kids to grab either me or Sammy. Those hairless rat tails would slide out of her hand and chew into our flesh, and it would be finished forever.

Behind us was the horde of customers, lurching closer and closer, each with their own pair of palm snakes. Running that way sounded like the worst game of junior high flag football ever. Trying to slip through that crowd without getting touched was the same as trying to run through a blizzard without letting a snowflake land on you. We wouldn't make it.

Then there was the goddamn hair. If we stayed on the floor much longer, it would eventually get long enough to really grab hold, and once it truly caught you, you'd be finished.

The mom was almost on top of me. I had a split second to make a choice to either keep holding the father at bay with the shovel or jerk it away to use against the mother. I tried to kick the mom instead, same as how Oskar had smashed the first few baby rats crawling along the wall. It didn't work. For one thing, I didn't have boots like Oskar, and his legs hadn't been covered in baby rat bites yet. My foot glanced off her stomach, pushing her off to the side. My other leg, weak and trembling from all the bites, slipped in the hair, and I went down sideways.

The mother's arms snapped shut on empty air above me.

The father reached down.

Another few inches, and he'd have me.

Then I heard Kiko flicking her Zippo and VOOOOOM.

Mom and Dad's heads went up in twin fireballs. Mom stopped moving forward for a moment, wobbling a little on her feet, like a bobblehead on fire. Dad took a step backward, still working on his balance. He knew something had changed, just not quite sure what, other than that his entire head was now consumed in raging flames.

But right then? I'd landed in that fucking hair, and that's all that I cared about. I'll wear cargo shorts 'til the day I die, but at that moment you better believe I was thanking the baby Jesus with everything I had, immensely grateful to be wearing sweatpants. If nothing else, they covered my bare legs. And that gave me a crucial second to scramble to my feet, which trust me, isn't easy if you're a big guy, and you can't use your arms.

Mom and Dad stumbled around for a bit, still not fully appreciating they were now on fire. They held up their arms but couldn't seem to see us anymore. The boys didn't pay any attention to their parents and kept struggling to free themselves from Sammy's broom. Dad bounced off the stack of the Indonesian DVD players and went down. Hair immediately curled over him. The fire went out. He rolled around for a moment, but not long. Except for the smoke, he never moved again.

I went to move and found the hair had me again, and this time it was trying to get inside, over the tops of my shoes, into my socks. I kicked and stomped, scraping the soles off on the stacks of tires. Then, a gift. Something went right for once. I found myself in front of the boxes of giant imitation snakeskin cowboy boots. I grabbed the closest box without looking at the size. That didn't make any difference. They were all absurdly huge. The stereotype of many, many Americans being grossly overweight is, by and large, one hundred percent correct.

I dropped them upright at my feet and stepped inside. Since I was still wearing my hiking shoes, they felt a little tight and awkward, but I'd be damned if they didn't give me better protection than just my own shoes. "Yeehaw, motherfuckers!" I started throwing boxes at everyone. Pretty soon, they'd all slipped into their own pair. The hair couldn't get through the imitation snake scales, and would buy us some time, but if we took any longer, the hair might still grab your leg and hang on. You might not get loose.

Hank approached the struggling boys, still pinned to the tires by the end of Sammy's broom. Once again, he held the fire axe by the end of the handle, deftly hooked the bottom of the pike around the older brother's ankle, and gave a quick yank. The boy went horizontal, much like I had, dropping flat into the hair. He thrashed a few moments in fits and starts, mostly still trying to reach Sammy, but eventually his movements subsided and stopped altogether.

Hank repeated the process with the youngest. Without waiting for the spasms to stop, he spun and gave Mom a gentle push with the head of the axe. She fell over like a candle that hadn't been secured to its base.

He wiped his eyes and faced the mob of customers shambling toward us, saying in a thick voice, "Stand back." He hefted the axe. "And get ready to run."

"Hold up," Gloria said, pointing. "Look."

It took me a second to figure out what Gloria meant. I couldn't see very well through the customers. It looked like the hair was growing in waves, starting in Front End and creeping to the back. It had begun growing out of the concrete up near the registers first and was just now reaching us. Anyone that went running through the registers would quickly find themselves in ankle-deep hair, maybe even knee-deep. If you were on foot, you probably wouldn't make it to the break room.

"Let's back up a minute, rethink our plan," Gloria said. "This, this won't work."

We retreated back along the center aisle, everybody getting used to walking in the awkward boots, looking to get some distance from the customers mindlessly trudging after us. That made me feel a little better until I remembered we were just moving deeper into chicken bug territory, and Back End was still infested with baby rats. We were running out of places to hide. At least the floor here in the center of the store was still only concrete.

"These boots are a good start, but they won't get us all the way," Hank said. "Unless we grow wings, I don't know how we're gonna get to the break room."

The customers kept coming. Some of them moved faster than others. It wouldn't be long until they reached us. We couldn't keep retreating. If we got backed up against the doors to Receiving, then we'd be completely trapped.

"If the remoras are this active, the emergence is coming. Soon. There must be another entrance to the basement!" the Professor insisted.

Gloria shook her head. "It's outside."

I got to thinking that this sounded like every other damn thing in my life where'd I'd been close to some kind of success, so close I could just about taste it, until life stepped in and said *nah,* not you, not today. The basement was right under our feet, right fucking *there,* yet we couldn't get there. Close, but no cigar. Even with Hank's fire axe, it would take days to chip a hole in the concrete floor big enough for Kiko to fit through, never mind me or Sammy.

"Then we have no alternative," the Professor said. "We must go through them. If we cannot reach the basement in time, it is all over. Over!"

"Hard to fight something you can't touch," Hank said.

Kiko shook the can of hairspray. "Not enough," she said.

Gloria sighed. Shook her head. "Was hoping it wouldn't come to this," she said and pulled out the Professor's handgun. I don't know where she'd been hiding it, maybe next to the pepper spray, but she'd had it the whole time. My hopes soared. This was America, and if you had a gun, then any goddamn thing was possible. A firearm could solve whatever problem came your way. Finally. We could send all these fuckers straight back to hell.

I don't know a whole lot about guns, mostly just what I'd seen in action movies. This one looked awfully small, small enough to be a joke, maybe what they called a .22 caliber. She held it like a toy she hadn't seen in some time, but the familiarity was still there. After she hit some kind of button near the trigger, the magazine slid out of the bottom of the handle. She checked to make sure it was full. Then she racked back the slide and a fresh shell popped out of the top. She deftly caught it and fed it back into the magazine like she'd done it a thousand times. It wouldn't have surprised me if she'd been a goddamn SEAL or Ranger, some kind of special forces.

Then again, maybe it was just the south side of Chicago.

Once she'd slapped the magazine back into the handle, she drew the slide back again to load a fresh shell. I think Gloria knew if she hesitated, she would never follow through. So before anyone could really react, she took a few steps toward Front End, settled into a comfortable position, feet shoulder-width apart at a slight angle to the approaching customers, brought the handgun up, holding it with both hands. Gloria's hands weren't large, but they swallowed the firearm.

The closest customer was a short Hispanic guy with dead eyes and a slack face. He was built like a barrel and his short legs swished through the growing hair on the floor. Ten feet away, Gloria took careful aim and squeezed the trigger.

A small, disappointing crack. Nothing like the big booming explosion I was hoping for. I had nothing against the customer personally, but I really wanted to watch his whole head explode like an M-80 in a watermelon. I didn't realize how much I craved some kind of oversize reaction, like his skull vaporizing or at the very least getting to watch him get blown out of his shoes, flying a dozen feet backward to smash into more customers.

Instead, his head waggled a moment, like he was avoiding a troublesome fly, and then he kept walking forward. I could now see a small hole, about the width of a ballpoint pen, in his forehead just over his right eye. Blood didn't even have the decency to leak out. Gloria might as well have used a hole punch on a piece of cardboard.

I wished the gun was bigger. Like a goddamn shotgun. Or bazooka. I wanted to see how well that sonofabitch would walk without a fucking head. Gloria coolly observed this lack of reaction to a brand-spanking new bullet in the head, then tried again. Another pitiful, anemic pop. A second hole appeared in his forehead. He barely even moved that time. Still no blood. However, he only managed two more steps before he lost his balance, falling onto the hairy floor.

Gloria didn't wait to see what happened. She fired again at the next customer, a woman close to her own age. The first shot was another right in the center of the skull a couple inches straight above the nose, giving the woman a spiritual third eye. The only difference this time was that the woman turned to look at Gloria with a confused expression. Gloria put another one in her head and a few seconds later, the rest of the woman's body got the message and she dropped.

The presence of a gun made no difference to the rest of the customers. They kept coming.

Gloria restricted herself to only two bullets per customer and fired six more times, shooting another three people. On the fourth customer, she pulled the trigger but only got a crisp click in reply. It was empty. It only held ten shells. She'd taken care of five. And they weren't even quite dead. The hair wasn't all that long back here in the middle of the store, and there wasn't enough to grab them firmly. So those that had been shot kept kicking around the floor.

At least thirty or forty customers remained, trickling slowly from the Front End, forcing us down the center aisle, straight back to the goddamn baby rats. Not only would we have to get through the customers, dodging the writhing, biting appendages, but we'd also have to somehow rise above the waves of thick hair that grew from the floor, following us. I had to look twice and confirm, the hair was actually growing in thicker clumps where we'd stepped, emerging thickest from our footprints.

The cowboy boots wouldn't be enough.

I considered briefly climbing up onto the racks, jumping from one to another, like using the rocks across a stream again, to get off the floor and get to Front End, but that idea crumbled once I really thought about it. Most of the racks wouldn't be able to withstand an extra hundred or so pounds, never mind two fifty, and would fall apart instantly, sending me and anyone else crashing to the floor where the hair would seize us.

We couldn't catch a break. One step forward, five steps back.

Something tickled my brain. Something that seemed important but wouldn't reveal itself. I couldn't grab it. It squirted out of my grasp like mercury.

Hank said, "We got maybe thirty seconds to figure out something."

Wanda said, "We could crawl up into the steel. Hide up there." She indicated the back of the store, where steel racks holding pallets of excess merchandise stretched up to the ceiling. It would solve our immediate problems, getting us away from the customers, hopefully avoiding the baby rats, and getting us off the floor away from the hair. It didn't sound that bad, kind of appealing actually. A clear, decisive way to retreat and if not escape, at least get out of the reach of the customers for a while.

"Then what?" Hank said. "Might buy us some time, but that's all. What if they learn how to climb?" He thrust his chin at the approaching customers. "This hair, it's everywhere. And it'll get up there. Easy. Then we'll really be up shit creek without a paddle."

The term paddle pinged something, something brewing, but again I couldn't pinpoint it.

"Okay, what else?" Gloria asked. I could tell she'd been holding off using the handgun as a last resort. Now that she'd been forced to use it and found it was all but useless against large numbers of customers, her hope and optimism had taken another serious blow. And when Gloria ran out of hope, she ran out of life.

Hank rolled his shoulders, then his wrist, spinning the fire axe as he got loosened up. "I'll take out as many as I can. You guys run like hell to the break room."

Before Gloria could protest, Oskar turned away and doubled over, vomiting blood. It exploded out in great clotted chunks, drenching the hair in front of him. I didn't need my glasses to see how the blood was thick with the fine grains of white rice. The wet hair grew excited, wriggling through the blood until it was a frothing red foam. Oskar vomited again.

"Give me the axe," he said, reaching for it, blood spilling from the corners of his mouth.

"Oskar, you—" Gloria started.

"No time," he snapped, spraying bloody saliva. He bit down, chewed a moment, then spit. "They're in my mouth," he said. Nobody needed or wanted an explanation. "Give me the axe," he repeated.

Hank held the axe out handle first, and Oskar snatched it. He turned to face the oncoming customers, doubling over again. More blood and white flecks sprayed out, settled over the hair. He gave us one last look, then staggered toward the horde of blank people, axe up and ready to meet their upraised arms.

Our retreat had stretched the customers out, giving Oskar a minute to deal with each one individually, instead of being overrun immediately. However, they would eventually catch up and swarm him. He knew that. He'd buy us some time, but there was no way he could get through all of the customers. Not with just a fire axe. And while puking blood.

We needed weapons. If the clothing racks would collapse if we tried to use them as stepping stones to the registers, maybe we could still use smaller ones as clubs or spears, like how I'd kept the dad off me with the shovel. Maybe if we circled up, shoulders together, our backs to the center in a kind of ring, we could keep the customers far enough from us as we moved as a group to get to the break room. That was a big maybe, though.

And there was still the hair, getting deeper every second.

The closest rack to me was garbage for something to climb on, but as a possible weapon, it was better than I could have hoped. It had a wide, round base about a foot in diameter that supported a metal pole about five feet tall, where a thin spiral arm stretched gracefully out to hold the merchandise. I ripped the clothing off and hefted the entire rack, checking the weight. It felt solid. A hell of a lot better than my shovel, anyway. I handed it to Hank. Gloria had already caught on and had gone to work grabbing another display rack.

Oskar got close to the first of the customers, the hipster, and didn't fuck around. The axe came down, and the hipster was suddenly missing half his head and mustache, axe buried in his neck. There may have been a bit of blood, but nowhere near enough, seeing more than half his skull was gone. He still grabbed at Oskar though, still kept coming. Oskar was in no mood to deal with that bullshit. He yanked the axe out and would've happily chopped both arms off if he could. He lacked the strength and leverage, and the axe simply wasn't sharp enough. The heavy blade did slice down to the bone though, knocking each arm aside. Oskar drove the axe forward, smashing it straight into what was left of the hipster's head, knocking it into an odd angle. The hipster wandered around for a while before losing his balance and going down.

Oskar figured out the best method for dealing with customers with the next one, a young woman. As she came at him, arms outstretched, palm snakes writhing in eagerness, Oskar swung the fire axe horizontally, like it was a baseball bat, and he was going for a home run. He twisted his body, whipping his hips and arms around, and sunk the blade deep into her neck. The blow slammed her to the floor, six inches of steel blade still jammed in the meat and bone. When she landed, the handle jutted straight up.

Oskar vomited more blood. He wiped his mouth, then put the snakeskin cowboy boot on her jaw. His own boots had fit nicely inside the giant, imitation snakeskin ones. He yanked. The axe came free with very little blood.

I picked up another spiral clothing rack and simply shook the clothes off, tossed it to the Professor. Now everyone had one except me and Gloria. We went to grab our last two, and out of the corner of my eye, I saw Sammy make a little, unimportant motion, jabbing his rack at the floor, testing the strength of the base. The simple gesture collided with the word "paddle," and an idea exploded behind my eyes.

The answer had been in front of us the whole time, but I hadn't made the connection until now. I had to deal with them every second of every day at work, and I don't even know if I consciously saw them anymore. Or if I saw 'em, they didn't register, and I was so used to ignoring them, they may well have not existed.

The fucking carts.

I could have kicked myself for not figuring it out sooner. And they were all over the place. Most were up in Front End with the customers, but there were always plenty scattered around the store. People abandoned them all the time for the slightest reasons, including employees. Luckily, this FOOD4U! had inherited the giant carts from the Crafty Beaver, able to hold hardware and lumber, not like the tiny ones in the Jewel or Aldi down the street. These could hold one of us easy, probably two.

"Hang on!" I shouted and darted back through New Arrivals to House Shit. The family's cart was still next to the bunk beds. They hadn't gotten far with their shopping. The basket was empty. I pushed the cart back to the center aisle, using it as a battering ram as I went. It felt a little like what we used to dream of when we got bored or irritated at work, smashing into merch, destroying property. What do they call it? Cathartic.

I found two more along the way and slammed the

three of them together. Racing back, I shoved them at the group. "Hop in."

Gloria had been breathing fire, psyching herself up, gathering energy and the determination to go running through the customers armed only with a clothing rack. Now I was yelling at her to redirect, to toss that plan out for something that involved carts. "What's that?" she asked.

"Get in!" I yelled.

Meanwhile, Oskar dropped another customer. Two more came for him, reaching desperately at his arms. He swung the axe wildly. I saw a few ragged severed fingers go spinning away.

"And then what?" Gloria asked.

Sammy appeared with another two carts. That gave us five total. It might just be enough for seven people and a dog. I couldn't bring myself to count Oskar, although if he could last another minute or two at the most, I might be able to grab him on the way. "Wanda, you and Kiko share this one," I said, bumping a cart their way with my hip. Wanda dropped Peaches in first. Everybody dumped supplies into their baskets.

Gloria still didn't like it, didn't see what I had in mind. "No. Someone will have to push. I'm not willing to sacrifice anyone else."

"Don't have to," I said. "Look." I really wanted jumping into the cart to be cool, like the Duke boys sliding across the hood. I don't know if you've ever actually tried to climb into the basket of a shopping cart, but it's not as simple as you might think. It was old and wobbled unsteadily, and the edges of the basket felt like barbed wire. In the end, I can't say I was terribly agile, or it was all that graceful, but I got my butt inside.

"We're running out of time," Gloria said. "I don't know if—"

By then I had gotten to my knees inside the basket and grabbed my empty rack, using it as a pole to push me along like Huck Finn on his raft. If my attempt to clamber into the cart wasn't exactly nimble, more fodder for *America's Funniest Home Videos,* then me sailing off in the cart was smooth as silk, like I was a regular goddamn captain of a gondola. I cruised off down the center aisle like it was a gentle, if kinda hairy, stream.

I didn't look back to check on everyone else because I'd rolled fifteen feet down the aisle in no time and had to go around a few of the prone customers that had already been introduced to Oskar's fire axe. The filaments tried to grab at the wheels, but after years of rolling through hair nets and leaves, the ball bearings were more like gravel, grinding the hair into black paste.

As a vehicle, I can't recommend the cart. It shook and rattled like hell, veering wildly. Settling into a halfway comfortable position was impossible. Steering and propulsion involved the entire body. I found I had to brace my knees against the sides, steering with them really, using my torso to twist, generating power from my shoulders as I slammed the base against the floor with a CLONK every time I dug in for another thrust forward.

I was too late to save Oskar.

One of the customers got hold of the axe handle, and when he reversed his grip, the palm snake thing had shot out and attacked the webbing between Oskar's thumb and forefinger. He didn't yelp or jerk away or anything. No, in true Oskar fashion, he grabbed the thin appendage with his bleeding hand and yanked the customer toward him. They both lost their balance and went down. Hair covered them, and they were gone by the time I got there. I couldn't even grab the goddamn axe.

I couldn't worry about it because I found myself suddenly in the thick of customers. They came at me from all sides. I whipped the clothing rack around in a circle, heavy base knocking reaching arms away. Then Boris the Rattail was right there, right in front of my cart. His crutches hung from his forearms as he held his arms out, but his legs seemed to be working at least as well as the rest of the customers. At the time, I kinda felt like everything had all started with his temper tantrum, and while I wasn't exactly thrilled to be smacking old ladies in the head with the base of my clothing rack, I fully admit I went after Boris with a fucking vengeance. When I was finished, his head was oatmeal, and I'd broken the damn base off my rack, leaving me with more of a spear.

The convoy of carts caught up, and next thing I knew, Hank was swinging his own clothing rack in great sweeping arcs, knocking the customers down and back. The rest of the employees saw a chance to get through one of the open register lanes and rushed for it, driving off the occasional customer as they went. Sammy followed Hank and the Professor through, and I brought up the rear and saw Tim. He'd followed us partially out into the store with the rest of the customers, gradually turning back when we sailed past

’em in the carts. Even though he now had those palm snake things, I couldn’t bring myself to whack him with the rack. So, I pushed myself past his register, pausing just long enough to reach back and draw the chain across the lane, snapping it closed on an eyelet on the opposite side.

Tim bumped into it and just kept pushing forward, not seeming to understand something was holding him back. I left him behind and pushed my cart through the registers into the open area in front of Customer Service. The rest were straining hard, struggling to move forward in hair as thick and luxurious as a goddamn shampoo ad.

All I can say was thank fuck the remoras still weren’t getting along because that was what ultimately allowed us to get into the break room. The hair couldn’t tell the difference between customers or employees. It would grab hold of the customers and wouldn’t let go until enough strands had crept up under their slacks and jeans and touched bare skin. Once it realized their corrupted flesh wasn’t what it wanted, it let go. This didn’t stop the customers totally, but it did slow ’em down.

Sounds weird to say, but I don’t know as we would’ve made it into the break room without the hair.

The break room had no door.

There was nothing to stop the customers from coming inside.

And hair was already growing from the concrete floor as well as the outer cinderblock walls. I’d been thinking we might be able to use some of the tables to maybe barricade ourselves inside, buy some time while we drew or painted on the sheets or whatever the Professor needed, catch our breath, you know. But now with hair growing up through the concrete, we might need the tables to stay off the floor.

Soon as she was inside, Gloria jumped out of the cart and ran down the hall to the basement doors, keys out.

Everybody else climbed out of their carts and gathered up their supplies. Hank set his five planters on the nearest table, each with its own can of vegetable shortening inside. Wanda gathered up Peaches. Kiko still had her hairspray. Me and Sammy pushed carts toward the break room entry to slow down the customers who were already spilling through the doorway.

When we got back to the hallway, Gloria had the locks open. This time she ripped the second door open on her own. The tearing sound of the rubber seal took me back to that morning. It felt like years.

Kiko lit Hank's torches. The coated towels sent up a fair amount of black smoke, but it wasn't as toxic as smoke from the hair. The way the vegetable shortening torches lit up the short hallway was impressive. Hank took his over to the FIRE EXIT but only needed a quick glance to know hair clogged the gaps.

Gloria held a torch out over the stairs and peered down into the flickering darkness.

"Wonderful," she said.

"Wait!" I said, as the image of the water bottle rattling down the garbage chute hit me.

This new idea also involved a cart, and I dashed

back into the break room, best as I could in the giant cowboy boots. Customers were spilling into the break room, bumping into carts, sending them ricocheting in slow motion back into the tables. I threw chairs at the closest customers and didn't have to dodge anybody to grab a loose cart. I rolled it right back into the hallway and up to the open doors. Gloria stepped back to give me room.

"We don't know what's down there," I said. "Let's send this down first. See what we wake up. If nothing else, these carts are tough; should still work so we can use it to haul all this stuff."

"Now that's an action plan," Sammy said.

We didn't high-five, but I kinda wanted to.

I got it centered at the top of the stairwell, and everybody crowded around. The torches sent looming and jumping shadows down to the center landing. Beyond that was absolute darkness. It was still strangely warm. I stepped away, gesturing at the cart, telling Kiko, "You gave me the idea."

She flashed a surprisingly bashful grin at me and squared up behind the cart. She kissed her fingertips, glittery black fingernail polish flickering in the torch-light, and gave the pale-blue handle a soft nudge. The front rolled off the first step. They dropped, but didn't hit the next step yet because the bottom frame of the cart scraped along the top step instead. Once the cart started to tilt though and slide forward, the front wheels only nicked the steps as it flew along, until they caught fast, flipping the cart end over end, filling the stairwell with thick clouds of fine dust. The cart crashed onto the landing in the middle of the stairs, where it bounced twice and stopped.

We held our breath.

Nothing happened.

Silence from the darkness at the bottom.

Dust settled.

The only sounds came from the break room as customers shuffled through, pushing past the carts, chairs, and tables. They had almost reached the hallway.

We all looked at each other. Gloria said, "I suppose we may as well get it over with, though Lord knows I'd rather not." She held her torch out to the Professor. "Your idea," she said.

"I suppose it is," he said and took the planter, the torch momentarily lighting him from underneath, and I knew if I made it through this, I was gonna be seeing that gaunt face in my nightmares for the rest of my life. Still, I was ready to follow. With any luck, the Professor's plan would work, and we might just get out of this building.

Then I remembered Oskar. Vomiting blood. And little white specks.

I had the same goddamn things in me. So did Sammy. And Hank. The Professor. The only choice I had was to hope that the Professor's plan worked, and once we sent that thing back to wherever, it pulled everything, all the remoras with it. If it didn't, I supposed the least we could do was try and save the damn world.

Starting with Gloria, Wanda, and Kiko. And Peaches too, I guess.

So once we'd all stepped through the doorway and started down the stairwell, me and Sammy pulled the doors shut. Of course there were no keyholes on this side, only knobs that popped out of the handle. We locked them by pushing them in and prayed they'd hold, then headed down the landing where the others had gathered around the upside-down cart. The torches didn't seem so impressive in the limited space and thick dust of the stairwell. The darkness was so oppressive it felt solid, like you might bang your head.

We held all five torches as far out as we could and could just make out a cement floor at the bottom, strewn with debris. "One more time, Kiko," Gloria said, but she gave me a quick glance. Sammy got the cart upright, and we positioned it at the edge. Kiko set it on its one-way journey once again.

It bounced and crashed down, this time maybe even louder.

Once it landed, nothing moved but the settling dust.

We heard nothing but the customers trying to get through the doors at the top.

Despite telling the Professor it had been his idea and sending him down the stairs, once we were on the landing, Gloria went first, leading the rest of the way. The more steps we descended, the worse I felt. Dread flooded my mind, making it hard to think straight. Maybe I should have just been thankful it didn't feel like I might shit my pants anymore. I knew from experience not to get too excited because that could make a surprise appearance at any time.

At the bottom, the torches showed us we'd descended into a ghostly forest of a dead factory, where rusted hulks loomed over us in contorted, painful looking shapes. I had no idea what they could have been used for. This place could have been making anything from tractors to bombs. The massive equipment was shrouded in cobwebs and darkness. The torches did their best, but the space was crammed with so much machinery, shadows lurked everywhere. Hank explained it was a good thing the ceiling was so far up. "That hair's been growing up through the floor. Now it might be growing *down* at us."

We turned the cart upright and put the sheets, paint, markers, and Peaches inside then pushed straight into the abandoned factory. These assembly lines or whatever were arranged in rows, about five yards apart, so Gloria had us spread out, and whoever carried a planter went down their own aisle. We moved along as evenly as possible, a bobbing line of flickering torches. Ever since Hank had mentioned the hair growing down, I couldn't stop checking the space above me, even though I could only see utter blackness up there. Not seeing anything should have made me feel better, but it just made things worse. Darkness can hide most anything. I was so jumpy and jittery I half-expected the asymmetrical machinery to reach out and grab us.

By the time we'd reached the end of the rows, I was drenched in sweat. It wasn't just me and Sammy either. Everyone was panting and wiping at their eyes. The further into the darkness we went, the hotter it got. Ten feet past the last of the assembly machinery, we came upon a brick wall. Hank wandered a ways down to the left, holding his torch out and examining the bricks, while me and Sammy went to the right.

Soon enough, we came up a large black hole in the wall, big enough to drive a VW bug through, a gaping, hungry mouth that couldn't wait to swallow all of us.

"Hey, Professor," I said. "This what you're looking for?"

Sammy held his arm through the opening, using the torch to get a sense of what was on the other side, but the smoking flames revealed nothing but utter blackness. It was too dark, too vast. Everybody gathered around the opening. Hank held his torch out low, looking for some kind of floor on the other side of the bricks. At first, it didn't seem like there was anything, just a vertigo-inducing drop. He worked a brick out of the wall and dropped it.

It struck the ground almost immediately and we all exhaled in relief. It wasn't a bottomless pit. Hank crawled through, moving slow, sliding through feet first. He took a few steps, holding the torch out and around. We could see that he was standing on rough stone, about a foot, foot and half below the factory floor. Everyone piled through. Sammy and I lifted the shopping cart with our supplies and Peaches through the hole.

I guessed we were in some kind of massive cavern, perhaps far under the store. I took a deep breath. There was a change, you know? I don't know exactly how to explain it, but the air, it tasted thick, like you could almost chew it. We were standing at the edge of something like a cliff or ocean that I couldn't see, but it was there, visible or not.

My ears popped, and I had to swallow to equalize the pressure.

The Professor started out into the blackness, and I

couldn't help but feel he was walking out onto a frozen lake, and there was no telling when the ice might break and plunge him into the abyss. "Yes," he said, his words weirdly muted in heavy, dead air. "This is... promising." We followed, our torches feeling smaller and smaller against the overwhelming darkness.

"There!" the Professor nearly shrieked in triumph. "The dais!"

We'd reached what I first thought was a flat pile of boulders. We got closer, and I saw it was a circular platform, painstakingly constructed out of rough-hewn rocks. They looked like they'd been carried here and reassembled. The whole thing was maybe two feet high, and we could see it was around a dozen feet in diameter when Hank and Gloria got around the other side.

In the very center rose a slender, though gnarled and twisted form, maybe seven feet high. I thought it might be a stunted tree without branches until the Professor jumped on the dais and held his torch out to get a better look. Kinda like the air, I can't explain why, but I got the inescapable feeling that this thing was ancient, like it might have been carved out of solid meteorite. "The altar," he pronounced.

I've only been dragged to church a couple of times in my life, but it didn't look like any altar I'd ever seen. A small plume of impossibly black smoke curled above the skeletal stone structure. We could only see the smoke against the darkness above when the Professor held his torch high and close to the tree. Maybe that's why it gave me the impression of a limbless tree with the tip on fire. The smoke or whatever it was moved in slow motion, as if rising through water.

"Is that it?" Gloria asked, pointing at the sluggish dark wisp rising from the apex.

"Ben and I called it the pilot light," the Professor said. "Observe how it is growing. We must hurry. I don't think we have much time."

"Is that what we'll see?" Gloria asked doggedly.

"I will do my best to explain, but please, right now we should really begin the preparations," the Professor said. "I'd hate to be caught with our pants down, so to speak." He grabbed the finger paint and began to drag it along the sweeping lines on the dais itself, applying it in thick dabs, using two fingers to drag through the dust as he circled the twisted form in the center. He used blue paint for the outline, then red for the individual runes and sigils within. Hank followed along with his own container of yellow paint, outlining and emphasizing the Professor's original lines.

While they painted, Kiko and Wanda spread out the white sheet next to the dais. The Professor had shown her the page in one of the notebooks with the symbol, and she began to recreate the sun and eye image in a much larger scale on the sheet with the thick Sharpie markers.

I couldn't help noticing how much energy the Professor had. The weird, dense air had energized him, and he jumped around the dais like a monkey who'd eaten too many Frosted Flakes. It was almost as if the closer this thing got our universe, the happier it made the Professor. This observation led me to a startling question. What if the Professor had misled us? What if he'd been lying? What if, instead of stopping it like he claimed, what if he and his partner Ben had been part of the cult? What if they'd been trying to call it all along, trying to pull it into our universe? Now he had us helping him bring it here.

But I had no way of knowing. And even if that was true, I had no idea how to stop him. I decided to trust him. There wasn't much choice.

"How will we know it is getting close?" Gloria asked.

"You'll know." The Professor nodded.

"How?"

The Professor paused, looking for the words.

"What will it look like? What will we see?" Gloria demanded.

"It isn't anything that we can see. Not with our eyes. How would an ant know what the earth looks like?

"Then how will we know it is coming?"

"You will know. You feel this, do you not? The sensation of this air?" the Professor said. "The pressure has already changed here. Can you not sense it? Perhaps the most obvious thing you will notice is heat. You cannot ignore how the temperature has been rising."

"Figured it wasn't the furnace," Hank said.

"And what causes heat?" the Professor asked like he was in a classroom.

"Vibration," I said. A bit of high school physics had stuck.

"Exactly," the Professor said. "Motion and vibration of atoms. They're getting ready for the transformation, growing more and more active."

The slow-motion plume of black smoke was longer now, stretching up another three or four feet. The Professor said, "Yes. Can you feel that change? It is almost here." He turned and looked down to Kiko and Wanda. "How much longer?"

"Almost to the—" Kiko began.

"Shhhh!" Hank hissed. He stared out into the darkness.

"What is it?" Gloria whispered.

Everyone held their breath, sending their hearing out to the edges of the light, probing into the gloom. We heard nothing.

"You must hurry!" the Professor whispered to Kiko.

"Thought I..." Hank shook his head. "Guess not."

For a long minute, the only sound was the faint squeak of the Sharpie as Kiko dragged the big marker across the sheet. Wanda kneeled next to her, arms outstretched, hands flat, keeping the fabric taut so Kiko could work. I took a quick glance at the plume of smoke. It was almost five feet long now.

Then a chittering. A scrabbling, claws over stone.

Something exploded out of the darkness.

At first, I thought it was a big dog because of the size. But this was no dog. It wasn't a big cat. It wasn't a capybara. It was a rat. A goddamn giant rat. A rat the size of a fat German Shepherd.

Sammy instantly moved to put himself between the giant rat and Kiko and Wanda at the sheet. I jumped off the dais, glad I'd held onto my broken clothing rack. It wasn't all that sharp or heavy, but it might be halfway effective if I went for those gleaming red eyes. I tossed it to Sammy, saying, "Get ready. Spear that fucker. I'm gonna use the cart as a shield."

I grabbed Peaches out of the cart and tossed her up on the dais to Gloria.

The rat was nearly on us.

Both me and my stacks of carts had been struck enough times by slow-moving cars to grasp the consequences when that rat hit my cart at nearly fifteen miles an hour. If the cart was more or less resting in place when I got in the way of the rat, the momentum of the running animal would knock me and the cart back into the dais, leaving Kiko and Wanda open to attack. So I ignored the pain flashing up my leg and launched myself and the cart straight at the rat.

The rat tried to dodge the cart at the last moment, but I had rage on my side. The front of the basket slammed into the rat's right shoulder. The impact sent both the cart and the rat spinning. Sammy was right there though, right on my heels, and he leaped at the rat, foregoing the uncertainty of striking the rat in its eye, going instead for guaranteed results, driving the clothing rack deep into the rodent's heaving side, jamming the pole between its ribs.

The rat screamed.

It flopped and rolled, ripping the pole out of Sammy's fingers, squealing in agony, a horrible piercing sound that filled the vast cavern. It scrabbled around, huge teeth bared in retaliation. But then I crashed into it with the cart again, aiming for the pole still stuck between ribs. The rat scurried away, back into the shadows of the cave, and I felt a sliver of hope. We'd driven it away. We still had a chance.

Then I saw more of them, absurdly huge rats, creeping out of the darkness.

Kiko finished scribbling the last few lines on the

sheet, stood back, frantically comparing the image on the sheet with the one in the notebook. The Professor eyed it critically as well, pointing and starting to say, "Perhaps a bit more—"

The stone floor vibrated.

"We must start the ritual!" the Professor shouted. He held his notebook in one hand, a torch in the other. "Hurry! Prepare the symbol! Get it up here!"

While Kiko and Wanda joined Gloria and the Professor and Peaches on the dais, Hank, me, and Sammy each took a torch. I put mine in the middle of my cart and faced the darkness. Hank had his pocketknife, but these rats were so big it might as well have been a toothpick. If they rushed us, it would be over. At least they were still keeping their distance, wary of the torches and any more spears. Soon, though, as I watched dozens of rats swell into the hundreds, maybe even thousands, basic animal cunning would recognize the power of overwhelming numbers, and they'd swarm us.

The floor shook again.

The Professor held his notebook to his chest and began chanting something in a high, breathless voice, reciting it from memory. The words weren't recognizable, certainly not English, nothing I'd ever heard, something thick and guttural. It seemed to be nothing but harsh consonants, like the forklift driver's name I could never remember. At the end of the first line of the prayer or invocation or whatever, the Professor took a quick breath, and before he could continue, a deep, thunderous cracking filled the cavern, so loud it shook my bones. He screamed at us, "It's coming!" and pointed to Kiko and Wanda.

They raised the sheet with the symbol, holding it up to the skeletal structure. Neither of 'em was especially tall, and I had the ludicrous impression that they hadn't gotten the stone tree's attention. I wondered if Sammy and I should take over and raise it higher.

The floor shivered again, this time so violently I nearly went to my knees.

The rats were getting closer, less and less afraid of the flames.

Another thirty seconds, and they'd be all over us.

The Professor started back in with his incantations, and with his next line, the black plume of smoke crackled and sparked. Another tremendous crack, and the floor shifted sideways a few feet. Everyone went down. The air began to swirl around us in long, sweeping curls, gentle at first, then growing stronger and stronger.

I heard the rats coming for us, the claws scraping on rock, the excited squeals, before I saw them. Me and Sammy jumped onto the dais, backs to the stone tree. I figured I might try and rip the lid off the vegetable shortening when the rats got close enough to touch, just shoving it into their faces, burn as much as I could before they tore into me with those giant teeth. Hank climbed up on the platform as well, and we prepared to make our last stand.

With every word out of the Professor now, the crackling and sparking above the black smoke from the tree grew more and more violent. At the end of one particularly eloquent part of the incantation, the Professor's chanting elicited a burst of sizzling pure white lightning that erupted out of the top of the tree and shot to the roof of the cavern, somehow far, far over our heads. The distance didn't quite make sense, because this stretched far above the parking lot or whatever was directly overhead. We were somewhere else. I don't know how else to explain it. It's like when we'd crawled through the hole in the brick wall we'd slipped into a pocket outside or time and space.

The winds kept rising.

I couldn't worry about it because the rats were twenty yards away.

The Professor shouted hoarsely into the winds that whipped his clothes, threatened to tear the pages out of his hands. His voice found new strength. Some of the chants sounded familiar, and I wasn't sure if he'd started again, repeating it for emphasis, or if this was just a new stanza that mentioned some of the same stuff.

The rats were ten yards away.

I got ready to dig my hands into the burning vegetable shortening, trying to tell myself the torture of lighting my arms on fire was worth the satisfaction of taking some of the rodents with us, at least making them suffer with our deaths. And if I burned any of the goddamn parasites out, so much the better. Maybe I could jam my thumbs into a rat's red eyes, each about the size of a mandarin.

The Professor's chant rose to a feverish pitch, flinging the words into the roaring air. Wild gusts tore around the dais, as if a tornado was forming around us. Another stunning explosion of pure white lightning split the abyss, bleaching out the shadows for a split second.

The rats were almost here. Five yards now.

It was nearly over.

The Professor's voice kept building until he hit a crescendo, and he flung the final line of the incantation straight up into the utter blackness that had totally reclaimed the cavern after the sudden interruption of lightning. Then, for a split second, right there at the end, everything seemed to pause, holding its breath. The wind died. The rats stopped creeping forward. The smoke from the stone tree died out almost completely.

We had almost an entire second of stillness and silence.

Just enough to think maybe we'd won.

Then the thunder and cracking began again, this time making what came earlier seem like practice. It was so loud I thought it might burst my eardrums and wouldn't have surprised me to find they were bleeding. After a moment though, the shaking subsided dramatically. A few rumbles followed, but that was all. Everything grew still once again.

The rats had stopped and wouldn't get any closer. They scrabbled around each other, keeping their distance. reluctant to cross the last open five yards to the dais. The rats lifted their heads as one, sniffing at the air. Suddenly, as if there was some unheard, invisible signal, the rats scattered.

In less than five seconds, I couldn't see a single rat. They'd utterly vanished back into the gloom.

"Is that it?" Gloria asked. "Did you stop it?"

The Professor hesitated. He looked up at the plume of black smoke, now back to only around three feet high. Another rumble shivered through the cavern, but then the Professor said, "I think, that yes. Yes! We have—"

Something massive moved in the darkness above us.

Several somethings.

I had no real idea of what was out there, just the inescapable sense that something gigantic with endless legs was unfolding, unfurling itself out in the total blackness, just beyond the light. The darkness above us became alive, as shapes swung and rolled through the absolute night, things solid and real, shrouded in darkness.

A long, dark cylindrical tube shot out of the void, wrapping itself around the Professor's head, cutting him off mid-syllable. Another whipped out, grabbing his leg. And another, curling around his limbs and torso. Another. They stretched out of the darkness from every direction, curling around his limbs, torso, anything they could snare.

Tentacles.

Huge, each perhaps several feet thick, and seventy, eighty feet long. At least.

They encircled the Professor, squeezed, then easily ripped him into a dozen pieces.

A sudden cloudburst of blood drenched the dais.

The tentacles withdrew, shrinking back into the blackness, taking chunks of the Professor with them as they went. The winds died. Everything grew quiet and still once more, as if nothing had happened.

We looked at each, stunned, gasping for breath.

There was nothing to say.

The plume of smoke billowed up again, growing with an unchecked eagerness now that the Professor was no longer shouting at it. An inner pale green light began to seep from within this plume, as if glowing inside the smoke, where the sickening, greenish light revealed a hint of a hazy window, as if you could reach through the smoke and touch somewhere else.

"He didn't stop it," Gloria said.

"Doesn't look like it," Hank agreed.

"What now?" Wanda asked.

No one had an answer.

"There's gotta be something we can do," Wanda insisted.

"Something," Sammy echoed.

"I'm sorry," Gloria said. "We tried."

The nauseating, putrid light grew brighter, squeezing through the smoke like chicken fat through a fine colander, pushing the crushing darkness back, banishing it to the deep reaches of the jagged edges and pits of the cavern. The light wasn't constant, it flickered. Shapes of varying shades danced and weaved in the murk, like creatures swimming through sunlight straining through an algae-choked pond.

I wiped sweat out of my eyes. The temperature hadn't stopped climbing. After being outside through ten midwestern summers, I knew damn well the cavern was now over one hundred degrees, at least. If it kept climbing, we'd start to suffer heat exhaustion, then heatstroke. And if it kept going, our brains would boil in our skulls. I couldn't help it and got to thinking about how it would probably be for the best if I died fast.

If we all did.

Gloria clapped once and said, "Y'all circle up. Grab hands. Come on."

So, with nothing left, we gathered around the stone tree and joined hands to pray. On my right was Sammy. Wanda was on his other side, and she held on to Kiko. Peaches stayed between Wanda's feet. Kiko had hold of Hank, and Hank tenderly grasped Gloria's left hand. She reached out with her right and took my free hand, and we completed a ring around the ancient meteorite structure.

"Oh, Lord." Gloria's shockingly powerful voice echoed out into the sickly green light. "Hear our plea. Gonna keep this short, 'cause we don't have much time. We're all your children, and a little mercy would go a long way in your infinite wisdom. I don't ask for much, Lord, but this time I'm begging. In Jesus's name. Please. Amen."

A smattering of "amens" around the circle.

Gloria turned her head to Hank. "I'm sorry you happened to have the bad luck to have gotten yourself caught up in this. I hope you find your wife." She moved to Kiko. "I'm sorry that you are so young. I hope that reincarnation is real. You deserve another chance. Wanda, I am truly sorry I failed. You deserve peace." She smiled at Sammy. "Samuel. I am sorry because you're awful young too. None of this is fair." She squeezed my hand. "And Joseph. I'm sorry I never invited you to church. I don't think I wanted to face the 'oh, is it bring a White boy to church day?' comments. I'm sorry. I wish I could've been stronger. I know praising the Lord is not high on your priorities, but I do know you enjoy good old-fashioned Gospel music."

I wanted to say I wished I'd been able to see her as something beyond her badge this whole ten years. I wanted to say that I was sorry. I wanted to say that she was a daily reminder that life was important when everything around screamed otherwise. I wanted to blame the store but knew deep down, I hadn't been strong, like Gloria.

I squeezed her hand. She seemed to understand.

She turned back to the group and smiled. It was tired, it was scared, it was honest. "I know some of y'all don't believe, but we're all, all of us, going to a better place. One way or another."

Part of me wanted to sneer at her like the Professor. Like I said, fear makes us all assholes sometimes. Because that speck of hope was enough to kill me if I let it. It was easier to stamp it out, ignore it. We weren't going to a better place. We were most likely going to die in horrible fucking agony. And that'd be it. Even as she'd been speaking, the light had been building, infecting the shadows with its toxic green illumination and was about to spill out into our world. We were finished.

But it was Gloria. No different than Sammy. I couldn't bring myself to protest, I just nodded once instead. We dropped our hands, watching the smoke not just going straight up anymore, but billowing in all directions, spreading out with a purpose. Wanda gathered up Peaches, and nobody said anything for a while.

Gloria noticed the twisted form of the sheet where Kiko and Wanda had dropped it when the tentacles came whipping through the darkness. She bent, picked it up, tilted her head as she idly examined the various sigils and runes. She looked up at me and Sammy. "Gentlemen, will you do the honors and hang this sheet up there." She gestured at the top of the stone tree.

"It'll burn right through it," Hank said.

"Most likely," Gloria said. "But I never had much patience. I'm getting tired of sitting around waiting for this thing. Let's get it over with."

Like with Gloria's prayer, there didn't seem to be much harm in her idea. We each took a corner, and making sure Kiko's art would be on the inside, lifted it up, dragging it over the tip of the tree, diverting the smoke for a moment and as it spilled through us I almost cried out and dropped the sheet, but held on as Sammy flicked his corner over, and we finally draped the sheet over the tree.

The effect was instantaneous. I had no more released the cotton when another massive shiver ran through the cavern, this one picking us up and dropping us several feet. Smoke, dust, and an immense cracking began to reverberate through the abyss. The green light blinked out, then came back. Stronger for a moment but then faded quickly.

Everything shook. I didn't know what was happening, if it was an earthquake or what. I've never experienced an earthquake, and if it's anything like that, I hope I never do again. Everything was shaking, the very air, the very molecules, even the goddamn atoms. I couldn't breathe. Couldn't see. We clutched at each other best we could, crouched on the dais at the base of the meteorite tree.

The tremors got worse.

Then the world collapsed into darkness.

The first thing I saw was warm light from Kiko's Zippo bouncing off broken stone.

A few moments before that, I wasn't sure if I was dead or alive. I gradually became aware of rocks or something rough pushed hard into my body along my legs and left shoulder, and someone's knee was in my stomach. I couldn't tell what was up or down. Some snippet of avalanche survival tips jumped out, something about using your spit to figure out gravity so you didn't end up digging the wrong way. Right then though, this was absurd. First, there was only absolute darkness and dust. Forget spit, I don't know if I was even breathing for a while.

Someone hacked and coughed. I heard rustling, things moving.

"What on Earth…" Gloria's voice.

More movement.

"Hello?" Wanda.

"I'm here," Kiko said, and a moment later, her lighter sprang to life.

It wasn't much, but it was enough to get a sense of our immediate surroundings. As best as I could tell, at least part of the cavern had collapsed. I couldn't understand why we weren't dead, crushed to a pulp, nothing more than juice trickling through cracks in all the rocks. I was starting to think that maybe Gloria's prayer might turn out to be the only explanation I might find for our survival and then looked up to find the stone tree still intact, amazingly still standing. Nothing remained of the sheet except a few glowing ashes. The strength of this tree was out of this world. It must have blocked or knocked away anything that may have crushed us, protecting us from falling rocks.

That still didn't make a whole lot of sense, but I wasn't gonna question it too hard. I was glad to be alive. I realized part of my confusion came from one missing lens in my glasses. Once I figured out I could still see through my right eye, I started to get a better idea of our surroundings. The knee in my stomach belonged to Sammy. He scooted away, working his way up through the broken rocks. In the faint glow of Kiko's Zippo, I also saw Hank wiping dust out of his eyes, working his way clear of bigger boulders. I even saw Peaches and Wanda, climbing to higher ground. No one seemed to be seriously injured, just covered in dust and scrapes, no more than a few bruises.

As we worked our way up through the rubble, I could also see faint light from somewhere far above. It spilled down through the jumble of rocks, and I realized it might be late evening sunlight, as it didn't get dark in the summer until eight thirty or nine.

The cavern had not only collapsed into a jumble of boulders the size of Hummers and small houses, but great swaths of the western edge of FOOD4U! had also tumbled into the pit. Pieces of the cinderblock walls had been scattered near and far, like somebody'd upended a bucketful of Legos. The entire department of House Shit landed off to our right, merchandise spilling everywhere through chunks of concrete and rebar. Farther away, I saw what looked to be the twisted remains of the chicken rotisserie machine.

Then I realized it wasn't just sheer luck we were alive.

The meteorite structure was still giving off an enormous amount of energy. The force field or whatever had driven off anything that came near it. That's why we were still alive. Smoke shot upward, already reaching all the way up to the exposed mass of wires and pipes left hanging under the store's cracked and broken concrete floor.

Lightning crackled up and down the smoke.

The sick green light began to spill through once again.

The only thing we'd managed was to postpone it.

Something else above us shifted and gave way. Another twenty or so yards of the floor split from the rest and fell to the rocks below. More racks and displays and merchandise fells into the pit, crashing around us. This included the wind chimes, the steel framework display with all those models and a few hundred boxes, in an explosion of dense, off-key jangles and loud bangs.

I felt the light react. It blinked at the sounds.

I thought of the moths and how they flinched when Gloria dropped the gates. I thought of her clapping. I thought of how my music used bone-vibration technology. I thought of the Professor, explaining how vibration makes heat. I thought of how the needle on my turntable picked up the minute vibrations hidden within the grooves of the vinyl record.

"Gloria," I said, "Sing. Please. Sing at it!"

"Sing what?"

"Anything," I said. "It doesn't like sounds from here. Sing your heart out." I reached down and pulled Sammy to a standing position with me. "We're gonna go grab the biggest goddamn wind chimes we can find." We scrambled through the wreckage, Hank following, as Gloria began to sing. I figured she'd go for something like "Amazing Grace," but instead I heard the first wavering bars of "Will the Circle Be Unbroken?" rise hesitantly into the clouds of dust and piles of debris. As she got rolling, her voice gained strength and grew louder, until she was barreling along like a train under full steam.

Meanwhile, the light began to pulse. It didn't look like it was getting stronger, as if the sunlight was keeping it down. The billowing smoke faltered, stopped.

Wanda joined in with Gloria. She knew the words too.

Me and Sammy didn't have to go far to stumble over wind chimes. We kicked away smaller boxes, looking for the truly gargantuan ones. A few still hung from the steel frame, but most had been sprinkled around like some children's game. I found one almost four feet long and tossed it to Hank, big around as a hefty branch. He immediately started back to Gloria. Sammy found one six goddamn feet long, wide enough to roll a basketball from one end to the other. Better yet, it still had a loop of wire hooked through two holes at one end, where it had hung from the steel.

I found another chime almost as large a few seconds later, but lacking the wire. I shrugged out of my hi-vis vest, twisted it tight, then fed it through the two holes, wrapping it around my fist. This way I could hang onto it without dampening the vibrations.

We huffed and puffed back up to Gloria and the girls. Hank didn't waste time, just took his wind chime and swung it over his head into a ridge of rock. There was a reasonably impressive bang, but nothing like the explosion of sound I'd been hoping for.

Gloria was just about out of song.

As she faltered, the light grew steadier and stronger.

We found a halfway level area just above her and spent a moment kicking away debris so there was nothing to trip over. I nodded to Sammy. He nodded back. We each took hold of our respective chimes, holding them from makeshift handles at the ends, turned until we were almost facing each other, then with a quick, "Go!" we spun. I whipped around, holding the chime as far out as I could. Sammy did the same.

They struck each other with an impossibly deep GONG, resonating so much that we both dropped our chimes and clutched at our ears.

The light went berserk, throbbing spastically.

We nodded at each other. Again. This time, with the benefit of a practice swing, the impact was harder, louder, stronger. The shapes within the green light swam with more frantic and jagged movements. We caught each other's eyes and nodded one last time, regathered the chimes. We looked to the others, Gloria, Wanda, Kiko, and Hank, mimed covering our ears.

The third time shattered both chimes.

The stone tree seemed to suck all the green light

back into it. And for a moment, there was nothing but darkness yet again.

Then, an explosion of overpowering bright, white light.

And that's all I knew.

4

INTERVIEW TRANSCRIPT-SUBJECT:-REDACTED-

Transcribed by: Ofc. -REDACTED-, Berwyn, IL PD

AGENCY: DEPT. HOMELAND SECURITY

DATE: 29 July 2026

LOC: Berwyn Police Department, 6401 W. 31st St, Berwyn, IL 60402

TIME: 7:58 AM

CASE: 47-5190-0043

PRESENT:

Special Agent Fred Jackson—Department of Homeland Security (DHS)

Joseph Sutter—FOOD4U! Employee

Unnecessary sounds, such as "um" and "ah" have been omitted from the following statement for the purpose of making this statement easier to read.

SUTTER: I blink, and paramedics were strapping me to a board. Wrapped me in aluminum foil and gave me a protein bar and a bottle of water. Then you guys brought me here.

JACKSON: And…and that's what you think I should put in my report.

SUTTER: Up to you. It doesn't matter. None of this does. I tried to tell ya, remember?

JACKSON: I guess I don't.

SUTTER: Told you nobody's gonna read it.

JACKSON: Why not?

SUTTER: I told you straight up you wouldn't like what I had to say, and ultimately, it didn't matter, you know? None of us are getting through this.

JACKSON: I don't follow.

SUTTER: Don't you feel it?

JACKSON: I know it's been a long night—

DE LA IGLESIA ENTERS.

SUTTER: Peaches! Where'd you find her? Come here, girl.

DE LA IGLESIA: Found it wandering around the parking lot. Fred, can I talk to you outside a minute?

SUTTER: Good dog, oh you're such a good dog.

JACKSON: Can it wait? We're almost finished here.

DE LA IGLESIA: I don't think so. Things are…

SUTTER: Things are getting weird out there, aren't they?

DE LA IGLESIA: Shut up. I'm speaking with Agent Jackson.

JACKSON: I don't know if I understand. This is…

DE LA IGLESIA: You need to come outside and see the sky. Trust me.

SUTTER: Told ya.

DE LA IGLESIA: Shut up! No one wants to hear from you.

SUTTER: Don't you get it?

JACKSON: Apparently not.

SUTTER: It's like the store. We all should've read the fine print.

DE LA IGLESIA: Fred, please. Come with me. You need to see this.

SUTTER: Told ya all we did was postpone it.

DE LA IGLESIA: Shut up!

SUTTER: Feel it?

JACKSON: Did you hear…wait. What the fuck was that?

SUTTER: You guys usually sweat this much?

JACKSON: Something's wrong with the AC. That's all.

SUTTER: Sure. Meantime, me 'n Peaches, we're gonna—oh shit. Right there! Saw you both swallow.

JACKSON: Okay, Joe. Fine, whatever.

Glad you're having fun, but we need to-

SUTTER: Come on man. You feel it right now, don't ya? The air pressure changed and you know it. Better equalize your ears before your eardrums burst.

DE LA IGLESIA: Fred, please. Come outside. Something… it's all wrong.

JACKSON: Art, just–

-GLITCH-

SUTTER: -too late.

DE LA IGLESIA: Did you hear that?

SUTTER: Take a deep breath while you can, guys. You spent your whole life thinking you were in control of your own destiny. Everything neat, proper, in order. Hate to tell ya, but that's done. And you know it. I can see the fear in your eyes. Good news is, a panic attack won't kill you. Bad news is, something else will. And it's here.

DE LA IGLESIA: I'm going to make sure you face the consequences of your actions, I promise you.

SUTTER: We're all facing the consequences. Before we're gone, though, I need to see everyone else. Where'd you take them? Are they here?

DE LA IGLESIA: You-

-GLITCH-

JACKSON: —isn't according to protocol.
SUTTER: I know. It isn't fair. Here's the thing, though. See, you guys haven't had time to get used to the idea. I have. And you know what? It's gonna be okay. That's what I've decided. Like I said at the start, when did it all begin? Hell if I know. The whole cycle of life thing. Same with the end. Hell if I know.
JACKSON: —I can't—

-GLITCH-

DE LA IGLESIA: —something! Fred! Come on, please!
SUTTER: Everything ends, man. Everything. I asked you, twice I think, if you wanted to know when you would die, and you ignored me. Never answered me. Well, guess what? Hate to say it, but it's now. Yeah, now.
DE LA IGLESIA: Don't listen to him.
SUTTER: You both know I'm telling you straight. I get it. Most of us, we don't want to die. It's scary. Too much unknown, out of our control. Sure. It's a lot. But when you gotta stare at in the face for a while, like I have, you might start to see it

makes sense. Feels right. Everything ends. Everything. Shit, listen to the math of the universe, you know…music. Think about songs. Every song ends. That's a good thing. I don't care what your favorite tune is, you'd get sick of it if it never stopped. It'd become…hell, fucking torture, right? If it just kept going and going. Like a goddamn Grateful Dead song, when they're too stoned to realize the song should've ended twenty minutes ago. Nobody needs that.

DE LA IGLESIA: You're so full of shit you squeak when you walk. I'm gonna—

-GLITCH-

JACKSON: —this can't, no, no-

SUTTER: Me 'n Peaches are gonna go find my friends.

SUTTER LEAVES.

JACKSON: -no-

EN D

RE COR

D

IN

G

A LOOK AT: COMBUSTIBLE BY HUNTER SHEA

POST-APOCALYPTIC HORROR MEETS THRILLER IN A DYSTOPIAN NIGHTMARE OF FIRE AND ASH.

The world didn't end with a bang or a whimper…it ended with people bursting into flames.

Across the globe, spontaneous human combustion (SHC) is turning ordinary citizens into living infernos. Governments collapse, cities fall silent, and the air itself tastes like ash. Society burns while the lucky few are left to wonder: *When will it be me?*

Sam and Aja were already falling apart before the fires came. Now, trapped in a crumbling apartment and suffocating under the weight of isolation, their love feels just as doomed as the rest of humanity. But when whispers spread of a small Canadian town called Consumption, untouched by the inferno, hope flickers.

Stealing an RV and refusing to leave Aja behind, Sam sets out on a desperate, ash-streaked journey through a burned-out North America. With his best friend in tow and a growing crew of strange, unforgettable survivors, they chase rumors through a landscape warped by horror, madness, and the heat of human combustion.

AVAILABLE NOW

THANK YOU

Thank you for taking the time to read *FOOD4U!*. If you enjoyed it, please consider telling your friends or posting a short review. Word of mouth is an author's best friend and much appreciated.

Thank you.
Jeff Jacobson

ABOUT THE AUTHOR

Jeff Jacobson is a writer and teacher. He writes slightly ridiculous novels and the occasional scary short story. Born in Northern California, he has lived in Australia, Taiwan, and now lives in Chicago with his wife. He has two kids that are a lot cooler than him.

www.ingramcontent.com/pod-product-compliance
Lightning Source LLC
LaVergne TN
LVHW100516110826
845146LV00002B/656

* 9 7 9 8 8 9 5 6 7 9 1 9 7 *